LIGHTNING CAUSED

Book Two in the Ada Reed Mystery Series

Roger Lynn Howell

coffeetownpress

Kenmore, WA

A Coffeetown Press book published by Epicenter Press

Epicenter Press
6524 NE 181st St.
Suite 2
Kenmore, WA 98028

For more information go to:
www.Camelpress.com
www.Coffeetownpress.com
www.Epicenterpress.com
www.Rogerhowellbooks.com

This is a work of fiction. Names, characters, places, brands, media, and incidents are either the product of the author's imagination or are used fictitiously.

Cover design by Scott Book
Design by Melissa Vail Coffman

Lightning Caused
Copyright © 2024 by Roger Lynn Howell

Library of Congress Control Number: 2023951896

ISBN: 978-1-68492-189-8 (Trade Paper)
ISBN: 978-1-68492-190-4 (eBook)

To Susan, my life-long best friend.

Acknowledgments

I THINK ADA REED IS MODELED, at least superficially, after Nina (rhymes with Carolina) Montgomery—my 4-H instructor when I was about ten years old. Tall and slim, Nina would don a jean jacket over her flowered blouse, tuck her slacks into western boots, and wade out into the cow shit. There she would rope and wrestle calves or demonstrate proper milking of cows. After class, Nina would hose off her boots, toss the jacket, and straighten her bolo tie. Then, resetting her pink Stetson, she would drive into the sunset in her beat-up old pickup. I loved Nina. I think I love Ada, too.

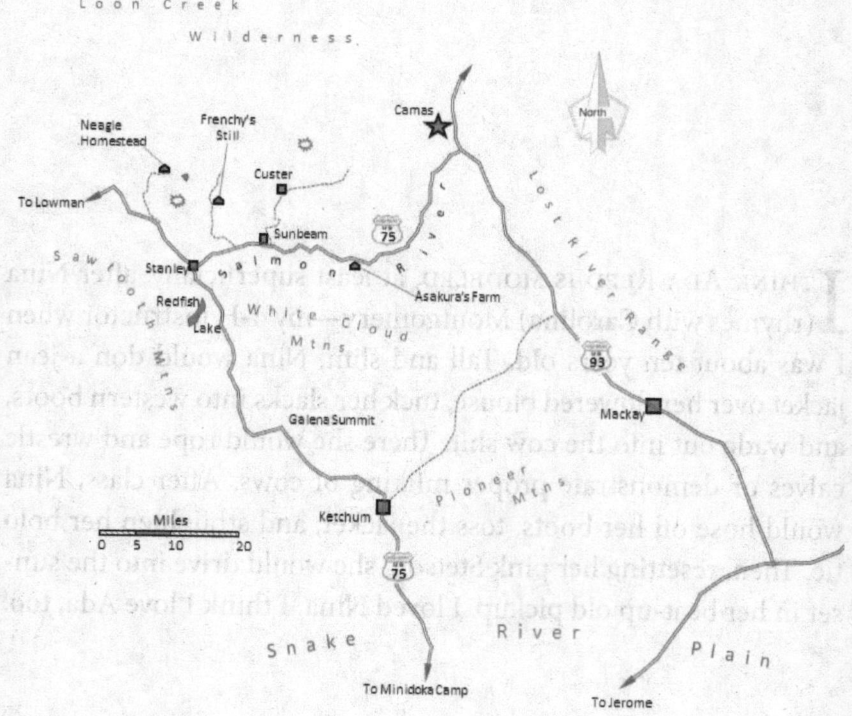

Central Idaho and the Salmon River Headwaters

CHAPTER ONE

17 September 1951,
The heart of Idaho

Two hounds rounded a bend of a forest lane. Their backs bowed in long strides and their paws threw up grit clawing through the turn. The dogs bayed as they ran, as hunting dogs do, but their yelps were lost in a howling wind that bent the trees and sent sand and pine boughs swirling. The pair were followed by a third hound just seconds behind.

The sun made barely a red disc in the sky, and that darkness started crickets to chirp and fooled prairie dogs from their warrens to forage. Deer darted in front of the baying dogs, and rabbits scurried between the legs of coyotes—all prey to the forest fire roaring and rushing behind them. Grouse and chukars feigned broken wings in a ruse to lead the danger from their nests. The hens would take flight, but too late, and the heat and smoke would drop most of them. The prairie dogs were last to retreat, and deep in their warrens pushed up dirt to wait out the fire passing over them.

It was the hounds' nature to run, and they were well-fed and strong, all three. They ran for miles; they ran until they simply couldn't.

Update 9:00 a.m. – Surveilling Valley Creek Fire

POLICE CHIEF KELLEN MUNSON MANEUVERED THE pickup truck down the hard-pack highway a little faster than was safe, while Acting Sheriff Ada Reed tried to update her duty log and keep watch on two vehicles following behind. Heavy smoke from a shortgrass prairie fire made it difficult for them to breathe, let alone see, and neither officer was doing well at what they were doing. But a swirl of clear air showed their small caravan to be holding together, and in fact, another vehicle appeared to have taken up in the rear.

The three trailing vehicles were evacuees fleeing the Valley Creek forest fire, whom Munson and Reed had driven in to help. They'd all been caught off guard by a shift in the winds, which had spread the fire from the forested hills to the grasslands. The two rigs directly behind were an old station wagon and a beat-up GMC flat bed. The third, she believed, was an early model Oldsmobile. All three were loaded to the gunwales with baskets and boxes, pots, and kids. Mattresses piled atop were tied and held down with shovels and axes.

Chief Munson was following as closely as possible a timber company pickup truck, while a Forest Service Power Wagon with a green flashing light led the whole anxious evacuation. Sheriff Reed kept a watch to see that the cars behind stayed together, although she was not sure what they could do if one of them broke off. It was too dangerous to stop for anything in their present situation. Smoke was swirling heavy and black, and Munson could hardly see to drive. He and she had wet their bandanas and tied them over their faces, but though the bandanas filtered some of the stench of dying marshes and willows, they did little to make the air more sustaining.

They had met up that morning in the crossroads village of Stanley: Acting Sheriff Ada Reed, Chief Munson, and District Ranger Ben McGann, the driver of the green-flashing Forest Service rig. They were friends, the three of them, but more importantly that morning, they were the persons most in charge of the fire burning through the heart of Idaho, and of its fallout. They'd gulped coffee and toast on the porch of the Stanley Hotel, laughed nervously, and conferred regarding the still-distant blaze roiling and billowing in the yellow morning light. It was another forest fire, much like the one before and the one before that. For three months, from Montana to the Oregon border, fires had flared up and scattered deer by the herd, dirtied the winds, and poisoned fish right out of the water. This one was designated, Ada learned, the Valley Creek fire. The name meant nothing to her then, and the distant inferno gave no indication of being any different than the others.

"It's blowing toward Lowman, isn't it?" She had asked. Even then she'd tied a bandana over her face to help her breathe, and under her Stetson the bandana made her look like a bandit. From the neck down, though, she wore the official gray duty shirt and badge, olive tie, and olive trousers of the Yellowpine County sheriff. She wore western boots but had not buckled on the heavy utility belt and gun.

McGann, the Forest Service ranger, tried to assure her. "Lowman's a good thirty miles down canyon," he said. "I've not seen the fire that could stay together through that kind of country."

"I'm more concerned for Stanley, here," Munson had said. Munson was Chief of Police for the town of Custer, Idaho, half an hour east of Stanley. The Sheriff had her office in the county seat of Camas, about an hour further east from Custer. She and Munson had driven out together to check the progress of this new fire.

Munson's words had sparked an uneasiness in her, a twinge, and it must have been then a young firefighter hurried over to them with a note for McGann: a report of evacuees trying to turn west out of Valley Creek. The message had come over the two-way, and McGann jumped up and ran straight to his truck.

Ada had chased after him. "Are you sure it's safe?" she called.

"It's safe for me, not for you, *bandito*," he'd told her with a big grin. "The fire is blowing due west. I'll be okay by miles." She returned his smile, although hidden by the red bandana it hadn't been much. Still, her eyes had given it their best.

He'd driven off, and although she told him she wouldn't, she'd followed behind. Munson would not let her go out alone, and so there she and he found themselves at Trapper Creek, eight miles above Stanley. They hadn't noticed the wind swing around and had only stopped when they were choking on the smoke. McGann, with the timber company truck following behind, was alarmed and angry when he'd busted out of the swirling wall of smoke to find them stopped in the middle of the road. He'd told them to fall in behind and keep their asses close.

And that's exactly what they were doing. The other vehicles had swung in out of the smoke at Sheep Trail to join the convoy. The wind, Ada saw, was blowing the grass fire in a southwest direction, and they were driving southeastward, not quite perpendicular to it. She couldn't see far enough ahead to judge whether they would clear the line of the fire, but she was confident McGann would get them through it. She couldn't stop coughing, though, and her head felt light, almost floating at times. Swinging around to watch the other cars was becoming more dizzying each time.

She was glad Ben McGann was in the lead and they had only to follow, but also sorry she'd caused him extra worry, and concerned she might screw up in front of him. She and McGann had known each other since high school. For a short while they'd known each other very well, but they'd gone their separate ways. He'd recently returned to the Salmon River country to take the district ranger job.

Now and then to her left, flames danced in a thin line at the base of the black smoke. The flames were getting closer, and that couldn't be good. But then the smoke would close in and all would go gray again—and dizzying. Behind them, the vehicles were barely keeping up, with the mattresses on top bending back and slapping in the wind as their speed hit fifty miles an hour. But Munson, hunched over the wheel and white-knuckled, shook his head and said they couldn't slow down; they had to keep moving.

About then Munson must have hit the brakes because Ada was thrown backward into the passenger side footwell, banging her head hard against the jockey box. She didn't hear their tires skidding over the road nor feel the truck swing sideways and come to a stop. But Munson slamming the truck door roused her, and she found herself stuck in the footwell and unable to move for what seemed a long, clumsy time. She managed to find the door handle behind her back and kicked the door open, then wriggled and twisted and fell onto the oiled and packed gravel of the roadbed. From between the pickup's wheels red flames were approaching from not two hundred yards away. For the first time she felt the heat of the fire on her face.

She staggered to her feet but had to brace herself on the front fender. The lumbermen's truck in front had stopped and was blocking the road. Munson had barely managed not to slam into it. The station wagon behind had missed ramming into them both but had come to a stop on the shoulder of the road. The flatbed and the Oldsmobile stopped short of the snarl, but the drivers looked panicked. Ada stumbled forward to see what could be done, too confused to panic, and just then McGann returned. He'd seen he was alone and had circled back.

The ranger slapped the hood of the station wagon and waved that car on, yelling to get to Stanley and not look back. That car disappeared into the blowing smoke. McGann backed his rig up to the stalled truck and in seconds had a tow chain hooked on. Munson helped Ada into their pickup and, coughing and tearing up, they were under way again before she'd completely taken in the situation. Her head pounded, and when she felt the knot in back, there was a bit of blood on her fingers. The rabbit's foot on the mirror was swinging like a pendulum, and Munson was saying something to her, but her thoughts fluttered and she barely followed him.

They'd met up in the sunny village of Stanley that morning—she was sure of that, although some of it was hazy—she and Munson and McGann. The morning air had made her shiver although the sun, just topping the ridge, was warm on her back. And there was something she'd heard . . . or something she'd not heard. "Wait a minute, what does that mean?" she had asked. She looked from one to the other. Was there worry in their eyes—a flash of concern? "Will it turn; will it come toward Stanley?"

"There are miles of grassy meadows between us and the fire," McGann had assured her. He wore his uniform to code, as she did, and his fit him nicely. When he'd taken off his Smokey Bear hat, she'd had to smile at the shock of sandy hair he never could keep off his forehead.

"September meadows," Kellen Munson had argued. He was not in uniform except for his hat. Kellen, as per always, wore a pearl-snap western shirt—blue and fuchsia—too cheery for the work at hand and too colorful on any day for his plain mien and manner. He said, "September meadows, after a hot, dry summer."

So, what in hell did any of that mean? Lives were at stake, for God's sake, and she was in charge . . . sort of. Ben, Ranger McGann, was calm and reflective, and she liked that about him— loved it about him. But cool reflection, damn it, is not so comforting when you're sort of in charge, and you don't know whether to spit or go blind.

"Stanley will be okay, then?" she had pressed. She was sort of the sheriff: 'Acting Sheriff Ada Reed,' whatever that meant. What it didn't mean was an afternoon in the garden listening to the radio bulletins, confident whoever the hell *was* in charge was in charge.

McGann had run to his truck and driven out of town toward the fire, and she shouldn't have, but she'd felt left behind, and scared for him, so she'd run after him.

The rabbit's foot slapped and twisted on its string, and Munson in his bright plaid shirt hunched over the wheel, focusing on the road. Her head pounded but her mind had cleared enough to see the road bent gradually south as they drove, and that was enough to gain them a few yards on the flames, but they were going too slow.

Neither of them said a word, but the pickup truck under tow was slowing down the whole convoy. They hadn't gone a mile, however, before McGann swung the Power Wagon off the road into a broad, roadside gravel pit, pulling the broken-down lumbermen's truck swerving and bouncing behind him. Kellen Munson stopped, and the rigs behind him stopped, but McGann was out in an instant, waving them to keep going.

"Get these cars to Stanley," he yelled. "Kellen it's up to you! We'll sit it out here between the gravel piles."

Ada couldn't believe what she was hearing. She opened her door and yelled, "Get in, Ben, we can take everyone!"

But he was already hurrying away. "We'll be all right behind the gravel piles," he yelled back.

"No, you can't!" she screamed—she must have screamed, it sounded like a siren in her ears. And she must have jumped out and run to him because he caught her, roughly around her middle, and she was hauled back to the truck and pushed in.

"Go, Kel!" McGann shouted. "Don't stop!"

Munson had her, had hold of her belt, and he pulled her into the cab. The truck lurched, the door slammed shut, and they sped away with the two trailing vehicles right on their bumper. She peered over the seat back and saw darkness closing in until a clear gust showed four hunched figures staggering toward the piles of road gravel.

The flames had gained on them. Munson, on the hot side of their cab, had to hold his arm up to shield his face from the heat, but he somehow kept the truck between the borrow ditches. Ada didn't notice, but slunk down onto the seat coughing, dizzy, and numb.

They'd not driven another five minutes when they broke out of the smoke and flames. Like passing out of a tunnel, they drove blindingly into sunlight and saw the low, timber buildings of Stanley in the distance. The chief pushed it another quarter mile before pulling over and waving the others on. The flatbed and the Oldsmobile continued to town, with the mattress atop the Oldsmobile smoldering.

Munson stayed to look back on what they'd left behind, and to wait—just in case. He burned his hand on the door handle getting out, cussed loudly, then came across to help Ada. She fell to the ground, and he sat down with her. They watched silently as orange flames leapt the highway a couple hundred yards back: delicate, orange, dancing little flames. It was a whirling cauldron of flame and smoke, however, between them and where McGann had pulled out.

"We have to go back," she said.

"We can't, Ada," not till the fire burns through."

"He'll die, Kel."

"He'll get those lumbermen low between the gravel piles. They'll be safe there from the flames. He won't park the vehicles nearby in case, you know . . . the gas tanks."

Ada walked off a ways and stood with her back to the police chief, her arms wrapped tightly around her. Munson yelled something about staying close-by in case the winds changed, but she didn't give a damn. Snow fell around her and gathered on her shoulders and in her hair, and she held out her hand and laughed. It was ash, for God's sake! Just ash, and it was trickling down all around. She closed her eyes tightly, but no tears wet them. She'd used up all her tears running through the smoke.

When she opened her eyes again, the flames were gone. Magically, as quickly as they'd overtaken the road, the flames were racing off southward catching afire small trees and bushes and leaving behind miles of flat, featureless, coal-black meadow. Wisps and twists of smoke rose everywhere. "It's hell," she said, quietly.

Munson started to walk over but decided she'd probably rather be by herself. He stayed back by the truck and packed a pinch of tobacco in his cheek. "It ain't hell, but maybe hell's front porch," he said, also quietly. The highway from where they'd come, as far back as they strained to see, smoldered and smoked. It was an oiled-gravel road surface and the oil, in places, had caught fire.

They stood for forty minutes waiting for the road to cool and watching great, roiling columns of smoke rise from the main blaze. Their grass fire had scarcely been a sideshow; the main forest fire by then was consuming the heavily treed hills between Kelley Creek and Knapp Creek. Those flames were a good four miles distant, but the plume had risen and flattened on the winds aloft, spreading a ceiling over them. Hence, the snow-like ashfall. "It's just hell!" she cried.

"They'll be all right, Ada."

"They won't be!" And neither would she. They'd met again after years, she and Ben McGann, and worked together a little on the Yankee Fork case. They'd had a few beers and some laughs, a steak dinner or two, and they'd teased about old times. But there was nothing serious about it, they were the oldest of friends; and there was certainly nothing untoward. And yet, watching the gray smoke billowing up, climbing bulge over bulge like an atomic blast, she felt her heart would break.

Another half hour passed as a column of blue-white smoke swelled and twisted in front of the more distant wall of brown. It was another grass fire; some other meadow burning. In other times she might have laid back and enjoyed the awful beauty of it all. But now in those roiling, mushrooming columns she saw nothing but death and heartbreak. He had no goddamned right to do what he did!

She didn't see the Forest Service Power Wagon emerge from out of the smoke. But there it was, moving silently through shimmering waves, coming toward them so matter-of-factly she could scream. Her head throbbed, her eyes burned, and her throat was too dry to make anything but a croaking sound. He was towing the pickup truck behind him, moving slowly like a goddamned parade. She climbed into her truck and motioned for Munson to get in on the driver's side. "Let's get going, Chief," she shouted. "There's work to do in Stanley."

He jumped behind the wheel and started to turn the truck around. "We need to help them," he said.

"Hell, no! Ben has it under control." She pulled out her note-book and pen. "The redoubtable Ranger McGann has it all under control."

Update 2:45 p.m. – To Stanley Village
with Chief Munson, documenting the evacuation.

CHIEF MUNSON WAITED ANYWAY, OF COURSE. Or at least he moved slowly enough for McGann's small convoy to catch up to them, and they drove into Stanley in tandem. When they arrived in the tiny, crossroad village in the meadow it was to a round of handshakes from the drivers whom they'd led out, and from half a dozen others who'd made it out on their own. One side of the Power Wagon, the folks all noted, was Forest-Service green, but the paint on the other side was blackened and blistered. McGann, himself, was singed and black with soot, but in one piece and smiling broadly, the son of a bitch. The timbermen's pickup had blown two tires, but they'd changed one of them and limped into town on the rim of the other.

Sheriff Reed let the congratulations proceed without her and slipped into the log-framed grocery to beg a glass of water, then took up a position under the bulletin board outside and started her paperwork. She took down the names of each family that had made it out of the burn zone, and she listed what they were driving, how many family members they had along, and who else they might have seen.

The screen door slammed, making her jump. But it was only Chief Munson, who joined her with two bottles of orange Nehi and a box of Cracker Jack. He opened both bottles against the edge of a post, gave one to Ada, then sat on the porch near her. A little ash was falling, and he brushed it away with his hat. "You're doing great Ada," he said. "But it wouldn't hurt for you to step out there and meet with those folks."

She almost laughed at him. "This is no time for electioneer-ing—in a disaster, Kellen?"

"They'd like to meet with the sheriff in charge, and . . ."

"I'm trying to do my damned job!" She turned and wiped her eyes. She was trying to do the job she was sort of in charge of—Acting Sheriff of Yellowpine County. She'd agreed to take the job, to put on the badge and the ill-fitting uniform, to keep the position open for her husband, Montgomery Reed, who'd been called back to the Army for the Korean conflict. But it had already been six months, and flush with notoriety following her handling of the Yankee Fork murders, she had been convinced to stand for election in her own name.

"Ada, I know you're doing your job. You're doing it darned well. It just wouldn't hurt to let folks know it's you who's doing it darned well." The Yankee Fork murders had occurred in Munson's town of Custer, and since then he'd become her self-appointed campaign manager.

She shook her head, then glared at Ranger Ben McGann who walked up to join them. Munson said, "Maybe you can't help folks directly, but you can encourage them. They want to see their sheriff and hear what she has to say. It's exactly the wrong time to stand off and not at least show some sympathy."

"Empathy."

"Though maybe not so much correcting their diction."

"It isn't only campaigning," McGann offered. He held his hat in his hands. "It's the calm reassurance folks need sometimes from the authorities."

"Calm, clear-headed reassurance." She scoffed and refused even to look at him. For the rest of the afternoon Ada stayed on the porch under the bulletin board and marked down the people's names. She asked and answered about neighbors and family members she or they may have seen, and generally relayed what information she could. When her bandana was down and her Stetson pushed back, the people greeted an attractive woman in her mid-thirties—attractive but bone-weary that day. Sun-tanned and blue-eyed with a sharp jawline, her face was leaner than it had been a few months earlier, and with maybe a line or two at the eyes and the corners of the mouth. And those eyes . . . well, they were a little red and moist from time to time, but that was mostly from the smoke in the air.

Every half hour or so a truck or a station wagon rolled from out of the western haze toward town. The vehicles were invariably loaded down, often carrying chickens, pigs, even calves in with a lot of wide-eyed children. They were the ranchers, the small-time loggers, and the part-time miners who lived up Knapp Creek and upper Valley Creek. Each group in its turn stopped at the general store to check the names on the bulletin board and give their own names for Ada to add to the lists. The women would set down their children and, straightening their hair and aprons, step inside to buy loaves of bread and rings of bologna. The men gassed up the rigs, checked the tires, and gazed with hands in pockets at the burning country from where they'd fled.

After checking in and gassing up at Stanley, the refugees generally turned right—south toward Ketchum if they had friends there or money for a hotel; or south to the forest service campground at Redfish Lake if they were short of both. Most headed to Redfish.

About mid-afternoon, a station wagon stopped in front of Ada fully loaded with bedding, dishes, and children inside, and mattresses and tools atop. Ada greeted them as she had the others. They had come out Valley Creek ahead of the fire, droving cows and pigs as far as the meadows, where they'd left the animals to fend for themselves. The children asked Ada to take a dog they'd come across, because they were going to a cousin's place where there wasn't room for a dog. They handed her a rope tied to a bluetick hound singed on its back and burned of foot. The poor thing was frightened and groveled when she kneeled to it.

"We found him running loose, scared as all heck," the man told her. He thought it was surely one of Mooch Neagle's dogs. "No one else runs coon hounds in this country," he said. "I thought

Mooch'd leave his own mother behind before he let them hounds out of his sight."

Ada thanked them and accepted the leash gingerly. She had no idea what to do with a hunting dog. Munson fetched it a bowl of water, and then another.

At around five o'clock, a plane dropped out of the gloom, circled the town once, then landed on the airstrip above town. McGann had been expecting it. He stopped by Ada's bulletin board to explain that the plane had come to take him to check the fire's progress from the air, and then would fly him straight to the fire command center in Boise.

"Have a safe trip," she said.

"Ada . . ." In the smoke-tinted light, the broad brim of his hat cast his face half blue and half orange.

"I won't keep you, District Ranger."

"Then, I'll be sure to keep you apprised, Sheriff."

"'It's acting sheriff,' but yes, please do."

McGann caught his plane, and Ada kept to her lists. By early evening most of the back-country residents were accounted for. The few who weren't, Munson agreed, probably had evacuated the day before and turned west for Lowman and Idaho City. The red disc of the sun was on its final descent, and the pillars of smoke, now with the light behind them, churned and billowed a hellish orange. Ada and Munson packed to go as evening was distinguishing itself from the murky day.

They were gassing up for the drive home when one more loaded-down farm truck stopped. A solid matron in a surprisingly gay, ribboned, and daisied hat came by Ada's pickup truck. She asked them to take another dog.

"You have a veterinary there in Camas," the woman told Ada. "And this poor fella got singed pretty bad." It was another bluetick hound.

CHAPTER TWO

Tuesday, 18 September, 7:00 a.m.
Yellowpine County Courthouse, Camas, Idaho

SHE'D FALLEN INTO BED WITH HER throat and lungs raw from coughing all day, her feet cramping from dehydration no matter how much water she tried to drink, and the knot on the back of her head swollen to where she couldn't lay it properly on a pillow. Whenever she did doze off, the flames woke her, and the screaming and running. The two lost dogs had come home with her due to the late hour, but thankfully had flopped themselves down on the bedroom rug and slept quietly—till five a.m. Their moaning and kicking and scratching as they slept woke her.

But a pot of coffee helped to revive her, and she managed to get the dogs out to the backyard in time to save her living room carpet from a soiling. She barricaded them in the kitchen with her, after that, and spent the rest of her morning thumbing through *The Science of Wildfire Suppression, 2ⁿᵈ Edition* with the dogs' claws clacking and sliding over the linoleum floor.

Seven o'clock came, and she hadn't found a way to keep butter on the dogs' burned paws. They kept licking it off. She tried Vaseline, but they liked that too, and the same went for an application of Montgomery's honey-glycerin shaving tonic. Now she'd be damned if she was going to give them any of her cosmetic hand cream. She'd missed the Avon lady two months running and was nearly out of her cream as well as bath soap and everything else. The dogs waited, staring up with raised brows. In the end, she wrapped their paws in wet linen and took the poor things to work with her.

THE SHERIFF'S OFFICE WAS LOCATED on the first floor of the Victorian stone and brick courthouse on Main Street. Hers was the third door on your left after you passed around the wide staircase in the main foyer. The room was appointed with desks and file cabinets and squeaky chairs older than Ada, although she didn't mind the antiques so much. She was less fond of the paint on the walls, which was old and cracked and faded to several unpleasant shades of green. She kicked the door closed behind her, hung up her duty belt, and said good morning to Harry Truman, who gaped down from the olive drab wall above her desk.

Once she'd got a pot of coffee perking, she started compiling the evacuation lists made the day before. But with dogs unaccustomed to linoleum floors and walls and desks, she was getting very little paperwork actually done.

At five past nine, Mayor Ephraim Applegate stopped by to visit with the sheriff, and to help himself to his customary cup of her coffee. He mopped his face with a handkerchief and said by way of greeting, "They full up at the dog pound?"

"No, Uncle Eph. These dogs belong to one of the evacuees from the Valley Creek fire. They're hurt and the veterinary is too busy with a hoof and mouth running through the county to see them right now. She pushed one of the dogs aside to get to the file cabinets. "They got lost, I expect, in the excitement. I'll run out and see if I can re-unite them as soon as District Ranger McGann tells me it's safe."

"Ben?"

"District Ranger McGann."

He shrugged. Ephraim Applegate was married to Ada's Aunt Corrine. A man just entering his sixties, he was medium tall and a little more than medium wide, with thinning, mostly gray hair worn longer than the fashion of the day. Applegate was well liked around town and had served as district attorney for years before being elected to the mayor position.

He started to ease himself into Ada's chair but caught himself in time and stepped back to the guest chair in front of the desk. His niece had been getting touchy about that sort of thing. She was a bit touchy, too, about something as simple as fetching him a cup of coffee. And so, he heaved a sigh as he settled into the groaning oak chair, and with his eyes on the pot across the room, rocked himself forward again.

"Sit," Ada said. "I'll bring you a cup. Two sugars?"

"Thank you, sweetheart. Three." He fell back into the chair.

Her desk was piled with cardboard signs printed variously with the theme of electing or re-electing Ada Reed to the office of Sheriff of Yellowpine County. Some had her picture printed on them, smiling but serious, she hoped. Some had the relevant text in blue and red against a white background. Some of the signs had been nailed, double-sided, to pointed stakes while others were left flat.

"These aren't doing you a lot of good here on the desk," Applegate said.

"Are you concerned for my re-election? You don't even want me running, Uncle Ephraim."

"No, I don't think you should."

"You want me to concede and let Jeff Banning have the job?"

"No. But if you were to pull out now, we could run Wickers in your place."

She had thought about pulling out of the race. There were days when she thought of nothing else, and yesterday had been front and center among those. Besides the frustrations of the job, she was not a good politician, and her instincts, if she were to base them on an inability to express even to herself why she should be the one doing the job, told her to get out. But the County Board wanted her out so dismissively she found herself staying maybe a little to spite them. And then there was Debbie Lynn, who was in trouble at home and needed her; and Ethel would be disappointed; and Maggie Li, whom she'd promised . . . She had to stay in it.

"You'll vote for me though, won't you Uncle Eph?" She cleared a space on the desk and set a cup of coffee down for him.

"Ada, I don't think you should do the job for your health, honey."

She hunched her shoulders, waiting to hear all about the danger she'd brought on herself by racing in front of a wildfire. But apparently, thank heavens, he'd not yet heard about that. He leaned forward and added, "Nor for the health of your marriage."

That was an easier argument. "What there may or may not be between me and Montgomery has little to do with this job," she said. "It's a lot older than that." *And deeper*, she thought. She'd gotten a letter from Montgomery a week earlier from somewhere near Incheon, although he couldn't say exactly where. The letter was just more of the same: more yelling, if that were possible in cursive script; more bullying. He didn't want her running for sheriff—it was an unattractive streak of self-importance, and damned embarrassing, besides. She had no idea of the realities of the job, and had she gone right out of her mind with the Yankee Fork business? Ada had heard and felt it all before; if not in those words, in others much like them. He might as well be scolding her from across the room as from across the Pacific.

She marshaled a smile for her uncle. "Besides," she said, "I don't think you should stay in your job for your health, either, Mr. Mayor, but that never stopped me from voting for you." She talked while wrangling the dogs, trying to get collars and leashes on them.

Applegate watched but did not help. "How many times did you damn-near get yourself killed in the Yankee Fork investigation? And no, I'm not apologizing for my language. You *damn*-near got yourself killed four times."

The dogs were not accustomed to collars and leashes, and she had to answer while chasing them around the office. "Uncle Eph, I . . . hardly think . . . I was near death."

"You were ambushed and shot at; your brake line was cut; you got yourself lost in a mine . . ."

"I wasn't lost."

"Hundreds of feet up rickety ladders in a goddamned crumbling mine; and you nearly got your brains smashed out with a boat gaff. That's four times in one investigation!"

"The ambush shouldn't count either. Whoever pulled the trigger either wasn't aiming to hit me, or he was such a poor shot I was never in danger."

"I'm serious young lady."

She got the dogs harnessed, stood with a bit of a lurch, and raked her hair back. "Got to go Uncle Eph. Turn the hot plate off when you leave?"

SHE STUCK A FEW CAMPAIGN SIGNS AND HER LUNCH behind the seat and put the dogs up in the cab of the pickup with her. It was not Ada's nature to ride with dogs, but Chief Munson had been concerned, the night before, that the low sidewalls of her pickup truck wouldn't keep them safe in back. They settled down on the seat after a while and didn't interfere so much with her shifting of gears.

The highway took her south out of the town of Camas between green pastures of the Salmon flood plain and the red, rocky cliffs of Buffalo Jump. Five miles out of town the pastures and woodlands pinched out and brown, sage-covered hills closed in around her.

Highway 75 through the canyon was not as hot as it had been the previous few days, but it was warm enough to soften the hard-packed gravel so her wheels drifted a little in the turns, and to vaporize the road oil so her eyes and nose burned with the fumes. At a straight stretch west of Clayton she downshifted and passed a flatbed piled high with junk cars, thought about stopping to ticket the guy, but let it go.

Her Uncle Ephraim worried for her, and he had a good heart. He just didn't know how to cope with a niece who wore boots and a badge. The truth was, she wasn't sure, either, how to reconcile what she was doing with who she thought she was, and there were long nights when she could barely remember how she'd come to be driving a pickup truck and wearing a gun.

Her uncle had been right in a way, she supposed. The Yankee Fork case had put her in danger, although the gold mine shouldn't count either. She'd scared the hell out of herself underground, but she was never in any real danger. The cut brake line was a different matter, though. That was real. And when the suspect had swung that gaff at her . . . She shuddered and told herself for the hundredth time she'd had no choice but to shoot.

An hour out of town she lost the oiled and well-graded surface when she turned north at Sunbeam Junction. From there, it was ten miles to Custer and she had only to deal with dust, rocks, and washboards. The valley opened after a few miles into the broad, flat dredging grounds of the Yankee Fork, where stacked tailings stretched for hundreds of feet on either side of the road. Her truck rose and fell and splashed through pools and runs of the broken river.

Once she rounded the gravel terrace above the town, Custer lay before her, jumbled as by a flood in the narrow pinch of the valley. The gold dredge floated silent and dark, its bucket line plunging down into the dark water six feet from shore, a high-water line already rusting on the sides of the barge. She drove through torn up and desecrated Bonanza—the Chinatown neighborhood—past the ashes of the roadhouse, and stopped at last at the town jail.

Chief Munson met her out front wearing yet another painfully bright western shirt. "Hope it's a better day today, Ada," he said. He met the dogs with a drink of water and half a spam sandwich for each. While Ada made use of the toilet facilities, Munson treated the paws of the two dogs with witch hazel and bag balm, then wrapped them up properly with gauze. The dogs didn't like the taste of witch hazel. They licked Munson's face.

He took a few of the campaign signs from her truck and pounded them into the ground on either side of Main Street. Munson seemed convinced Ada was the right person for the sheriff's job, and she wondered how he could be so free of second thoughts. She wished she could be.

Update 11:45 a.m. – Riding with Chief Munson.
Reconnoitering the Valley Creek burn.

THERE WOULD BE OVER-ANXIOUS RESIDENTS who wanted to see what was left of their places after the fire, but who could find themselves in trouble. And there would be the curious, of course, and the part-time opportunists as well. She and Chief Munson had to get back into the burn to let folks know the law was watching. They also had to get the hounds back to Mooch Neagle, who would be worried about them. As a consequence, the two law officers and the wayward dogs piled into Munson's pickup and headed west. They took Munson's rig because the sideboards were higher and safer for the dogs, he explained, and he owed the Sheriff's Department a tank of gas for the other day, anyhow.

Kellen Munson proved to be an inattentive driver when he was not being chased by a prairie fire. His way of looking at you when he conversed, though engaging when sitting on a bench or at a table, was less so in the tight curves of the lower Yankee Fork. The habit would not be compromised, so Ada found herself watching the road for him and pointing out the sharper curves, chuckholes, and other road hazards.

"Mooch is alright for being one of the Neagles," he was saying. "A little slow on the uptake, but a good kid. His brother Dolf is a little fast, and a troublemaker."

Ada kept her eyes on the road as she answered. "What kind of a name is Mooch?"

"Oh, heck, I think his real name is Murray. I'd change it too, if my name was Murray. Mooch is a good kid, though. Treats his dogs right, and that's okay in my book."

"What about his . . . . the gravel's pretty soft around this bend here."

"His brother Dolf?"

"This bend right here!" She waited until they were through safely, and asked, "What is Dolf short for, then?"

"Dolf is short for pain in the behind."

The rear end came around a little in a washboarded curve, so Munson slowed a fraction. He said, "Dolf is short for Randolph or Rudolph, I suppose. Or more likely Adolf, the way he carries on drinking and fighting."

The tight curves continued for another couple of miles before they made it safely to Sunbeam Junction, and there Munson took a right turn onto State Highway 75, toward Stanley. Once on the packed and graded surface, Ada took up a folder of reports which, she said, needed reading, and that kept the Custer police chief mostly quiet and mostly focused on the road. Half an hour later, they were back in Stanley, where they checked the bulletin board again and got the dogs a bowl of water.

Lettie Nance ran the grocery and gas station in Stanley, and she always caught Ada up on the high and the low gossip. She was also the mayor of Stanley and pretty much the town council, as it were. A short woman with coal black eyes and a salt-and-pepper bouffant, she'd caught Kellen Munson's eye, although he was the kind to play his cards close to his chest. She'd stalled out in Stanley some twenty years earlier and so far had outlived two Stanley husbands. She knew Munson liked her and was fine with it.

From Lettie's store, the two lawmen took their soda pops and headed west toward the Valley Creek burn and the Neagle farm. They started out on the same road they had limped into town on the previous day and were not enjoying that part of the drive. In any case, they got no farther than two miles from town before they were stopped by a roadblock manned by a half dozen firefighters. A blackened and sweat-streaked man of twenty or so waved them down.

The young man warned them the conditions were not yet safe and told them of a whole team of smoke jumpers who'd been out of contact most of the night. They'd only just been found, thank God, hugging boulders in the Payette River, where they'd had to scramble to escape the flames. Picturing it made Ada sick to her stomach. Munson argued where they were going would already be blackened, and therefore safe from fire. But the young crew chief advised patience. The embers were still hot enough to blow tires, he explained, and the unpredictable whirlwinds could set a gas tank ablaze.

With that in mind, and because their principal interest, the Neagle family, could not yet have returned to their farmstead, Ada and Munson headed back to Stanley. They were both okay, after the excitement of the previous day, not to push things.

Ada had packed a lunch of ham sandwiches for the two of them, so they stopped again at the log-and-timber general store and bought a couple more Nehi sodas and a bag of Clover Club potato chips. Lettie threw some bologna in the bag for the dogs, too, inasmuch as the refrigeration was on the fritz and the meat wouldn't keep. She let Ada and Munson know there had been trouble up at the Redfish campground, to which Munson touched the brim of his hat and told her they would see to it straight away. Ada was not at all eager to visit Redfish Lake, but she kept her misgivings to herself and started a new log entry.

Update 2:15 p.m. – South to Redfish Lake.
Trouble reported at the campground.

THE HIGHWAY SOUTH OUT OF STANLEY carried them hard by the river along willowy banks and broad rocky bars; it cut through tall-grass meadows and wound them between thickets of aspen and pine. Ada rode quietly for the most part, picking at a sandwich and watching out the passenger window where jagged peaks high above the valley haze caught the afternoon sun.

She'd grown up in the Salmon River country and, but for a few years away at college, had lived there her whole life. Nevertheless, she'd not been to the Salmon headwaters for some years except to drive through to Ketchum, and now the forests and waters along their route brought back a flood of memories. The truck swayed around bend after bend where she was able to pick out fishing holes and picnic sites she knew from those earlier years. But the memories themselves were colorless somehow, as though made of the same grey haze they were driving through.

Without a strong wind, days of stale forest fire smoke had pooled in the southern part of the valley and breathing got more difficult and mountaintops more shrouded as they drove deeper in. Forested moraines and broad, stream-stitched parks vanished into the gray pall. Green meadows faded too, and places Ada had camped with family years ago—places where tall, hardy people with tall tales built warm fires. There had been raft trips, too, and salmon so thick you could cross the stream on their backs.

Chief Munson kept glancing over his shoulder to check on the dogs, whose heads were stretched out over the railings and into the wind. Ada had barely conversed since they rolled out of Stanley. Munson asked, "Is there a problem?"

"No, of course not." She gathered her fine, fair hair out of the wind and watched the highway scroll backward in her side mirror. There was no problem, but no sense to it all either, and the vague misgivings she'd harbored at the outset of their drive returned. Those tall people and warm fires had gone away, and she'd some-how woken to find she was pretty tall, herself, and wearing a badge and a gun—and all alone. And there was nothing she could hold up and compare between then and now. It was like two uncon-nected lives, and the gap between them was only getting wider.

She slouched back in her seat and let the highway recede. A convoy of Forest Service vehicles passed them headed north; army-surplus trucks rumbling by with young men holding shovels, waving, and mugging from the sideboards—boys all much younger than Ada. She slumped down further and put her foot up on the dash.

Munson waved back to the trucks. "No problem, are you sure?" he asked.

"None at all."

She'd brought Montgomery to the Sawtooth Valley when he'd followed her from college with a diamond ring. That was ten years ago; maybe eleven. She taught him to fish in the rapids and beaver ponds of the Salmon, although he'd pretended he knew how. She'd been sweet and let him pretend. They were both like that then: nice to each other—back in the good times, whenever they were.

"It's been a while since I last visited Redfish Lake is all," she told Munson. "No problem."

The truck rose onto a rocky, sage-covered flat, then dropped again to the grasses and scattered stands of pine. A couple of miles rolled under them, and her butterflies grew stronger as they drew nearer the turnoff. She leaned her arm on the frame of the open window and her head on her arm and let her hair go. There had been good times with Montgomery; of course there had been—a full share of them if she was to be fair. She never would have married the man or followed him to Fort Benning if he hadn't swept her away as he did. He could be a million laughs when he wanted to be; and handsome, Good Lord! Not so handy with a fishing pole or a plow, but who could care when the guy looked like the damned Arrow Collar man. They'd honeymooned at Redfish, pitched their tent and cooked on a driftwood fire. God, they'd made love under the moon! But that was all part of the other life; the unconnected life.

Fifteen minutes out of Stanley, Munson turned in toward the hazy Sawtooth Mountains on a dirt road crossing through dry meadows. They had to roll up their windows despite the heat for all the dust billowing under their wheels, and Munson took it slowly for the dogs. It was all dying right in front of her: pine trees rusting, creeks drying up, grasses brittle and brown.

"Where's it all go?" she whispered.

"Is something up?" Munson asked.

"Let's just get there."

Montgomery had come back from Europe a different man after the Second World War ended. Or maybe he was the same man, but it took four years getting by on her own for her to see who he really was all along. And now he was off fighting again, and she had agreed to wear his badge, to hold the sheriff job open for him. Everyone said it would be only for a short while, but the war in Korea was dragging on, and Montgomery had written that he was duty-bound to extend his commission. She didn't write back to argue or dissuade, just as she hadn't argued when he accepted the re-instatement in the first place. He could have fought the recall. She could have fought with him about it. But maybe they'd both seen things falling apart at home; maybe they'd both felt it.

Munson bounced the pickup truck to a stop in the Forest Service campground on the east shore of the lake. Ada had wasted the half-hour drive. She had not come up with a single thought as to what to tell folks if they asked about food, or shelter, or fuel. Her worries grew as soon as the parking brake was set. Wall tents, canvas tarps, even blankets staked in front of open car doors made up a hobo jungle of forty or so displaced families scattered through the yellow pine and the boulders.

Munson got out and stretched, but Ada sat a minute longer with her arms crossed and her head leaned against the side window. The dread in the pit of her stomach she'd felt since they turned south out of Stanley now made her look around for some place she might run to and throw up.

"You ready?" the Chief asked.

"Sure." The lake breeze and all the memories of it hit her as soon as she stepped out. The sky above was a putty gray, and the water looked black and greasy. But it was a cool breeze from off the high peaks, and the lapping of the waves just a few yards away eased her jitters.

She grabbed her notebook and pen. "Let's get started," she said.

Update 3:05 p.m. – With Chief Munson:
interviewing displaced families at Redfish Lake

THE REFUGEE CAMPERS STOPPED WHAT THEY were doing and stared at the two lawmen as they entered. Even with the lake breeze there was a crowded, unwashed smell to the place. A dozen wood fires were burning, where women bent to prepare early meals, and the smoke swirled up and added to the pervading greyness. Ropes strung between tree trunks held diapers that flapped in the breeze, and she and Munson ducked them as they ventured through the shanty camp. Calves, sheep, and goats tethered to trees bawled; children ran loose, wailing; and men shouted angrily from somewhere back in the brush.

A few campers rose and followed them, but not closely. Some of the campers Ada recognized as refugees from the Twin Peaks fire three weeks earlier; a few others had been there since the Mill Creek fire. Most of them had nothing to return to: houses and barns were gone, crops gone, even the streams ran black with soot and silt, too thick to drink.

There was no center to the camp, no real gathering place, so she found a large, flat boulder, climbed up onto it, and waited for a small crowd to gather around. Marshalling a smile and as much confidence as she could pretend, she touched the brim of her hat, and asked the folks how they were getting on.

Well, there was no paper in the pit toilets, it turned out; there was no firewood left to be gathered; and there was no drinking water except in the creek, which flowed out of the lake where half the people did their wash. Ada took it down in her field book, writing as fast as she could and glancing up from time to time to see who it was adding a detail or a concern.

The shouting of the men back in the brush grew louder, causing Munson, with the dogs in tow, to disappear into the woods to check it out. Ada found herself alone in front of a growing crowd. The ones who'd followed and now stood around her were mostly the newcomers, and mostly women. They stood in jackets against the lake breeze if they'd remembered to grab them when they ran, or with blankets over their shoulders if they hadn't. They tried, even living out of boxes and car trunks, to look decent: they straightened their dresses with their hands as they walked up, and tucked strands of hair behind ears or under scarves.

A lot of men didn't come forward but stayed sitting—on the ground leaned against the yellow trunks of pine trees, or on running boards resting forearms on knees. They watched her with the look of country folk who asked little of their government and were used to getting it. The women stepped up with worry in their eyes. The men's eyes showed worry too, but that's where the sexes parted company. The men had let their clothes cake with soot, their hands and faces crust with dirt. The men looked angry more than anything—scared, yes, but angry and ready to fight someone. The women were not angry, and not scared but maybe a little, and Ada understood them to her core. They looked heartbroken more than anything; maybe even betrayed, and she knew that feeling as well.

An ache rose up in her chest and wouldn't go away, and she wanted to jump down off the rock. It wasn't right that she, of all people, should talk down to these folks. But she stayed, taking down names and making notes.

Although a little shaky in her voice, she said, "Uhm . . . yeah. Get drinking water from up-lake and do your wash downstream in the outlet creek." She cleared her throat. "Everyone—that's a rule now."

She lifted her hat and wiped her face on her sleeve. The cooking fires and the smell of too many animals and too few toilets had grown thick and was making her queasy. But she stayed up on the rock listening to one story of loss after another and offering what advice she could. Over the people's heads, smoke was pouring through the passes and settling in the long glacial basin, and wisps and strands of it snaked over the water. Redfish Lake was miles long, and deep and cold. It was crystal blue, usually, and she'd run barefoot on this beach—God, years ago as a child. But that had been the other life, now unconnected from where and what she was.

"Pool your labor, gas, and tools and haul firewood from the beetle-kill area near Alturas," she told them. "No permit required; I'll talk to Ben . . . to the Forest Service."

Somewhere in the trees not far from where she stood, she had honeymooned with Montgomery. But that, like the barefoot child, was gone—every smile, every fond memory she might have had of it, because this was also the shore, maybe just up the beach a ways, where she had camped alone; where she'd cowered really—when he was on a drunk, and she wasn't safe in her own home.

To the people she said, "You're on your own for toilet paper. I've heard equally good things about skunk cabbage and wooly mullion." She re-set her hat and tried to smile but crossed her arms over her breast.

"Is it safe to go back?" someone asked.

"No, it isn't safe . . . It, uhm . . ." She took a deep breath, and then another. "It is not yet safe into Valley Creek. Maybe soon, but they're blocking that off for one more day. If you're going to Knapp Creek, they want you to hold off for maybe a couple more days."

"You still have the dogs, I see." It was the woman with the flowered hat, whom they had met at the Stanley store.

Munson had returned and stood with the dogs in the back of the crowd. Ada gave him a smile and a shrug. He answered, "Yeah, we were hoping to get them back to their owner. Has anyone seen Mooch Neagle?"

Ada stuffed her hands in her pockets and looked aside while Munson talked with a couple of men who thought they might have seen the Neagles continuing on southward. Someone else said no, they more likely headed west toward Lowman. The words all jumbled together, though, and she didn't follow most of it.

The flowered woman said, "We're running out of anything to eat, Mrs. Reed." Folks nodded. A few stragglers sidled closer, and even those who'd stayed sitting turned their eyes up to her.

Ada nodded and took an extra moment to make sure no one heard the doubt in her voice. "There are USDA surplus commodities warehoused in Boise," she told them. "I'm talking to the bureau chief about getting some trucked up here."

She braced her hands on her hips and tried to look upbeat. "The fishing any good?" she asked. "Don't worry about a license. Hunting too, if you managed to save a deer rifle. I've already talked to the Fish and Game."

In the end, she was fine and the crowd disbursed in a better humor, although she wished she could have done more for them. She and Munson patrolled the length of the campground, speaking to as many folks as greeted them, and sharing what information they had. No one else had seen or heard from Mooch Neagle or his family.

They left Redfish near dark. Ada pretended to sleep against the door but, really, her mind and heart were too unsettled. Ever since she'd taken the sheriff job, her friends in town had been telling her the badge changed her, but they couldn't understand it had done nothing of the sort. The woman she used to be could never have put on the badge—not until she first had changed. Somehow, she had become a different person, and the trembling she still felt told her back there on the beach was where everything had begun to turn. She'd hidden out for three days the last time: another refugee sleeping in another goddamned car. That was five years ago, but it might as well have been fifty for the change in her. She couldn't sleep, but she was content after a while to lie against the door and listen to the road under their wheels.

CHAPTER THREE

Wednesday, 19 September, 7:00 a.m.
Back to Stanley.
Getting into the Valley Creek burn today.

IT WAS ANOTHER LATE START WITH dogs underfoot. She fed them, barely managed a poached egg and toast for her own breakfast, and left Camas under clear skies and a golden sunrise. From there westward, however, she and the dogs navigated a canyon thick with river mist and stale smoke. Chief Munson waited for her at Sunbeam Junction this time, and again she rode with him in his inattentively directed truck with Mooch Neagle's hounds riding in back.

They drove through Stanley without stopping this time and headed west to Valley Creek. Ada suggested they drive the dirt road on the north side of the meadows to keep an eye out for livestock and stragglers. And that was entirely sensible. But she also didn't care to take the highway again, past the place where they'd sat and waited for Ranger Ben McGann, and past the place where they'd left him surely to die. They drove the north side road slowly for about four miles and, around 11 o'clock, crossed the knife-sharp line between green meadow and bare, blackened prairie. Munson drove and Ada watched out the window without a lot of conversation between them. The forest fire was smoldering in the canyons far to the west, but the wind blew from the east, so the sky above had cleared. The cab of the truck quickly warmed under the full sun.

Another two miles of dirt put them in the deep canyon of Valley Creek. There, the foothills were charred as far as they could see. Underbrush was burned down to stubble, and the taller pines and aspens had lost all of their foliage if not most of their branches. Ash whirled across the hillsides, and cinders smoked in places. Munson drove slowly up the road, speechless for a mile or more. When he finally spoke, he said, "Lifeless," and that almost under his breath. But a slight movement caught Ada's eye, and she turned to see two prairie dogs hurrying about and digging in the baked soil.

The low ground cover was burned all the way to dirt in places, so that yellow and ochre soils banded the hillsides. A plume of gray ash followed in their wake, and with the breeze swirling around, they had to keep the windows up in spite of the heat to keep from being choked by it. The dogs in back fared poorly.

Only one other vehicle had gone in ahead of them, leaving tracks pressed into the ash. The tracks went just one way, so whoever had been on the road had either improbably survived the fire and driven out or had driven in after the fire burned through. The road crossed Valley Creek three times in three miles; twice fording the shallow, sandy-bottomed stream, and once crossing dangerously over a blackened timber bridge. The brush along the creek bottom was partly alive in places, although it was singed brown and red.

Munson stopped at a fourth crossing—another shallow ford of the channel—and they dropped the tailgate to let the dogs cool off in the water. Ada brought out a lunch she had packed. There was no shade whatever, but the splashing of the water sounded welcoming, and Ada felt a lifting of some of the gloom she'd felt since entering the burn. When she finally gave in and took off her boots, the cool water on her feet made the mid-day heat almost bearable. She only nibbled at a chicken leg but ate an apple to the seeds.

Munson rolled his shirt sleeves up to above his elbows. He said, "It's just a darned hot day, is all."

"It's a darned hot September." She soaked a bandana and spread the wet cloth over her head.

"What have you heard from Korea? Munson asked. "If you don't mind talking about it." He pressed the top of an orange Nehi against the edge of the tailgate, popping the cap, then handed the bottle to Ada.

"I don't mind." She pulled the tie from out of her collar as she talked and unbuttoned the top button of her duty shirt, then rolled up her pant legs and stuck her feet deeper into the creek. "They've been saying all summer they were in peace talks, but now I read they're only in talks about maybe holding peace talks. And in the meantime, China is sending ten divisions at a time across the Yalu."

"Wherever that is." He opened a bottle for himself.

"It's the river on the border." She rolled up the tie and stuck it in the picnic basket.

Munson said, "They've changed the draft, I hear. Every boy from eighteen to twenty-six has to register. Doesn't sound like they expect it to end soon."

"Jean Esker's son—he bags at the IGA—got a low number; she expects he'll have to go." She squinted into the sun. "Mont signed up for another tour, you heard."

"Yeah. And the Russians keep testing atomic bombs. I wonder how long before they enter the war." He wiped his hands on his jeans and opened the Cracker Jacks, then noticed Ada looking away into the distance. "Oh, shoot. I didn't mean nothing, Ada."

"Don't worry about me." She took a long swallow of the Nehi and a handful of Cracker Jack.

Munson said, "It's a hell of a war, I hear. But Montgomery knows what he's doing."

"It's not even a war but a police action. I don't think it makes a lot of difference to the boys."

It didn't make any difference to her, either. There were a

thousand ways for a man who knew what he was doing to get himself killed, and calling something 'merely a police action'—or 'simply a grass fire'—didn't lessen the chances.

Ada and Chief Munson and their canine companions continued north, where the canyon got deeper and steeper sided. The car tracks they'd been following eventually turned off to the right and crossed a charred bridge before twisting out of sight up a draw. At that point Munson suggested they turn around, inasmuch as there were no other tracks in the ash, which meant the Neagles could not yet have returned. Ada agreed, but before they could find a wide spot to make the turn, they came across a dead animal in the middle of the road. It was a blue tick hound. Munson got out and pulled the remains to the side of the road, shaking his head the whole way and looking sick about it when the two dogs in back began to whine.

When he got back behind the wheel, Ada said, "We have to keep going, Kel. I have a bad feeling."

"Yeah."

In another mile the canyon bent hard to the east, and all there was in front or side to side was black ash and red volcanic rock. There were no colors at all but those and the blue of the sky. Munson turned up a narrow track and nodded ahead. The forests all around were reduced to scattered black spikes sticking up out of the soil, devoid of branches and burned down to half their heights. With nothing else to obstruct the view, the Neagle place could be seen nearly a half mile up the slope.

He crawled the truck slowly into the barnyard and eased it to a stop. Ada stepped from the pickup into a couple of inches of light gray ash that puffed and eddied when she shut the truck door. They hadn't walked but a few steps before they'd kicked up clouds of ash around them. The ash, with a light swirling breeze, choked them so that they had to tie bandanas around their faces to breathe.

The house itself was easy enough to identify by its stone chimney, which stood above a rectangular foundation filled with smoking cinders. Counter-clockwise from the house were what might have been a tool shed, then a stone water well with the wooden frame and windlass mostly intact. An expanse of corrugated tin sagged over a high concrete foundation, marking the barn, she assumed, while pens and corrals outside were outlined by burnt posts and a few pieces of charred fencing. A horse carcass lay against one fence, blackened and oozing, and starting to bloat, but without flies yet gathered to it. Counter-clockwise from the dead horse was the road they'd driven in on, and then another ash-covered two-track trail leading a few hundred yards into a field. The homesite looked primordial to Ada as she turned to take it in. It looked as though all the husks and vestures had been shed and the earth showed itself bare as the day it was created.

"No one's home," she said through her bandana.

"I hope you're right."

"What do you mean?"

"Well, there's a car here that didn't make it out." Munson shuffled over to what once had been a Studebaker sedan—1941 or older—but was now a heap of burnt and already rusting tin. Ada followed slowly. The car was parked squarely in the middle of the farmyard. The interior of the car was gutted black and was empty, thank God, and no keys hung in the ignition. The back end was ruptured from what must have been the gas tank exploding.

"It was gassed up," Munson said.

"Maybe it was broken down."

"Saw it in town last week, I'm pretty sure."

Ada called out, "Anybody here?" then stood still to listen, feeling a little foolish. She heard only her own and Munson's breathing. With no trees or even brush to rustle in the breeze, and the ash muffling their footsteps, the place returned an ear-ringing silence. The dogs in the back of the truck, though, paced nervously and just then started up a low moaning.

She shuffled over to the collapsed barn and peered through a gap in the bent and broken tin. There were tools hanging from blackened posts, and farm implements sitting on a wooden floor too thick and mud-caked to burn through. She saw no victims, human or animal, inside. Continuing to the corner of the barn, a steel gate hung open and steel cyclone fencing contained a good-sized dog run. A padlock and chain hung from the gate. The padlock was locked, but the gate had been opened by prying the chain off of the wooden post. An iron staple hung on a link of the chain.

"Mother of God!" Munson shouted.

Ada wheeled around to see him stepping forward again apparently after having jumped back several feet. He stood looking down in the center of the barnyard not twenty yards from where they'd parked the truck. She hurried over but stopped short at the sudden realization that an irregular, flattened lump under the ash blanket at Munson's feet was a body—a very unmistakably human body.

"Oh, no, no, no!" She sidestepped the last few feet, shivering head to foot even in the broiling heat. "Who is it?" she asked softly.

"Can't tell."

She raised her hat and swept back her hair, then dropped to one knee near the body. "Do you suppose we should sweep off the ash?" she asked.

"Well, we have to, or we can't, you know, identify . . . it."

"Identify him. It's most likely a man from the . . . you know, overall shape."

Munson nodded. "Sweep it how?"

"I don't know."

But she retrieved her camera from the seat of Munson's pickup and grabbed one of her cardboard campaign signs from behind the seat. She photographed the victim as found from several directions. Then, with her bandana tied tight across her nose and mouth, she fanned the air above the body with the cardboard. Most of the fine ash was swirled away in less than a minute, but the ash billowed around them and it took another couple minutes for the air to clear.

The victim's arms had been raised above his head, and bits of denim remained in the grasp of skeletal fingers and at the armpits, as though he'd pulled his jacket over his head against the heat and flames. It hadn't helped. The body lay face down, burned to bones and charred flesh on the back side. He wore western boots, which were largely melted.

Ada photographed the victim where he lay in place, and then Munson, with bandana pulled up to his eyes and a pair of heavy leather gloves, rolled the body over. Although logically as it should have been, the clothed and un-burned front side was a bit of a shock to both of them. The young man wore a green plaid western shirt and blue jeans, and an Indian-head dollar belt buckle. Although his cheeks were charred badly and the hair on his head was gone, the center of the face was untouched but by the dirt of the barnyard he'd tried to burrow into. He had full eyelashes and a pleasant mouth: a young man of maybe twenty-two or -three.

"Gosh darn, poor Mooch," Munson said. The moaning of the dogs in the truck rose to a howl.

"You're sure it's Mooch?" She took a couple more photos, clicking and winding and repositioning herself and clicking to help keep her stomach down.

"Yeah. Mooch was a good kid. Dolf would have a scar over the left eye—from a beer bottle. A fight a couple of years ago in Sunbeam."

On the ground where the body had lain, Ada picked up a steel implement: a pry bar. "He's the one who kept the dogs?" she asked. "Looks like he let them out just in time."

"Why didn't he use a key on the lock?"

"Good question." Ada stood and wiped sweat and ash from her face. Her head floated, and she had to drop a moment and lean with her hands on her knees. The baying, and now yelping, unnerved her—like the hounds of hell, she thought.

She caught as deep a breath as she could through the bandana and stood. "I guess we'd better check the house," she said.

"Guess so." Munson followed behind her, and they shuffled slowly over to the smoldering tangle of timbers, pipes, and cinder blocks laid out under the standing chimney. The covering of ash wasn't as thick over the remains of the house, possibly because the burning and smoldering there kept the air above agitated so the ash couldn't settle. And that's probably why they were able to spot the old man's remains as quickly as they did. The black, Pompeiian thing was in a sitting position, found among burned and cindery remnants of what had to have been a rocking chair, about where the front porch of the house would have stood.

It took a while longer to find Mrs. Neagle—Irma, Munson believed was her name. It took the Chief stepping cat-like amongst the ashes and half-burned timbers of the main structure, poking and prodding with the pry bar Ada had found, and testing the burned-out floor with his boot here and there. The old woman's deeply burned remains lay under a blanket of fallen ceiling plaster, upon the iron springs of her own bed. Ada was able to make her way in to photograph the disposition and state of the deceased, but between smoldering fumes, the heat of the day, and the hellish tableau, she had to let Munson help her back out.

There was no shade, the breeze had died, and the ash had so caked like sour-smelling mud to their bandanas they had to fight for each breath. Munson walked Ada back to the pickup truck and sat her in the cab. It was hot there too, but at least she was out of the sun.

She sipped from a jar of water, then handed the jar to Munson. "We have to get the bodies back to town, Kel."

"Huh-uh. Not today." He walked back and let the dogs lap water from his hand.

"We have to. They'll decompose in this heat."

"Ada, now listen. It would take the two of us hours to get the bodies out of the wreckage of that house, and in the meantime these dogs are already suffering in the heat. Plus, we'd do a poor job of recovery if it's just the two of us. We'd end up messing things up. We ain't got but one tarp with us, anyway. And hell, I ain't putting Mooch's body in the back of this truck where his own dogs will know him."

"They already know him."

Her head was spinning and stomach churning again, and she didn't argue further. "I guess they've been lying here two days already and they won't get any worse overnight. But I'll have to come back tomorrow. First thing."

"We'll bring help tomorrow. You sit a spell, and I'll look around for anyone else."

"For the brother?"

"Yeah."

He moved on and Ada stood, though she had to catch and steady herself on the door of the truck. The sun was high by then, and all around was smoking cinders and ash whirling up into twisters where the slightest breeze caught it. The hills behind the house were scorched to the yellow and red soils and dotted with coarse red volcanic outcrops. *Primordial*, she thought. She closed her eyes and coughed, then took another drink from the jug. . . . *Before the animals each of their kind*, she remembered from a Sunday long ago. *"Before the waters were divided . . ."*

"What's that?" Munson called back.

"Nothing. God, but it doesn't take much to undo it all, does it?"

Munson looked around for another quarter hour as Ada recuperated in the truck, her head resting now and then on the dashboard. He checked the barn, the corral area, and the tool shed, and walked the perimeter of the homestead for any sign of Dolf having panicked and run into the woods. There was nothing at all of the older brother; no sign he'd even been there.

Before leaving, Munson turned Mooch's body face down again and covered it with the tarp, then weighed the tarp down with chunks of cinder block. At the first stream crossing on the drive out, both Munson and Ada got down into the water with the dogs, and they all drank, and waded, and washed away the grit and the smell of death.

Chapter Four

Thursday, 20 September, 4:30 a.m.
Victim recovery in Upper Valley Creek
Joined today by USFS and State Police

The sky was pitch black at 4:30 the next morning. Ada treated the feet of Mooch Neagle's orphan dogs and left the two of them in her backyard with a bowl of food and a large soup bone to share. With her gear stashed behind the seat, then, she drove her cherry-topped county truck to the White Cloud Ranger Station, which sat across the highway from town. The early start was necessary, all had agreed, because victim recovery would better be done in the cool of the morning. District Ranger McGann would help, but Custer Police Chief Munson could not make it. Smoke from yet another fire was blowing up over Loon Creek Pass and had the residents of Custer in a panic. Instead, Sergeant Ken Blevins of the Idaho State Patrol would come along. Ada caught sight of his black and white Pontiac Chieftain in the parking lot and paused for a deep breath before putting on a pleasant face.

McGann was waiting with his Power Wagon loaded to the brim with tents, water cans, grub boxes and shovels: supplies for the crews mopping up in Knapp Creek. He would continue on from the Neagle place but felt it his duty to see first-hand what the fire had done there. The equipment was neatly stowed and cinched down tight, and there wasn't room in the cab, Ada noticed regretfully, for a passenger. That meant Sergeant Blevins would have to ride both ways with her.

Sergeant Blevins stared at the equipment in McGann's front seat with a look of disappointment matching her own. He threw his gear behind her seat, anyway, and climbed in as a passenger, his knees crowding almost to the jockey box. She thought about sliding the seat back to accommodate the six-foot-two trooper but decided keeping her own feet on the pedals was more important.

In the bare pre-dawn they followed McGann out the gate and up the highway toward Stanley. The pavement ended two miles out of town. "Got tarps and ropes?" Sergeant Blevins asked at the junction of U.S.93.

"Got 'em."

"Medical Kit?" he asked a mile farther down Highway 75.

"It'll be a little late for first aid."

"Rubber gloves?"

They were not friends, she and Blevins. He'd tried to bluff and bully her off the Yankee Fork case back in July, and she'd dunked his head in a toilet. Actually, she'd barely got his forehead wet, but she'd disarmed him and kneed his kidneys pretty severely.

"Got 'em," she said.

"Lunch?"

"You didn't bring a lunch?"

Little more was said for an hour and forty minutes. She kept the truck in fourth gear most of the way, and the two law officers watched straight ahead as their headlights swept the hills and the oxbow meadows. Only a few cars passed them coming the other way, and they caught only glimpses of McGann's taillights ahead on the highway. The engine purred and the rabbit's foot swayed below the mirror in rhythm with the bends of the road. It seemed to annoy her passenger. "What's with the rabbit's foot?" He asked at one point. "You're not superstitious?"

"Not even a little," she answered. The rabbit's foot had belonged to a young woman, Rose Braden, who had died in the Yankee Fork three months earlier. Ada never knew Rose when she lived, but the girl's life—how she'd lived it—changed how Ada saw her own life, and how Rose died had done as much to keep Ada wearing the badge as anything else she could name. She held onto the rabbit's foot although she really had no right to it. "I'm keeping it for a friend, is all," she said.

It was light by the time they made Stanley, although the sun had not yet climbed above the high ridges. Ada told the attendant to fill the tank, then ran to the restroom while Blevins popped into the store and bought a tin of tuna and a couple bottles of warm soda.

The roadblock had been moved to the west end of town, and two uniformed forest service personnel were explaining to the driver of a station wagon which roads were open and which were not. District Ranger McGann had a quick word with the crew chief and the barricade was pulled aside for the recovery team.

Lower Valley Creek Road had seen more traffic since she'd come out with Munson the previous afternoon, but the tracks, one by one, turned off or turned around, and there were no new tire tracks once the canyon walls closed in on the black and bare upper Valley Creek.

At the Neagle farm, the embers of the barn and main house had stopped smoldering, and the wind had blown the ashes around so that bare ground showed between drifts. The sun by then had topped the ridge. There were no clouds, and already the day was warm.

The state cop, Blevins, insisted on writing up his own notes and taking his own photographs before they could move Mooch Neagle's body. After that, it took them just a few minutes to wrap the young man in a tarp and stow him in the bed of the county pickup.

The old man's body was more difficult because he had been cooked into a sitting position. After due photography and a sampling of the wood pieces found under him—an oak rocking chair they eventually agreed—they tackled the wrapping issue. Blevins actually proved himself useful folding and tying the package, and they put the old man, Clifford, into the bed of the truck sitting up and leaning against the back of the cab.

Irma's body was the most troublesome. It had burned onto the bedsprings and would not lift off without falling to pieces. But District Ranger McGann found some wire cutters among his gear, and with a great deal of deliberation they cut the wires and springs one by one to sort-of free her. The half-cremated body thus extracted was fragile, and they took great care as they wrapped it. It was early afternoon by the time they finished with Irma.

Ada had drunk nothing the whole morning, but now gulped water from the Thermos jug. She was not hungry at all. She and McGann sat on the running boards of their trucks, leaning elbows on knees, facing each other although not looking at each other. Blevins sat up on the edge of the pickup bed, also hunched forward. He swigged his Coca Cola and McGann drank from a canteen, but neither suggested a pause for lunch.

Ada said, "The fire had to have caught them by surprise. Irma didn't even make it out of bed and Mooch didn't have time to find the keys to the dog run. He had to use a pry bar to open the gate."

McGann had spoken little all morning, perhaps sensing Ada's exasperation with his grass-fire heroics. He said, "I can't hardly believe that. They'd have seen the fire top the ridge three miles away. It would have been too loud to sleep when it was still a mile away. It would have roared like a freight train coming down the slope."

Blevins said, "Maybe they got themselves too drunk to see the fire coming."

McGann shook his head. "The fire would have burned through here between seven and ten Monday morning. I doubt they'd all have been so drunk that time of day they couldn't get in the car and try to leave."

Maybe they thought they were invincible and could hide behind gravel piles, Ada thought but didn't say. She looked from one to the other and stayed quiet with her elbows on her knees.

Blevins said. "Then they must have been dead before the fire, and the fire came in and overwhelmed everything else in terms of evidence." He took a long drink from his soda and shook his head. "No, the old man wouldn't sit down in his rocker as the fire was coming, and the old woman lie in her bed. I don't care how drunk they were. They had to have been dead prior."

He untied his bandana, shook it out, and rinsed it with a bit of the water. "I once came on a whole family dead from botulism," he said. "Five of them dead as doornails sitting around the picnic table. A jar of home-canned green beans is what got 'em—right there between the salad and the sausages." He ran the wet bandana over his head, rinsed it again, then tied it around his face.

Ada squinted at the sun and mopped her brow with her bandana. She said, "It's a possibility, Ken, but I don't know. Mooch wasn't dead, was he? I mean he pried open the kennel so the dogs could run away. He wouldn't have let them out ordinarily. He was letting them escape from danger. And just in time too, because two of the dogs were burned and another didn't make it at all. Mooch was alive until he was overwhelmed by the flames."

McGann said, "Murder then? Maybe Mooch hid when his folks were killed and came out after the killer had gone."

"Or maybe he was the killer," the State cop suggested.

"Hold on." Ada had loosened her tie, and she unbuttoned her collar. "We're assuming the folks were not alive when the fire caught them . . ."

"Ada, you don't sit down in your rocker with a forest fire roaring down on you . . ."

". . . and now we're assuming it was murder. Let's let the coroner weigh in on both those questions." She ran the wet bandana under her collar. Both men shrugged.

She said, "Munson says Mooch was a good kid. He loved his dogs. What I want to know is, where was his brother; where was Dolf Neagle when the fire came through?"

Blevins looked up and nodded. McGann asked, "How'd Dolf get along with his family?"

"Good question. Sergeant, I guess you should put a notice out on your wire for Dolf Neagle."

"Suspect?"

"Person of interest." She wiped her face and took another deep drink of water. "Right now, let's see what else we can find around here."

Blevins re-loaded his camera, and he and Ranger McGann poked around together under the fallen metal roof of the barn. Ada walked a perimeter around the place to see if maybe the older brother, Dolf, had panicked and run into the woods. The walking was no hotter than standing, and it calmed her stomach a little. She found an old root cellar on the hill behind the house, and with the sick feeling returning, kicked away the charred wooden doors. But when she looked inside there was nothing but a few digging tools and some ruined potatoes.

She finished her walk and was thirsty again, and that was probably why her eyes were drawn to the well. It was an old-fashioned stone well with a roof and windlass, both badly charred, and it stood out back about halfway between the house and the root cellar. Ada went to it and tried to pull up the bucket, but the bucket wouldn't budge. The windlass was not jammed, but the bucket was stuck down the well. She found a piece of window glass nearby, rubbed it clean against her pant leg, and positioned it to reflect sunlight down the well. She eventually found the right angle, and the beam of light reached all the way to the bottom, where it found Dolf Neagle staring up at her, glassy-eyed and open-mouthed.

Ada jumped back, dropping the glass and falling on her behind. She probably screamed as well, because the trooper and the ranger came tearing around the barn in a cloud of ash. She made it back to her feet before they got to her but could only point to the well when they asked what the devil it was. McGann shined the broken glass down the hole, and the three of them peeked over the edge. Dolf was still there, crumpled and wedged, and half submerged.

"Dead," Blevins said. "Looks like maybe the killer—somebody—threw him down the well."

"Uhm, not exactly."

"What now, Ada?"

"Well, I mean if he was thrown down the well, wouldn't it have been headfirst? He's jammed in feet first, and his head is above the water. My guess is he climbed into the well himself."

"Why's he dead, then?"

McGann said, "Probably suffocated down there from the smoke and gasses."

"Doesn't look smoky."

"Wind's been blowing."

STATE PATROL SERGEANT BLEVINS COULD NOT GO down the well to recover the body because he was too big around the shoulders to squeeze in next to the deceased in order to get a rope around him. It was possible District Ranger Ben McGann was slim enough, but he was a tall man, and the reach would be tough; plus there remained the question of whether Blevins and the acting sheriff would be strong enough to pull him out if he got into trouble.

"Ah, Shit!" Ada said.

Blevins didn't try to hide his grin. "It'll look good on your campaign literature."

"Thanks, Ken."

McGann looked from one to the other. "You're not going down there," he said. "Are you out of your mind? Wait for more help."

She eyed him for a moment and shrugged. "Have to get him up."

"It's stupid, Ada."

"Yeah well, we do stupid things in our jobs, don't we, Ben?"

"Ada, it's nuts!"

But she already had her utility belt off. She took off her tie, then took off her boots because they were thirty-dollar goddamn boots. She took off her badge for no apparent reason and put on a pair of leather gloves. McGann, silent and unsmiling, retrieved a sturdy rope from the Power Wagon, which he looped between her legs, not all that gently, making a climber's harness around her middle.

Handing her Stetson to Blevins, then, she eased over the stone wall and lowered herself hand-over-hand on the bucket rope while McGann belayed her with the harness rope.

The air cooled almost immediately as she dropped below ground level, and it smelled dank and a little smoky. A gloom surrounded her as she descended, but her eyes adjusted to it until the mouth of the well glowed like a full moon above her. The smell of smoke got heavier at about two thirds of the way down, so she yelled for McGann to hold her there for a minute. Bracing herself against the interior wall and taking her glove in her teeth, she pulled a box of matches from her shirt pocket and struck one. It burned bright yellow. She took a moment longer to marshal her courage, then yelled up, "Looks good. I guess . . . let's . . . take me down."

She was not watching below as she lowered herself, and she stepped on Dolf Neagle's head. The men heard her shriek and started pulling her out, but she yelled up she was okay and needed another five feet of slack. McGann obliged her, and she slid down to where she was eyeball-to-eyeball with the dead man. Her legs were in the water to her thighs.

Dolf Neagle was a young man of about twenty-five—*was*, Ada thought grimly. His face was so pale it almost glowed in the dim light, and there was a faint purplish marbling to the skin. The eyes were waxy and almost black. He did not smell badly of decay, though, as she had feared he would, and in fact he smelled like . . . pomade, for Christ's sake! His hair was slick with it. But although he'd probably been dead for more than two days, the body had been preserved—probably by the same chilly water that was causing her already to shiver.

"Colder'n a well digger's ass down here," she mumbled.

"What was that?"

"Um . . . it's cold down here. Sergeant Blevins, make a note, please."

There was bloody vomit on the young man's chin and shirt, which she also reported up to Blevins. "Rope burns on the hands. He lowered himself in here, but not gracefully." The examination and the reporting helped to keep her stomach down. "No signs of trauma. No bruising, at least in the front."

She needed to slide another two feet down to get to the end of the bucket rope, and when McGann accommodated her, she sank into the icy well water to her ribs. "Shit!" she cried.

"What was that?"

"Shit. Just shit! That's not part of the notes."

She was able, barely by pressing her head and shoulder hard against the man's stiffened arm and stomach, to reach between his twisted legs and pull the water bucket up a few feet. She was wet, at that point, from toes to shoulder, and she started shaking badly. But she was able, just barely between the shaking and the cramping of her legs, to get her pocketknife from her pocket and cut the bucket away. She pulled the rope free, then called to be raised two feet, from where she was able to snake the rope around the dead man's torso and under his arms and tie it off.

Her breaths were coming short and shallow, she was shaking violently, and her stomach ached like she would throw up.

"Okay, pull me up," she called, "Get me up!" No longer able to help, she held onto her belay rope and let the men heave her out.

Ada couldn't undo the harness herself. She let McGann help her, then stumbled a few feet and sat shivering in the dirt and ashes. The day was turning into another scorcher, but she was chilled to the bone and the sun felt good. Blevins dusted off her Stetson and stuck it on her head for her. McGann asked her if she wanted a smoke. She could only shake her head, then managed somehow to put on her socks and boots.

The men struggled to pull the heavier Dolf Neagle from the well, bending over the low wall and heaving hand over hand. They dropped him once with a distant, hollow splash, and Ada knew she should help, but she was too busy fighting the shakes and her stomach. She got to her feet, as the men heaved again, and staggered to her truck for a drink of water. But when she took the water jug and a cigarette to the tailgate for a break, she came upon the three tarped and tied cadavers, and she threw up after all.

"We got him," Blevins yelled from over by the well, "if you want to complete your exam."

"I'll rely on your notes, Ken," she called back weakly. She took her cigarette and sat down on the running board of McGann's Power Wagon, and there she cried and shook pretty hard. But she cried for just a minute, and she was fine by the time the men carried Dolf Neagle, in a tarp, to her truck.

Update 2:45 p.m. – Four victims recovered.
Transporting to Salmon Valley Clinic in Camas.

All down Valley Creek to Stanley, then all down the canyon to where the Camas Valley opened up, Ken Blevins argued for a murder case. Ada, still damp from cuffs to collar and starting to chafe, focused on the road and let him talk. "I think you can cancel the APB for Dolf Neagle," she offered at one point. But otherwise, she mostly let him talk.

"They had enemies, Candidate Reed. The Neagles didn't live on the edge of the wilderness because they were overly popular. They weren't trying to get away from adoring fans."

"I'll look into it, Sergeant Blevins."

"So will I."

"Jurisdictionally, I believe I'm lead on this case."

"If the suspect . . ."

"Suspect?"

"I have my suspicions," he said. Ada turned left onto Main Street instead of right into the ranger station. Blevins checked his watch, rolled his eyes, and said, "If the suspect crossed county lines to commit the crime or to evade capture, then it's my jurisdiction."

"Until then, I'll rely on you to keep our highways safe and passable." It was a wise crack, but her wet uniform chafed, and she had four dead people in the back of her truck.

The alley between 6th and 7th brought them to the delivery lot behind the green cinder block clinic. Dr. Dennis Mink opened the overhead door when she rang, and the three of them spent an hour carefully unwrapping the bodies and lifting and wheeling them into Mink's walk-in cooler. There were not enough gurneys for the whole Neagle family, however, so the old man, Clifford, was left partly wrapped and sitting on the floor, propped against the back wall of the cooler. Ada stuffed the other tarps into a large garbage bin in the alley, then pulled closed the overhead door and joined the men in the examination room.

"Why are you bringing them here?" Mink asked for a third time. "Don't they belong with the undertaker?" He looked not at all pleased.

"Sorry, Dennis, but there appears to be some question as to the circumstances attending their deaths." She glanced at Sergeant Blevins, who was scrubbing his hands at the sink.

Mink said, "Not much of a question, at first glance."

Blevins dried his hands on a surgical towel, making Mink wince, and said, "There's a good chance foul play occurred before the fire swept through. We need you to autopsy these victims and determine a cause or causes of death."

"Okay. And who should I bill?" the doctor asked.

"It's Yellowpine County's jurisdiction," Blevins said.

Update 11:00 p.m. – Home.
Left victims' remains with Dr. Mink and
dropped Sergeant Blevins at his black and white.

THE WANING HALF-MOON WAS RISING OVER the Pahsimeroi Hills by the time Ada arrived home. She'd forgotten about the hounds left alone in her back yard, but was reminded by Mrs. Winslow next door, who rang her phone not three minutes after she'd dumped her notebook, Stetson, necktie, and duty belt on the kitchen table.

"They barked all day," her neighbor complained over the telephone, "Wouldn't shut up for anything. Is this going to be a regular thing, Ada?"

"No, Karen. It's very temporary. The dogs are part of . . . the displacements due to the fire up in the Stanley area." She worked one boot off with the other.

"Because there are laws about that sort of thing."

"I'm aware . . ." She held the phone against her shoulder as she tugged the second boot off.

"Disturbing the peace not the least," Winslow went on. "I talked to Officer Stengel about it."

"Thank you, Karen, I look forward to hearing from Stengel . . . Yes, they're in for the night." She covered the mouthpiece and banged the receiver on her forehead. "I understand, Karen. Jeff Banning is a good candidate too. Good night."

She brought the dogs in—she had no idea what their names were—and opened two cans of Ken-L-Ration for them. While they wolfed the food, Ada threw the windows open to get a cross breeze through the one-story ranch-style house.

She'd wanted to wash off the grit and well water all day but hadn't been able to do anything but wash her hands and face in the creek driving out and her hands again at the clinic. She retired to a hot bath and scrubbed herself raw from head to foot.

A cold ham sandwich had to do for dinner, and she ate it while patrolling the house, picking up the magazines, doilies, and knickknacks the dogs' tails swept from the tables and chairs. A pile of mail lay under the slot, and she gathered it onto the kitchen table. Montgomery had written again from somewhere in Korea, and she sat at the kitchen table to read his letter with the dogs crowded around her feet. Montgomery's two brief, handwritten pages contained little more than another cussing out for her wanting to stand for sheriff in the election. Dave Wickers could take over the job, Mont insisted, and Ada was in way over her head. She sighed and stuffed the pages back into the envelope. "His letters have been a bit cold," she explained to the dogs, "Since I shot and killed his best friend." The dogs raised their brows but kept their chins on the linoleum. Mutt and Jeff, she decided, would do for names, but which was which?

The local newspaper, the Camas Currier, was two days old, but she shuffled through it for ten minutes anyway. On page one, *"Hellfire, and nothing short of it!"*—she rolled her eyes—was *". . .ravaging the whole of central Idaho like a harsh judgement of the Lord!"* Pages two and three were given to the Labor Day parade, which apparently had been *"A great success this year . . . thanks entirely to Cheryl Miller and Betty Hopson"*—bless their bony asses.

From the editorial page, Ada learned that the idea of *". . . Mrs. Reed wearing a man's pants and tie was an abomination, surely not unnoticed by a righteous God."*

"Well, bless my bony ass, too," she told the dogs.

She tossed the Currier into the firewood box and called Mutt and Jeff out for a final go at nature. The back patio was mercifully cool, and the Milky Way was bright, so she sat awhile in the folding chair with a smoke and a glass of brandy. The yard screeched, at first, with crickets and cicadas, but eventually just buzzed with them as her mind unwound the events of the day.

At the clinic, Dr. Mink's initial examination had found no bullet wounds or blows to the skull on any of the victims. "I can't guarantee bullets didn't enter elsewhere—through the torso," he had allowed. "Especially the older folks; they're just too messed up to say right now."

"What about other trauma?" Sergeant Blevins had asked him.

"You mean like broken bones?"

"Exactly," Blevins demanded. "No broken necks or skulls? No fingers broken in defense?"

Dr. Mink had seen nothing of the sort, but it was, he emphasized, a very preliminary exam. Ada had tried to stand out of the way and listen, although the jitters had returned by then. She'd washed her hands at the sink but felt gritty from head to foot with ash and sweat, and being too near to dead, burnt bodies. Blevins didn't want to have to come back tomorrow, so he had kept up the pressure. There'd been no ligature marks on the boys, although the two old folks, well hell, they were pretty messed up like he said. Stab wounds would be hard to see in the old folks as well, but the boys, again, showed nothing of the sort.

She had settled heavily onto a bench with her notebook and pen in hand, listening for something useful to jot down. "I give up, Dennis," she told the doctor. "How did they die?"

Mink sat as well, looking all worn out. The heat and the fires, he told them, had been hard on the whole county, and the clinic had been busy all week long—damned domestic trouble. He would run some blood tests on the Neagles, but his initial guess was immolation.

Blevins had remained standing through the whole exam. It was late by then, and he was impatient to get the information he wanted and to get on the road. He scoffed at the doctor. "They didn't just sit down and burn to death, for Christ's sake!" He snatched up his Smokey Bear hat, and with nothing further said, she'd given him a ride back to his cruiser.

The brandy burned in her throat and brought her back to the stars and the shrieking insects. She lit a second cigarette, not ready yet for sleep where she would almost certainly find Dolf Neagle waiting for her.

CHAPTER FIVE

Friday, 21 September 1951
Working in town today.
Follow-up at Salmon River Clinic

THE ANIMAL SHELTER HAD NO ROOM for the dogs, and no one she called had a place for them. She decided to lock the two blue tick hounds inside the house to head off a repeat with Winslow next door. A few minutes were given to elevating knick-knacks, lamps, and vases, and she spread an old quilt over the davenport. She made a lunch, filled a canteen with water, and drove to the clinic.

To Ada's relief, Dr. Mink met her in his office rather than in the refrigerated examination room. "What's that Sergeant's problem?" he asked as she sat down in the oaken swivel chair facing his desk.

"Blevins doesn't like me."

"Yes, I rather picked up on that." Mink wore a clean white smock, which he must have recently changed into, since he'd have been up to his elbows in burned flesh all morning. A small but fit man with prematurely-graying hair, Ada had known him casually from the golf course and from the occasional charity soiree in what seemed already a by-gone era. Never married, he dressed and groomed fastidiously and was always well spoken and polite. They'd not been close friends, per se, but she liked and respected the man now, and believed he felt the same toward her. In the harsh morning light he looked even more tired than Ada felt, and she knew it was from the trouble in the valley: the medical problems attending the domestic problems that seemed to amplify with all the hot weather and drought.

"I found no broken bones pre-fire," he told her. "There were some breaks associated, I'm pretty sure, with the removal and transport of the bodies. Especially with Mrs. Neagle—she was badly cooked and embrittled."

The remark caught Ada off guard, and she had to look away and grimace. He didn't notice. "There were no ligature marks I could discern," he went on, "nor penetration wounds—again as far as can be seen given the condition of the bodies."

"So how did they die?"

"My money is still on the fire."

"It's odd," she said.

Dr. Mink had to excuse himself to see to a live patient. It would only be a minute, he promised. Ada, in the meantime, sat with the doctor's handwritten notes and read through one victim report after another. Except for Dolf, who was not burned, all of the reports were nearly the same. Except—and this made her sit up— there was an awful lot of alcohol in the blood of Clifford, Mooch, and Irma, and hardly any in Dolf's.

That sort of explained it, then. Well, it largely explained it. Irma, Clifford, and Mooch had been drunk as skunks when the fire came through. Clifford's blood alcohol level was over point-one-five. Hell, that's three times the legal limit, and Mooch and Irma were not far behind. They'd just been too stupid drunk to run or seek shelter.

Mink returned with a pot of coffee, which he poured into two glass lab beakers for himself and Ada. They sat at the desk in a beam of morning sunlight, and Ada laid out her theory for the doctor. As far as Dolf went, she explained, he'd been sober, and had stayed too long trying to rouse his inebriated family. He was simply overtaken by the fast-moving flames. Dolf had taken refuge in the well as a last resort; Mooch had stirred himself at the last minute to save his dogs but was too drunk to find the key and had to break the lock.

Mink doctored his coffee with sugar and milk and listened patiently. He said, "Neat package, Ada. But I'm going to have to disappoint you. That is, it may well have happened like you say, but there's no medical support for it."

"They had up to point-one-five blood alcohol. It's not likely they could even stand."

He said, "Those bodies were sitting under the hot sun for two days before you got them down here to the cooler. Under those conditions there's an awful lot of endogenous alcohol production."

"Huh?"

"Their blood fermented."

She pushed her coffee away and fought not to gag. It took her a moment.

"So, they weren't drunk?"

"They may well have been drunk the night before. But so long as they lived and breathed, the ingested alcohol would have metabolized. Usually, it's gone by morning even after a serious bender. The amounts I measured in their blood samples were commensurate with postmortem endogenous alcohol."

"Then why in heck . . .? What about Dolf? His blood-alcohol level was low."

"Dolf was half refrigerated down the well. He could have had a good drunk on the night before, but it was mostly metabolized. He was not drunk when he died."

"How'd he die, then?"

"Most likely asphyxiation."

"If the others were not drunk that morning, then they had to have been dead before the fire. I have to agree with our friend Sergeant Blevins, they would not just sit down and burn to death."

Mink said, "There are other analyses I can do. I'll have to send blood samples to the State lab in Pocatello." He studied her over his beaker of coffee. "It's going to cost another twenty-four dollars, Ada."

Update 10:00 a.m. – Office work:
cataloging victims' personal effects

SMOKE FROM GOD-KNOWS-WHAT FIRE had blown into Camas Valley, and the morning sun was dimmed to just a pale disc. Under the orange haze, Autumn seemed fully to be claiming the town. Although only mid-September, the elm trees had lost most of their leaves, and the locusts stood bright yellow against the leaden sky. She drove to her office past lawns brown and dry, leaf piles, and withered flower beds.

Dr. Mink had given her a file box with the personal articles found on the four deceased Neagles. The contents, when laid out, barely covered the spare desk in her office. She fixed a cup of coffee, got her notes up to date, then started through the items.

In the old man's packet, she found an association ring of some sort emblazoned with 'WRA,' and '1942.' She made a note to look up WRA. She recognized metal hasps for suspenders, and the steel rims of eyeglasses. The glass lenses had popped out.

There was nothing but a wedding band for Irma; not so much as a bobby pin besides that. Ada had forced herself to look at Irma's charred body—back at the scene while McGann and Blevins packed up the others so matter-of-factly. She was a short woman, and slight from what must have been a lifetime of hard work. Ada had wondered what Irma's life would have been like, so far back in the sticks with a husband and two sons and no women folk around. Did she have friends? Did she ever sit and share coffee and cake with the girls? She had tried to cry for the woman, but there'd not been enough humanity left in the bones and charred flesh, and no tears had come. And now nothing but the ring she wore for her husband. It made Ada shudder.

Mooch had somehow retained a jackknife in the pocket of his mostly burned-off blue jeans, along with seventeen cents in coin. He wore no jewelry but the Indian-head dollar belt buckle.

The older boy's packet was more complete. She found a

tooled-leather belt fixed with a gold and silver trophy buckle. Dolf had fourteen dollars in cash held in a money clip: a ten—on the outside of course—and four ones. His pockets held a box of Sen-Sen, a few coins, and a set of keys to a Studebaker. *He had the car keys in his damned pocket!*

The money clip was jeweled silver—most likely paste diamonds in stainless steel. Except . . . it bore the initials 'HRM.' It took a couple seconds, but she whispered, "Uh-oh." HRM, if it was who she thought it was, would be a problem.

The Sen-Sen plus the pomade she'd smelled down the well suggested a lady's man—or someone who fancied himself that way. But then he'd dressed in a striped shirt with checked pants? The lady's man must have thrown on his clothes in an awful hurry.

The front of the trophy buckle showed a horse and rider in gold relief, a looping rope, and a running calf. The back of the buckle was engraved with '*L. Boniface, 1946.*'

Ada sat in her chair staring at the few items laid out on the desk, willing them to tell her something about the last hours and minutes of a whole family. They probably had seen their deaths coming, she realized. So, were they trapped by circumstances no one could have changed, or by failure of one person or another? And did they curse and shout blame, or did they weep and shout their 'I-love-you's' in the final moments? As to the deadly circumstances that left them prostrate before the fire, they weren't drunk, and they could not have been asleep. So, they were alert, or they were dead. But alert made no sense. Neither did dead, inasmuch as they hadn't been beaten, stabbed, strangled, or shot. Therefore, the answer was simple: they were either dead by an unknown means before the fire came through—the perambulations of the two boys notwithstanding—or they'd all gone stark, raving mad.

She filed the items found on Clifford, Irma, and Mooch in a cabinet marked Valley Creek Fire. The money clip and the belt buckle she carefully sketched into her notebook. With her notebook and pen in pocket, then, she took the two pieces to the Clerk and Recorder's office for a consultation.

County Clerk Ethel Grimes' office was high-ceilinged and stone-walled, and the wood floors creaked. As a consequence, the room echoed badly regardless the many begonias, geraniums, and philodendrons potted and festooned about. In addition to being the county clerk, Ethel was the keeper of records and the answerer of telephone and radio calls, all of which duties kept her the most informed person in Yellowpine County. On Ethel, Ada had learned to rely for any and all intelligence, official or grapevine. She spotted the clerk at her desk behind a potted primrose and said, "Ethel, what can you tell me about these items?"

The clerk rose from her desk like a middleweight answering the bell—but pleasantly, sort of, in her own way. She said, "Let's see what you have there, Fancy Badge."

"They're items found on a deceased person. You're not squeamish, are you?"

Ethel scoffed. "Really?"

"Item one," Ada said, attempting an inscrutable smile, "an apparent trophy buckle." She handed the clerk the gold and silver rodeo prize.

Ethel turned over the buckle and read the inscription: '*L. Boniface, 1946*'. She said, "Ada, Louis Boniface wasn't caught up in the fire, was he?"

"No, but this was found on one of the deceased: Dolf Neagle."

"Oh my, you have yourself a problem then, Sheriff." She sat with the belt and buckle and scrunched her lips. "What was that fool Neagle boy doing with a hundred-dollar buckle inscribed to Boniface?"

"Pawn shop?"

Ethel said, "Not likely, and Louis—Frenchy—Boniface and Dolf Neagle lost no love between them. In fact, Boniface fought with Neagle right out on Main Street in Stanley, back in . . . oh gosh, that was back before Montgomery's time. Lance Harding was still sheriff then. Boniface probably would have succeeded in killing the boy if he hadn't been so drunk. Landed the old Québécois in the slammer, though."

"Québécois?—Aren't we fancy. What were they arguing about?"

"Who knows? Boniface is Latin." Ethel looked over the tops of her glasses as if the man's Latin blood should explain any act of passion. "What else you got for me, sheriff lady?" Ethel folded her arms and gave Ada a scrutable look of satisfaction.

"How about a bejeweled money clip emblazoned HRM, formerly endowed with fourteen dollars in greenback." She handed the clip to Ethel, who held it to the window and pulled her glasses down from her forehead to her nose.

"Fourteen dollars? This thing would more likely hold fourteen hundred dollars."

"I know! It's Holland Riis-Moreau, isn't it?"

"Looks like something he'd own." She rubbed it with a Kleenex and pointed out a worn engraving on the back side: two stags with a bare tree between them. "That's Riis-Moreau's phony, mail-order coat of arms, I believe." She handed back the money clip. "Carried by the same dandy?"

"Uh-huh."

Ethel glared over her glasses. "That boy had some nerve, then. Rumor is, Holland only comes out to Idaho when the heat is on him in New Jersey. They say he's had people whacked."

"Whacked?"

"Greased."

Ada folded her arms and raised her brow.

"Dispatched; knocked up."

"Uhm, I don't think . . ."

"Knocked off. You know what I meant." She handed the money clip back to Ada. "From what I understand, Riis-Moreau only just got back to the valley. After the big dust-up last fall, Sibyl stayed on at the ranch . . ."

"At the Obsidian?"

"Wintered there. And Holland went back to New Jersey. I understand Mrs. Riis-Moreau wasn't exactly holding church services out there."

"Ethel, how in the world would you . . ."

"My niece dates a young man whose brother buckaroos for the Obsidian."

"Of course." She closed her notebook. "Well, I guess I have to start somewhere."

"You're not going out to the Obsidian, that den of depravity!"

Ada gathered up her things and started away with a grin. Ethel chased her as far as the office door. "And you'll let me know everything?" she called down the hall.

Update 11:35 a.m. – Not working in town after all.
To the Obsidian Ranch to interview Mrs. Riis-Moreau

TWO HOURS THERE, AND IT WOULD BE TWO HOURS BACK, clutching and downshifting around a hundred curves. It was a long way to drive to ask about something as unexceptional as a money clip. But a rich man's money clip made it interesting. And a rich man's money clip in the pocket of a poor man as dead as Dolf Neagle made the drive necessary.

The highway wound in and out of bright sunshine along the Salmon River, which tumbled white and wild in its narrow channel. Granite walls towered over the road, with pine trees clinging to the narrowest crevices. Though the mid-day was warm, it was mercifully unhazy in the deep canyon, and the air pleasantly breathable. Ada gassed up the sheriff's rig at Stanley, then turned south, once more down the Sawtooth Valley. A couple of miles beyond the turnoff to Redfish Lake, she steered left onto the Obsidian Ranch Road—Holland Riis-Moreau's summer estate.

The ranch road was marked 'Private,' and demanded 'No Trespassing' in bright red block letters. However, except for an iron-rail cattle guard, it was not gated. The dirt road headed straight up a broad alluvial fan, flanked by split-rail fences on both sides and a long line of poplars on one side. The trees followed a ditch engineered to look like a natural water course. At the top of the fan the road dove into a thick stand of golden aspen, which filled a gorge for another quarter mile before giving way to broad green fields under walls of black columnar basalt.

The ranchstead took up a low rise in the middle of the meadow, and was dominated by stables, a stout barn, and a three-story log and stone ranch house. All but the stones were painted white. She drove forward, but at the turn to the ranch house her way was blocked by a turnstile gate.

She wasn't at the gate for a minute, however, before two mounted cowboys came loping toward her. They were armed. The cowboys pulled up and doffed their matching Stetsons. One wore a cropped beard and looked to be the leader. The other was clean-shaven and, though somewhat vacant of eye, was somewhat handsome.

"Sheriff Ada Reed to see Mrs. Riis-Moreau," she said to the more intelligent-looking of the cowboys.

"Do you have an appointment?"

"It's official business."

"Uh-huh. Do you have an appointment?"

"It's going to be a damn site more official if I have to turn around and get a warrant," she said, now to the more handsome of the two. "You better ride off and ask your boss lady if she wouldn't rather see me informally."

Handsome nodded and rode off to the ranch house, while the more intelligent looking cowboy dismounted and waited with her. "You a real sheriff?" he asked after a minute. "I've never seen a sheriff look like you."

Ada nodded her affirmation, and wished she'd kept the handsome cowboy with her instead. "You ever see a guy up here by the name of Dolf? Dolf Neagle?" she asked. "He drove a '41 Studebaker sedan."

"Huh-uh."

Ten minutes passed, and then fifteen. At last, they heard a whistle and saw the second cowboy wave them up with his hat. Ada drove up ahead of the horse and rider and parked in the yard between the stables and the ranch house. Both cowboys followed her up the front steps of the house.

A lady under a bold pile of chestnut hair greeted her on the porch wearing a saffron colored floral muumuu. At least, it was probably a muumuu from what Ada had read in *Vogue*. She'd never actually seen one. The garment was supported by Mrs. Riis-Moreau's substantial breasts, leaving her shoulders bare, and it reached almost to cover her sandaled feet. She held a tall drink in her left hand that was, unsurprisingly, the exact color of the dress. "How can I help you sweety?" she asked with a deliberate smile.

"Sheriff Ada Reed. I would like to talk with you about a young man whom you might have known."

"Known, as in past tense?"

"I'm afraid so," Ada said. "It would be best if we talked privately, if you don't mind."

The lady slapped the handsome boy's butt. "Get along fellas," she cried. "Go do some cowboyin'!" She watched them go, then turned back to Ada with an open-mouth smile. "So, you're Montgomery's wife, are you?" Then looking Ada up and down, "If we were in New York, I'd have Frederick do something with that hair."

"Mrs. Riis-Moreau . . ."

"Sibyl. It means prophetess." She was forty-something, but a well-traveled forty-something.

"Mrs. Riis-Moreau, do you have any idea how this item may have come into the possession of Dolf Neagle?" She handed the jeweled money clip to Sibyl.

"Oh, no. Poor Dolphin?" She handed back the clip and sipped from the colorful cocktail. "Well, I suppose I gave it to him."

"For what?"

"For being sweet. Don't you have someone who's sweet to you, Ada, with Montgomery so far away?" She turned abruptly and pointed. "Look at those deer. Do you see them?" Three does had emerged from the underbrush at the foot of the basalt cliffs and wandered a short way into the meadow.

Ada glanced at the deer but kept her pen to the page of her open notebook. "Does your husband know you gave the money clip to the Neagle boy for being sweet?"

Sibyl sighed and swirled the ice cubes in her glass, still watching the deer. "Have we arrived at your main line of questioning, sugar?" She slapped where a pocket should be but found none in the muumuu.

"Neagle was found dead under mysterious circumstances shortly after your husband had returned to the valley."

Sibyl had turned and begun to sway toward the front door. "Well, come on," she said over her shoulder. As they walked through the house, she kept talking without looking back. "First of all, my husband is not mysterious, nor is he subtle. If he was going to have someone killed it would"—she laughed—"it would not be over me. But more important, it would be a bloody and most un-mysterious ending for whoever. You'll have to excuse the mess; I can't keep a maid around."

They crossed through a high-ceilinged living room to a lounge with a wet bar, where Sybil took several cigarettes from a silver tray. The stag-and-tree crest hung above the bar, and stuffed heads of game animals lined the walls. They continued down a hallway and through a well-appointed but dusty library.

"Watch the dog shit," Sybil said as they exited into the sunshine again, and onto a redwood deck rimming a swimming pool. It was the largest swimming pool Ada had ever seen, even counting the new municipal pool in Salmon.

A man of medium build and in an unmitigated state of nakedness lay on a chaise lounge near the edge of the pool. Sibyl said, "Holly, that lady sheriff is here to see you."

"The lady sheriff? Is she as pretty as the magazine pictures?" Holland Riis-Moreau scooted and twisted to look her way.

Sibyl clicked a jeweled lighter. "I guess, if you like the tall, authoritarian type." She lit a cigarette and exhaled into the breeze.

The man adjusted the lounge to a half-sitting position but didn't bother to pull an available towel over his exposed parts. He was tanned evenly, head to foot, and his browned skin hung a little loose. He would be Sibyl's senior by perhaps a decade. Half-graying hair covered his chest, and his belly was not as flat as he would have it look by holding in his breath. "Welcome to the Obsidian at long last, Mrs. Reed," he said. "How can I help you?"

Ada forced herself to get a description of his face: *High forehead; full hair, blacker than natural; Roman nose, broken once; wide-set, brown eyes like a cougar; square jaw* . . .

Sibyl smiled, mostly by curling her lip with the tip of her tongue between her teeth. She offered Ada a smoke.

"No thank you," Ada said.

"You don't smoke?"

"No, never."

The woman took a second cigarette to her husband and lit it for him. "One of my friends died, Holly," she pouted. "You didn't kill him, did you?"

Holland took the cigarette and reached with his other hand for the drink next to the chaise. "Which one?" he asked.

"The rustic one with the sandy hair and the German name."

"Adolf? I liked him."

Sibyl turned back to Ada and shrugged, then moved to an Adirondack with her cocktail. Ada conducted her interrogation for twenty minutes with Holland variously posing, scowling, and yawning, and Sibyl giggling in the background. "Why are you here," she asked several times, "with all this smoke and fire."

"We like it here—the fires are exciting," Sybil said from behind her. "It's always been a . . . a mountain of whiskey and romance!"

Riis-Moreau chuckled at his wife's answer. But Ada's tolerance for smarmy disrespect had been exceeded some time earlier. She asked rather abruptly, "Things get hot for you back in New Jersey?"

Holland at last pulled a towel over his middle and rotated his legs down to sit on the edge of the chaise. Ada was half turned from him anyway, facing the Sawtooth peaks, which appeared much taller and distant in the smoky haze. Holland said, "I hear it's gotten more dangerous for businessmen in the valley since last I was here. Do you shoot businessmen for fun, Ada Reed, or as a vocation?"

He was referring to the perpetrator in the Yankee Fork case, whom she had shot and killed—blew the son of a bitch right off the bow of a dredge.

She sighed. Fifteen minutes earlier she would have nodded and given a straight-forward answer. Now she said, "As a necessity of the job, generally, but exceptions can always be made." She wished when she'd said it that she hadn't.

Holland smiled broadly, but not pleasantly. "I always liked the gentleman you shot. We got along fine—with each other and with others in the valley. We had a regular poker game, you know, although it was usually our mutual friend, Montgomery, who made out like a bandit."

He rolled his head back and squinted into the sun. "I miss Montgomery. Is he coming back soon?"

"They're in peace talks."

"Uh-huh. Until then, do you also play poker Mrs. Reed?"

"Never."

"You should learn the game."

Update 5:15 p.m. – Got the naked truth at the Obsidian Ranch; going home to clean off.

THE COUNTY CLERK, ETHEL GRIMES, HAD told Ada she would check on her, and the cowboys let her know there was, indeed, a call for her on her radio. They escorted her out to the truck, where she leaned in, pushed a couple of buttons, and flipped a switch. She spoke uncomfortably into the microphone. After a moment of static, the receiver crackled and she recognized Ethel's voice. Ethel let her know there was nothing further needing her attention out west, and nothing much happening in the east part of the county either, "over." Ada answered that she was on her way back to Camas, "over." She leaned in again and hung up the radio receiver, then took a step back toward the main house. But there was nothing more, really, she needed or wanted from either of the Riis-Moreaus. She had left hanging what Holland meant about poker playing and Montgomery making out like a bandit, but she couldn't think how she might pose a question to him about it.

"Tell them I was called away," she told the cowboys as she climbed in behind the wheel.

The good-looking cowboy's eyes crinkled, and he touched the brim of his hat. "Shall I escort you out the gate, then?"

Ada shook her head, then shook her whole body. "No, let Einstein, there, do it." She started up the truck and followed the horse and rider to the turnstile gate, then raised dust all the way down the treed lane to the highway.

In fact, she had little doubt what Riis-Moreau was implying with his comments—that Montgomery was on the take and she was expected to fall in line. As the Yankee Fork case was wrapping up, the safe in the offender's office had been found to contain ledgers and lists. A lot of people, especially in Boise, had made a point of keeping the contents under wraps. She knew for a fact, though, that Montgomery's name had been on one or more of those lists. It had made her queasy when she'd first learned it, and now after hearing Riis-Moreau's creepy implications, it made her sick. But she couldn't think about that just then. She was having trouble enough holding her marriage together with the Pacific Ocean and her job coming between her and Monty, without dwelling on insinuations and unsubstantiated doubts.

Chapter Six

Saturday, 22 September 1951
Expense reports, paperwork, more paperwork.

"YOU HAVE A BIG PLACE, PETE. Heck, you've got twelve hundred acres they could run around in."

"I've got three dogs of my own, Ada," the voice on the telephone explained, "and they're working dogs. I run sheep, and I can't have a couple hounds running all the fat off my flock. Have you talked to Wardle?"

"He's stove-up with rheumatism and can't take on the distraction."

Ada had come home from the Obsidian Ranch to find curtains pulled down from the front window and the davenport quilt torn to shreds. Dog feces was tracked across the kitchen floor, and the back door was scratched nearly through. The beasts had, at least, taught themselves to drink from the toilet. But then they'd done the predictable, and marked most of the doorways, furniture, and corners. She'd cleaned till midnight. Breakfast came late; she locked the hounds in the garage and got to the courthouse a little after eight.

The morning sun worked its way slowly through the window blinds of her office, lighting bright green stripes across otherwise drab green walls. She gave up on the kennel calls and was typing out travel vouchers and a trip report when State Patrol Sergeant Ken Blevins walked in.

She took a deep breath. "Hi, Ken," she managed, pushing aside the Smith Corona. "Do you like dogs?"

He ignored the question. "I brought in a prisoner, Acting Sheriff Reed, and I'd like you to stow him in your jail for a time, it being your jurisdiction and all."

"What being my jurisdiction?"

"The Neagle family murders."

"The Valley Creek deaths."

"Is that what you call it?" He tossed his flat-brimmed hat onto the spare desk and ran his hand over his flat-topped head. In no apparent hurry to share how he'd cracked the case, he got a cup down from the wall and filled it from the pot, then unexpectedly carried the pot over and refilled Ada's cup.

"I may have mentioned the other day I had my suspicions," he said, returning the pot to the hot plate. "It turns out I had good reason." He stirred a spoon of sugar into his cup, taking his time. "And I—that is, the long arm of the Idaho State Patrol—apprehended the suspect last night trying to leave the state."

Ada stared at her warmed coffee, leaned back in her chair, and crossed her leg over her knee. "By all means, tell me what you have," she said.

Blevins took the chair opposite Ada and read from a small pad from his breast pocket. "One Eddy Asakura; male, 28 years of age; five-nine, one hundred sixty-five pounds. Of Japanese descent."

He sipped from his coffee, slurping so as not to burn his lips, then flipped to the next page. "Mr. Asakura was apprehended outside of Caldwell at twenty-one hundred hours, Friday, doing forty-five in a thirty-five. He was headed for the Oregon border."

Ada, still a bit flustered for his having poured her a coffee, took a slow breath and didn't answer immediately. The name was barely familiar to her. Asakura, she believed, had served in Montgomery's regiment in Italy. Mont had spoken neither ill nor favorably of the young man but had mentioned that he'd come to settle in the Salmon River valley after the war. There may have been the slightest apprehension in the mention of it.

Blevins slurped again. Ada asked, "What has Mr. Asakura to do with the Neagles?"

The highway patrol sergeant was working hard not to let a big grin belie his professional objectivity. "Well, you folks tucked up here in the mountains wouldn't have heard of it, perhaps, because it mostly played out down in Jerome County. But Mr. Asakura had brought legal proceedings against Clifford Neagle; had pressed it for years. The lawsuit was dismissed two weeks ago."

"Lawsuit for what? And why file a suit in Jerome County? That's two hundred miles away."

Blevins set down his coffee and crossed his leg over his knee. "One hundred ninety or so, either highway you take." He gave in to the grin, took his knee in his laced fingers, and leaned back.

"But Jerome County is the site of the Minidoka Internment Camp where Eddy Asakura was once confined," he said, now speaking to the ceiling. "Asakura claimed Neagle was responsible for the wrongful death of his parents at the camp."

"And Neagle . . .?"

"Clifford Neagle was a guard there, with the War Relocation Authority."

The WRA *on the ring*, Ada recalled. Her skepticism and her guard let up a little as she recognized a thread of logic running through Blevins' gloating and supposing. She sat up in her chair and listened closer, albeit with arms crossed. Blevins had been busy. Two witnesses had seen Asakura's old-model GMC pickup truck parked on Basin Butte Road, at the pass down into upper Valley Creek. That had been the morning of the day before the fire. A third witness—the gas station attendant—put Asakura in Stanley that same night, just hours before the fire roared through Valley Creek.

Blevins said, "The pass is not three miles up the canyon from the Neagle place, and there's nothing and no one along the way. That right there is motive and opportunity."

"And means?" Ada asked. "There was no sign at all of foul play. No strangulation, no piercing or cutting; no fatal wounds of any kind."

"I'm getting to the good part, Ada." He rubbed his chin and shook his head slowly. "Corporal Asakura was Special Forces: an army-trained killer. And that's not to mention his Asian skills. Ever heard of *Ninjutsu*? It's in his record. You should look it up."

Blevins presented a comprehensive argument. It covered just about everything—except, perhaps, direct evidence there'd been a murder. "So far, Sergeant, there's no evidence that . . . there was no shooting or bludgeoning, or . . ."

"Judo?" Blevins shrugged.

"No broken bones. Plus, everything you've told me sounds circumstantial."

"I don't give a damn if he used voodoo. The man has a strong motive and no alibi. He was a couple of miles up-canyon with nothing and no one between him and his victims. You got any other suspect?"

She didn't, but his insistence annoyed her. "I've not seen evidence yet a damned crime was committed," she said more testily than she probably ought to have. Her tone brought his chin up and narrowed his eyes.

She cleared her throat and more gently said, "But in point of fact, Holland Riis-Moreau had cause, vis-à-vis his amorous wife, to want Dolf Neagle dead." She didn't believe it herself. Holland had seemed to her neither surprised nor annoyed by his wife's infidelity.

Blevins didn't believe it either and he stood, retrieved his smoky-bear hat, and turned at the door. "Dolf was still moving around when the fire caught them; Clifford wasn't," he said. "And Clifford's who Asakura had it in for."

He stuck the hat on his stubbly head. "Look Sheriff, I brought the suspect to Camas—to you—out of professional courtesy. He was trying to leave the state and that gives me the authority to haul his ass back to Idaho Falls."

"No Ken, leave him here. I'll watch him." She took a deep breath and plastered on a smile. "And thanks. That's quite a package you put together in a very short time."

Update 2:45 p.m. – Preliminary Interrogation of Eddy Asakura

ASAKURA, NATURALLY, HAD A RECORD. Ada found an inch-thick folder on the young man in her file cabinet. The arrest report, for cattle rustling, was signed by Sheriff Lance Harding in April of 1946. He was accused and found guilty of stealing and butchering a calf. He'd spent three months in the county jail. There were other minor scrapes: he had—oh, damn!—he'd assaulted one Clifford Neagle; sent him to the clinic. Montgomery had jailed him for that.

EDWIN AYUMA ASAKURA WAS A YOUNG MAN in an older man's clothes. His white shirt was tucked into brown, pleated trousers, which broke evenly over a pair of brown shoes, worn but polished. He wore neither suspenders nor belt—they would have been taken from him along with his necktie. A linen jacket loosely complimenting the trousers lay folded on the bunk. Thick, black hair had not been cut for a couple of months, but was combed and showed the slightest hint of gray at the temples. The young man's face was a nut brown, and although he was no more than mid-twenties in age, it was lined from days under the sun. His hands were rough but scrubbed clean.

His was the last of three cells along one stone wall in the basement of the courthouse: the cell reserved for long term residents. It boasted, in addition to the bunk, a seatless ceramic toilet against the wall. Ada sat on a wooden chair outside the bars of the cell and took out pen and notebook. She asked, "Where were you going, Corporal?"

"I am no longer a corporal in the United States Army. I received my discharge six years ago."

"Honorable?"

"I try to be."

She made a note to look it up. "Where were you going, then, Mr. Asakura?"

"Chehalis, Washington. My aunt, my mother's sister, is sick. She is old and she is sick, and I wanted to say goodbye to her." His voice was not deep, but it was soft and resonant. There was a slight formality to his word choice and enunciation, but no real affectation.

"Do you mind if I sit?" he asked.

He eased down onto the edge of the bunk and sat with straight back and hands on his knees. Corey Braden, of the Yankee Fork affair, had sat in such a way in the jail in Custer; in his wheelchair, of course, but with the same proud air—at first. There was a difference in the eyes, though. Asakura's were as distant and brooding, but not as remorseful. Not remorseful at all.

Ada let a moment pass and asked, "Your family, your extended family, all live in western Washington. Why did you move here?"

"It's a free country." He dropped his head and smiled.

"Do you understand why you were arrested?"

"Apparently the country is freer for some than for others." His smile remained. "Where's your old man—Major Reed? Off shooting up Asia this time?"

It was a wholly impertinent comment, and it disappointed her. She had thought she might like Eddy Asakura. She'd immediately been drawn to his polite manner and the slightly exotic rhythm of his speech. But there was no call for that kind of disrespect. She raised her eyes, ready to make an angry answer, but before she could speak an image came to mind of Montgomery off in Korea shooting up people who . . . looked much like her prisoner.

It took a couple of seconds, but she cleared her throat and said, "He's near a place called Pusan. Does that bother you? He's fighting to defend more than America, you know. He's defending the whole Pacific, including Japan."

"You do understand I'm American, right?"

"Of course, I know that. I'm not prejudiced."

"Good to know."

The walls of the basement were of mortared stone, and the high ceiling was of hewn timbers with pipes and ducts suspended on metal braces. It was all newly painted white, and six bare lightbulbs in the ceiling made the place unpleasantly bright.

Ada wrote in her notebook for a minute, then shielded her eyes and asked, "For what did you receive your Silver Star?"

"For killing. Does that bother you?"

Her whole body tensed. But no, it didn't bother her. Killing was no more than pulling a trigger, after all—then seeing the realization of death come into a man's eyes and watching him rage against it; seeing the fear and the unbearable regret . . .

"Why should it bother me?" she said, "Killing is part of war."

"Killing is all of war. But I was killing Caucasian boys; Germans and Austrians, maybe a smooth-chinned Dane now and then. Blonde hair, blue eyes."

Ada had stopped writing. She was not going to like the young man, that was plain. But she didn't have to like him to do her job. "They were our enemies," she said matter-of-factly.

"Mine too."

Yes, of course they were his enemies too. The dark, narrow eyes and heavy jaw were straight off the old recruitment posters; his tawny glower she had seen in too many newsreels.

But those were bigoted thoughts and, thank God, she was not that way. "You were a machine gunner?" she asked.

"By summer of '44 we had more gunners than operable guns. I was a specialist." She'd put pen to page again, but looked up, curious. He explained, "I worked at night—outside the perimeter."

She'd never heard the term. Again, she had to look away as all sorts of possibilities for 'outside the perimeter' filled her mind. She put that aside, too, and got back to the case at hand. "What were you doing up on Basin Butte Road last week?"

"Fishing. There are decent-size trout in Valley Creek Lake when the fishing is right."

"Then you did, in fact, drop down into the Valley Creek drainage. Were you alone?"

"Alone . . . yes."

"And so, how was the fishing?"

"The water was too warm." He stood and walked the four paces to the end of the cell.

"When did you leave there?" she asked.

"We saw the smoke getting closer . . ."

"We?" She shielded her eyes from the glare.

He paused and leaned a moment on the bars of the cell. "A figure of speech. For me, the lake is a place of peaceful meditation. I visit with my ancestors there; converse with them. About mid-afternoon, I looked up to see the smoke billowing beyond the ridge, and I thought perhaps the fish were not worth the further risk."

"The fish you weren't catching."

He shrugged. Ada took a moment to catch up her notes. "Is that a ballpoint pen?" he asked.

"Yes. Have you seen one?" She stood to hand him the pen, then sat again.

"Amazing," he said. He rolled a line of ink across his palm. "It really goes years between fillings?" He clicked the pen a couple times and handed it back.

"You can't refill it. You throw it away."

"Hmm."

She said, "Clifford Neagle died a couple miles below that lake, and not long after you left."

"If I had known, I might have stayed to watch."

She breathed in and out, and continued. "Three years ago you broke Clifford Neagle's nose."

"I am ashamed of that."

Ada glanced up from her notes and was surprised to see genuine contrition on the young man's face. She said, "You spent years in legal proceedings against Neagle." The court records had shown that Eddy Asakura filed a lawsuit against Clifford Neagle in 1947, alleging wrongful death of Shirley and Hideo Asakura. The lawsuit against Neagle had been dismissed in '49, but Asakura had re-filed in late 1950—just ten months ago.

She said, "The new lawsuit, I understand, was also recently dismissed." Again, she looked up from her notes. "Lawyers aren't cheap."

"Neither is one's family disposable." The young man sat again but did not relax his formal posture. His eyes remained fixed on the wall behind her.

She said, "Neagle was employed at the Minidoka War Internment uhm . . . Center . . ."

"Japanese concentration camp."

She knew what the place was, and it assuredly was not a concentration camp. "Relocation Center. You were . . . relocated there?"

He twisted his lips in a smirk. "I was relocated, restricted, restrained, and repressed there. Yes, along with my parents."

For a couple of minutes Ada wrote in her book. She looked up and said, "I'm told your parents died at the camp. I'm very sorry. Can you tell me under what circumstances?"

"My mother died of whooping cough. Twenty-four people died of whooping cough in the camp that winter. There was not enough medicine."

"Your father was shot trying to escape?"

"That was the official report. Our fellow prisoners told a different story, although no one listened then or later. The willow became an oak. Hideo Asakura was shot breaking into the warehouse where the pharmaceuticals were kept."

Ada made a note in her book, then rose to go. "Can I get you anything?" she asked.

Asakura stood as well. "The last time I was in residence, they allowed me a writing table."

"I'll see if Ethel can come up with something."

Update 6:15 p.m. – ~~Finished for the day~~ Apparently not finished for the day. Campaign event, I am reminded.

She got the hounds out of the garage and into the backyard, although she couldn't imagine they would have any further need of the yard after their indiscriminate use of the garage floor. She was just settling into a hot bath when she was interrupted by a knock at the door. It was Ethel and she . . . "Oh, damn it, Ethel, is it tonight?"

"It's tonight. You're out of uniform, Sheriff."

Ada was in her pink bathrobe and slippers. "How much time do I have?"

"Chief Munson has already lit the fire in the grill."

A week's worth of dirty laundry overfilled a basket in the closet, and from it she retrieved her cleanest dirty uniform shirt and her least-wrinkled khaki slacks. She tied a half Windsor knot in the mirror as Ethel checked her watch, then leashed the dogs and grabbed the keys to the pickup truck.

"Are you sure you want to take the dogs?" Ethel asked.

"I'm sure I have to take the dogs." She dropped the tailgate and waved the hounds up and in. "Besides, these poor troublemakers have been cooped up at my place for days. They could use an outing."

Ethel led the way to the west end of town where the lights were on at the park. The grounds were picketed with *Ada Reed for Sheriff* signs, and the picnic awning was festooned with red, white, and blue crepe paper bunting. "Oh, jeez!" was all Ada could say. Forty or fifty people were already gathered in the picnic area, including a few whose names and faces she did not know. She blew a long breath, then leaving the dogs in the bed of the truck, put on a big smile and made her way into the crowd.

The Custer police chief—her erstwhile campaign manager, Kellen Munson—shook his head and gave an exaggerated sigh of relief as she walked by. He was wearing a crimson and nautical-blue plaid western shirt and blue jeans, and standing over a flaming grill. District Ranger Ben McGann was there in uniform, including his Smokey Bear hat, the brim of which he touched as Ada drew near and walked quickly by.

She was cornered almost immediately by a half-dozen people whose farmsteads had burned, and who were among the homeless left by the numerous fires through the summer. Ada knew the number was much greater than half a dozen, and it was growing, as witnessed at the Redfish campground. But there was not a lot she could do for them right then, she explained, until the County authorized some funds for her use.

"Jeff Banning is arranging the use of a whole warehouse of army surplus tents," one of the group told her.

"I know. But winter is coming," she explained. "You can't live in tents through the winter."

Chief Munson had wired up a microphone, and the tinny thing crackled as he began an introduction. It was a lead-in for her getting up to talk, and Ada felt herself gripped by a panic worse than at Redfish. Munson stood on the bed of a low-boy trailer and made a drawn-out but fair point that Sheriff Ada Reed had not been intimidated nor deterred in bringing justice to the Yankee Fork. She'd proven herself tough enough for the job. There was some polite clapping, then a few more words followed by more polite clapping. He actually spoke well, but instead of putting Ada at her ease it twisted her nerves a little tighter.

Up on the trailer, microphone in hand and thanking Munson, it felt as though her stomach had not made the climb with her. "Uhm, thanks." The microphone made her words sound like echoes from the bottom of a well. "Thank you, Chief Munson." She would have preferred to be at the bottom of a well, just then, or at least on the ground with Allison and Loretta in their picnic outfits and their new hairdos. The two ladies stood right below with several others in a half circle, and Dottie was with them and showing again although it couldn't have been five months since her fourth was born; and Cheryl . . .

They were all waiting. She blurted, "It's good of you all to come out like this." There was a smattering of polite applause, for which Ada touched the brim of her hat. Her head spun, and she wondered briefly what in God's name she was doing up in front of the whole town hawking herself like a dime-a-dance hustler. "Thank you," she said again.

She caught a big breath and started into her prepared remarks. The forest fires were on everyone's mind, and she was able to share some facts she'd learned from the Forest Service briefings. Then she said a few more words about the growing homeless problem—though nothing much of substance. "I've recently been informed a truckload of surplus commodities has made it up to Redfish from the Department of Agriculture warehouses," she said to enthusiastic applause. "But we still have a lot to do."

She really wanted to share some thoughts on the role of public assistance in a free society, but she'd been warned not to let her 'college' show because it might sound superior. Instead, she garbled an idea about the importance of respecting the county budgets. Finally, after a few more un-collegial words, she said, "Kellen tells me the chicken will be burned if I talk for too long. So, let's dig in, and I'll try to chat with each and every one of you while we eat."

Back at eye level—thank God—she nearly did talk with each and every person there. She reached out for hands and touched shoulders, laughed, and leaned in to speak confidentially. She worked the crowd like the hostess that she . . . well, until recently, she had been. She all but offered canapes and cocktails around.

She explained to the reporter from the Camas Courier that, "No, the housewife is not a relic of the past. The nuclear family is one of the great strengths of our democracy."

"No," she told half the neighbors who greeted her, "I am not part of any silly suffrage movement. I just want to see the laws enforced evenly." And to a few of the more curious, "Yes, I do have to alter the standard uniform. But just in a little here and out a little there."

To Reverend Farrow, she answered that perhaps the Lord didn't mean to promote meekness so much as compensate those who happened to be meek by offering up the earth as inheritance. At least she hoped it came out like that. "Besides," she said, sidling away, "I think I have a pretty good handle on *the Poor*, the *Merciful*, and the *Hungering for Righteousness*." She was hungering just then, having not eaten since breakfast.

"And *the Peacemaker*, Ada?" he asked.

"That's what my campaign is all about Reverend." She turned to go.

"And *the Pure of Heart*?"

She paused half a step. "I'm working on it."

Ben McGann held a chicken leg between the fingers of one hand and a beer in the other. He could only nod when Ada turned, and they found each other face to face.

His blue eyes were clear and innocent, although his lips were smeared with barbecue sauce. "You have my vote, as you know," he said.

She hadn't forgotten the scare he'd given her riding out the grass fire. "I'm angry with you, Ben."

He nodded. "I sensed that."

She rolled her eyes and hurried on. Her two closest friends, Betty and Cheryl, who had done such a wonderful job with the damned Labor Day parade, were at the center of a growing circle of ladies—both Junior League and VFW Auxiliary. Ada roundly congratulated the pair, and apologized for missing the parade due, it turned out, to an unfortunate mine accident in Bayhorse. There was a quiet moment. Some of the ladies weren't sure how they would vote, and they seemed nervous about it. It went beyond the political issues.

"After all, Ada," Cheryl reasoned, "are we all supposed to go out and get jobs?"

"Put our men out of work?" Betty asked.

Ada was light-headed with hunger by then, and the chicken and hot dogs were disappearing from the grill just beyond the klatch. "I'm running for sheriff," she explained with a smile, "because, uhm ..."

Because I couldn't clean that empty house one more time, she thought, *or sit all alone, or choose theme colors for another church social!* But she didn't say that. She cleared her throat and said, "Well, at least I don't have to worry about what to wear every morning, do I?"

That was met with a lot of raised brows, and the grill was empty by the time Ada dug herself out. But Kel Munson was swell and agreed to take the two hounds for a walk around the park. "You're doing great," he said.

"I haven't picked up a vote."

"You haven't lost a vote."

She probably did lose a vote or two among the league bowlers who were passing around a paper bag behind the bandshell. Lester Booley was among them, stumbling and talking too loudly and profanely for a public gathering. Booley was a young ne'er-do-well. Barely in his twenties, he'd been collared more than once by Montgomery, and Ada had fielded complaints about him as well. She marched up behind him and snatched the bag and bottle from his hand.

He wheeled and cussed her. "How tough do you think that badge makes you, bitch?"

She grabbed his shirt with her free hand, pulling him out into the center of the bowling-league circle. With her face stuck up so close she could smell the rum through his cheap cologne, she said, "It isn't how tough it makes me, Lester, but how tough it makes my deputies. Do you want to see a list of their names, or shall I have them stop by your place and introduce themselves?"

"I don't give a damn about no deputies." He said, although not convincingly.

"Call me bitch again and you will. You get yourself home now," she told him.

"Why should I?"

She jabbed her finger into his chest. "Because you're in a state of public drunkenness, and I have empty cells at the courthouse I wouldn't mind filling. Get on home, Lester." She tipped her hat to the rest of the young men standing around, who parted for her, and started away with the remains of their bottle.

"Hey, Reed," Booley called. "What happened to Dolf Neagle, I heard he was murdered by a Jap."

A number of others turned toward her and quieted. She said, "Not likely." She emptied the rum onto the ground, tossed the bottle into a trash bin, and started away again.

"Yeah." He scoffed. "I'd have bet he wouldn't've bought it like that."

"What do you know about it?" She turned back with her hands on her hips.

"I don't pretend to know nothing, bi . . . bi . . . uhm, sheriff," he said. "But it wouldn't have been the first time Neagle got his ass in a sling for banging the wrong girl." He leaned on a couple of his buddies, and they laughed as Ada walked back to her party.

The park quieted a little as all the barbecue and beer began to weigh down the attendees, and Ada managed to find the edge of the crowd, where she was spied by Margaret Li from the town of Custer. Li waved from a bench under hundred-year-old elms, wearing a matronly dress and embroidered silk jacket. Her long white braid hung over her shoulder and down to her lap. She'd watched from the bench the political rally begin and had observed it as it gained in enthusiasm. It had peaked and was now beginning to wane along a right-skewed energy distribution—much like an exothermic chemical reaction, she decided, or a nutrient-limited bacterial growth.

Maggie Li had been one of Ada's early suspects in the Yankee Fork murders, and then an important witness, a valuable advisor, and a friend, in that order of incidence. Ada brought a plate of potato salad, a couple dinner rolls, and two forks. "Help me out, Maggie," she asked, "Why am I running for sheriff?"

"Because you don't like to be told you can't."

"That's what I thought."

She joined Mrs. Li on the bench and laid the plates between them. "Kellen gave you a ride from Custer?" she asked.

Li nodded. "Yes, Munson is a nice young man. No Charlie Chan, but an honest cop, I think."

"The State police brought me a prisoner today: Eddy Asakura. They suspect him of the deaths in Valley Creek Canyon. It looks bad for him. He doesn't even claim innocence."

"Asakura, the young Japanese gentleman? No, he would not remonstrate and cry out his innocence. And so, you accept that as proof of guilt?"

"Certainly not proof, but neither does it bring to mind new-fallen snow."

"He is proud, and you do not understand him. Ignorance breeds fear, Ada, and fear breeds hate. Did you not suspect me of killing Rose Braden?"

"Only for a very short time, and only because she bore Asian symbols on her hands . . ."

"Which they weren't."

"No, but there were Asian symbols on the medallions she wore."

"Which you did not understand, and so you suspected a cult ritual, which you feared, and that caused you to hate me."

"Never."

The old woman took a small bite of the potato salad and made a face. "Always they put in pickles. Why not radish?" She slathered the roll with butter, though, and gobbled it down. "Bread is a luxury anymore, and it's easy on my teeth," she said. "I should bake more, and you should get to know your prisoner before you hang him."

CHAPTER SEVEN

Sunday, 23 September, 9:15 a.m.
Half day today.
A chance to catch up on paperwork.

SUNDAY MORNINGS WERE NOT THE BEST for Ada. In fact, they were . . . not the best. A day of rest sounds great unless you happen to live in a house that echoes. None of the shops worth shopping open on Sundays, the movie theater stays dark until two, and the girls would all have made their plans days before. And of course, weekends were for men only at the golf course.

Dolly, however, unlocked the café at 8 a.m. on Sundays, bless her heart, often to find Ada there on the sidewalk waiting. At Dolly's, just the clink of spoons and the rattle of dishes could make Ada smile. The café was always warm and smelling vaguely of cinnamon, and the talk at the other tables, though usually unintelligible, was soft and friendly.

Ada sat at the counter rather than take up a table. A girl watched her from a booth, standing on the bench seat and peeping over her mother's head. The girl's mother glanced Ada's way, glanced a second time, then whispered for the child to sit. Ada rotated her stool back to her hotcakes and eggs, tucked her tie into her shirt, and said 'yes, please' to another cup of coffee.

She'd known the waitress behind the counter since the girl

was a baby: Tom and Linda Hodge's daughter, Tammy. Now Tammy was not a day over eighteen and not a month from being a mother herself. She filled Ada's cup, and asked, "Then, are you a real sheriff?"

Ada closed her eyes and heard the bullets buzzing over her head and smelled the dust of the road and the hot oil dripping under her truck. She smiled and said, "I don't know how much realer it gets."

The girl picked up three plates of hashbrowns and eggs and carried them to the back table. The old men there took the plates from her and said something to make her giggle. When she returned, she took up Ada's empty plate and asked, "Aren't you afraid?"

"Of what?"

"I don't know. What if you make a mistake?"

More loud talk rose from the old men in the back. Ada dropped her head, thinking of half a dozen ways to answer the girl. She stood, grinning, and with a wink left a dollar bill on the counter.

THE YELLOWPINE COUNTY LIBRARY OPENED AT TEN on Sundays, and that gave Ada something to do into the early afternoons. On this particular Sunday she was shown how to use the new microfilm machine, where she found newspaper articles going back to pre-war years. Eddy Asakura, it turned out, had not been a quiet man. In addition to the troubles with Clifford Neagle, he'd sued the Potaman Ranch over water rights—and won—and he'd been barred from attending further meetings of the Salmon Valley chapter of the Veterans of Foreign Wars. The arrest and conviction for cattle rustling was covered daily in the papers for nearly two weeks. Ada remembered nothing of the story, but she'd been living on the farm with Montgomery then, and they'd had their own dramas to work through.

From the library she made her way to the courthouse, which was always cool and quiet on a Sunday afternoon. When she let herself in through the alley door, she saw one of the county trustees, Larry Marsh, exiting the council chambers on the second floor.

Marsh saw her at the same time, and he pulled the door closed, rattling the glass.

She let him descend the marble staircase before speaking. "I wonder if I can have a minute, Larry, to discuss the problem with the families burned out by the fires."

"Larry? Is it Larry now?"

She took a deep breath but refused to abandon her smile. "Of course, it's Trustee Marsh at meetings, but if you prefer . . ." She cleared her throat. "We have a growing problem." He was wearing a fly-fishing vest, and he scowled at having to detour around her. "I'd like to propose at the next Board meeting that we . . ."

"We?"

"That the County allocate funds to provide accommodations— nothing fancy—for twenty-five to thirty-five displaced families who have lost their homes. Some of these people don't even have . . ."

Marsh pushed by her and marched to the assessor's office, found it to be locked and slipped a manilla envelope under the door. He said, "I can't believe the famous lady sheriff of Yellowpine County can't solve a simple problem without spending thousands of dollars."

"What does that have to do . . .?" She'd followed behind him and had to turn again as he about-faced. Her smile was all but forgotten. "I know you don't like me, Larry, but these are real people, and they're in real trouble."

"Candidate Banning has a plan, and it won't cost the County a dime," he said over his shoulder.

"Jeff Banning wants to stick them in army surplus tents. But winter will be on us in a couple of months. They can't get by in tents."

"I like Banning's plan."

"You like the price."

He held open the back door of the courthouse, thought a moment, and said, "By the way, I've disallowed your last expense reimbursement. You didn't attach receipts."

"I bought sacks of potatoes and corn for the families at Redfish Lake. They don't give receipts at a farmers' market."

"Well, I'm sorry Ada, the rules are pretty clear."

"That was forty dollars of my own money!"

"Maybe you could use your TV connections." He grinned. "Hold a telethon—a benefit for the refugees. Figure it out; you went to college." Marsh wore his fishing vest out the back door, leaving Ada almost as baffled as she was angry.

A week's pay! She didn't have to figure that part out. It would be day-old bread and friends' home-grown vegetables—and don't even answer the door when the Avon lady rings!

THE TROUBLE FOR ASAKURA, SHE FOUND in the sheriff's files, had started before the arrest for rustling and before his confrontation with Neagle. Each incident file in the cabinet included a note from the FBI of his highly unexemplary conduct while interned at the Minidoka Japanese relocation center. He'd been a teenager there, but already tagged as a troublemaker. Each file included records of his military service, including both a silver star and a court martial.

Ada spent another couple of hours at her desk re-doing her remaining expense reports and travel vouchers to pass Marsh's sudden vindictive scrutiny. Satisfied with those, she drove home and got a load of laundry on the line, swept and mopped behind the dogs, and at last sat in the shade of her patio umbrella with a bottle of soda and a cigarette . . . but she had no matches.

There were no matches in the kitchen either, nor on the shelf above the washing machine. There was a book of matches in the glove box of the pickup out front, but her neighbor Karen Winslow was out in her front yard and Ada more than anything did not want to deal with her right then. She simply wanted a smoke.

She rifled through the pins and bobbles on her vanity, then looked into Montgomery's souvenir rosewood box of class rings, cufflinks, and military medals. There, at last, she found a lighter. It was a silver, bejeweled thing, and even under the forty-watt bedroom lamp she could see the case was emblazoned with the Riis-Moreau crest—that phony, mail-order design. The other side was engraved "SRM."

Ada grasped the lighter in a fist and leaned back heavily against the bedroom door. SRM—Sybil Riis-Moreau, bless her boozy, well-traveled ass—had no-doubt given the lighter as a gift to her 'sweet' friend Monty.

Update 4:15 p.m. – ~~Getting the hell out of~~ Patrolling south of the river.

SHE HAD THE DOGS FED AND LOCKED IN THE GARAGE and her gear tossed into the cab of the truck at a quarter past four. But where in God's name did she think she was going? To arrest a woman for having an affair with her husband? To shoot her?—the idea made her smile, but only for a moment, and besides, it would be more to the point to save the bullet for him. She only knew that things had changed suddenly and cruelly—everything had changed—and her life that was merely a mess that morning had become a train wreck.

She needed to get out of town to where no one could see her cry or see her break something or hear her scream. And so, she hit the highway with red light flashing and the siren blaring. But then that was too much like screaming, so she turned off the siren and the light after a mile or so.

Twenty miles south on Highway 75, she turned her sheriff's rig up the willow-choked East Fork, the valley where she'd lived nearly all of her life before Montgomery. The dusty road carried her up out of riparian woodlands, around low rocky knobs, and through small stands of scrub aspen. For a few miles the bumps and ruts kept her mind from wandering too far, and she was able after a while to get her breathing and her homicidal inclinations under control. She drove past wheat and barley fields where heavy combines were just bringing in the harvest, bounced and rattled through scattered remnants of forest, and raised dust over open meadows of sage and rabbit brush.

Five miles in from the highway, near Horse Canyon, the turns of the road, the fields, and the farm roads grew more familiar. Hayfields lay mowed into graceful contours matching the turn of the land, and coyote willow and alder brush in Autumn leaf bunched along the river and followed in rusty-orange clumps and yellow twisting hedges up every water course. A half a mile farther on, a gray timber hay stacker marked the corner of her father's north pasture as it had for as long as she could remember. A rail fence she and her father had built through a long, hot summer bordered the property. Now bleached and gray, the fence sagged with age.

At the turnoff to the farm where she was born, a broken-down hay rake sat overgrown with wild rose vines exactly where Montgomery had walked away from it five years earlier. The dirt lane seemed much narrower than she remembered. Her truck rumbled over the cattle guard and rolled to a stop in the yard between the barn and the two-story house.

It was Ada's house and her farm, left to her when her mother passed, although she hadn't been back for some time. She wasn't sure what had brought her back today, but she stepped out, staying close to the truck at first, with her foot on the running board and her arms draped over the side of the truck bed. The old farmhouse stood weathering under the afternoon sun, sagging here and there, half hidden behind overgrown honeysuckle. White paint peeled from porch columns, and the fascia and the siding hung dry and cracked. She sighed, closing her eyes and picturing every detail behind the shuttered windows: the upholstered furniture too worn to be hauled to town; doilies and tea tables; the dining set where her father said grace, too rustic for their new home in Camas; the souvenir dishes lining the walls—her mother's small pleasure—too old-fashioned for Montgomery's taste.

A low-angled sun stabbed her eyes when she looked up to see what bird sang in the big cottonwood. It was a robin, and the sun made her squint until her mouth formed a false smile. False or not, she wore the smile to the steps of the house, then onto the porch, then again when she found the key behind the shutter to unlock the front door. Inside, the floor creaked and the rooms echoed one by one. She set her rucksack on the kitchen table and worked open a few windows to air the place out, dusted a little bit, and turned down the bed.

The robin called her back out to the porch, where she sat down on the top step, leaned against the rough porch column, and closed her eyes for a few minutes. The late afternoon sun shined on her face and burned down on her legs and shoulders, and the tightness in her eased a little, although the feeling of being a damned fool didn't. She had bought a bottle of nice champagne the day Montgomery mustered to Seattle, and she'd been saving it for his return. But there on the weathered and leaf-strewn porch she worked out the cork, shooting it halfway across the barnyard. The drive from town had shaken the bottle, and it sprayed foam, which she caught in her mouth till it came out her nose. She wiped her hands, then lit a smoke from Sybil's engraved silver lighter.

A light breeze brought the smells of stream and woodland swirling through the barnyard, but not the smells of the farm she remembered. The manure of the calving pen had long ago dried, and the fields had not been turned, so the rich organic soils lay sealed under a dry surface rind. There was no musty grain, no pungent alfalfa, just the sourness of rotting leaves. Her father had scratched the farm out of the East Fork dirt and had lived his whole life there. To her knowledge he'd never been farther down the road than Camas. A blizzard up in the White Clouds one spring cost him half his herd and nearly his life, but he made it out of the canyon on the third morning, carrying a motherless calf up on the saddle with him. Ada, barely ten years old, had made the calf her own and nursed it twice a day with a glass bottle. "You'll make a fine mother someday," her father had told her—but of course, she never would.

She came home from college to help with the farm after he died, leaving behind the classroom studies, the parties, and pizza parlors. She left behind most of the laughter she could ever remember. But she was home and for a while that was enough, and her days had quickly filled with tractors and milk cows—and weeds. And then Montgomery answered her letters by driving all the way from Virginia to propose. He was tall and handsome, damn him; and he was gentle back then, too, and there was never a question but she would go away with him.

"Here's to you, Monty Reed," she said. "You big, sweet son of a bitch." She'd not brought a glass out with her, so she drank a toast from the bottle. Dust and bugs eddied in the yellowing afternoon light, and the air was warm and dry. She stretched her neck one way and the other and took another drink.

Montgomery moved her back to Richmond after a simple service, and he settled her in a neat little cottage near his parents, his brothers, and his brothers-in-law. He joined the Army and made captain even before the war started. Ada thought she would finish her degree at the local college, to fill the long days alone.

"But you already have a profession," her husband's family reminded her, "You're Mrs. Captain Montgomery Reed." So, she stayed home and learned to say "y'all," and to smile and be a proper hostess and wife.

She drank from the bottle, wiping her mouth with her hand and her hands on her pants, then wiping her eyes on her sleeves. She tossed her smoke and, as shadows lengthened, lit another and drew her knee up, hugging it in her arms to rest her chin.

Montgomery was called up after Pearl Harbor, and Ada was left alone in Richmond with his family who seemed not to give a damn if she was there or not. Her own mother needed her more than ever, so without asking anyone's permission, Ada caught the train back to Idaho—to the hayfields and calving pens, and the cold, clear waters.

And they worked together and waited, just the two of them,

though her mother grew weaker and weaker by the day. Her passing, at last, left Ada with nothing to count on but the dirt under her feet . . . until Montgomery caught up to her in '45.

The bastard! He stayed on the farm for not much more than a year—her dirt farm, he never let her forget, and her drafty, broken-down place way the hell and gone in the sticks. She refused to put her land in his name—it was all she had left of herself— and they'd fought over that, too. He asked for the sheriff job in town and was given it out of respect for his military rank, and he moved her to town with him—there was no discussion. Her livestock was sold off and her fields left neglected. There were not enough families after the war willing to work another's land; good workers left for highway and pipeline projects or for the factories of the cities. Her father's land—now her land—was left to ruin. They were her forsaken pastures now, overgrown with sage and rabbit brush; her hayfields gone to thistle, and her wheat fields gone to spurge and knapweed.

The cigarette burned her finger, startling her, and she flipped it down to the dirt of the barnyard and washed her mouth with another swallow of champagne. She stayed on the edge of the porch as the sun swept through the trees and the sky turned to gold and the air cooled. At last, the sun filtered red through a distant stand of locust trees, the golds and scarlets faded away, and a deep blue settled over the place.

She finished the bottle, leaning back against the porch post with the last sliver of the old moon rising red and hazy in the sky, then made it to her feet and fell down into her own bed for the first time in years.

CHAPTER EIGHT

Monday, 24 September, 9:00 a.m.
Late start this morning.
Follow-up interview with Mr. Asakura

THE COLD WOKE HER, AND A MORNING WIND that rattled the unheated farmhouse. The electricity was not turned on, nor the water, so after a stop in the bushes, she managed to make it back to town on a long drink from her canteen.

She arrived at her house on Fort Street—their house . . . Montgomery's house—in time to clean up a bit and put on a uniform not smelling of stale champagne. She got to the office a few minutes late, and after wincing through a chat with the mayor, was ready for a follow-up interview with Mr. Asakura.

Asakura stood from the table when she entered, and he bowed slightly. She reached through the bars to set a large cup of tea on the writing table, then pulled a chair over near the bars and sat with her own coffee. She said, "I didn't mean to presume, I just thought . . . I could get you a coffee if you prefer." A pencil lay on the table next to a few sheets of paper. He had been writing.

"No, please, this is fine; it was thoughtful of you."

They said nothing for a minute but sipped from their mugs. The windows were all closed to the street above and there were no other prisoners, so the cell block was quiet. There was just the creaking of the wood floor above as the courthouse employees arrived for work. Ada set her coffee on the floor and opened her notebook. "What are you writing," she asked.

Asakura remained standing. He rotated the paper on the desk, and read,

> *Wrought iron, wrought explanations.*
> *The flesh suffers chains,*
> *The heart, songs of the wren.*

"Is that a poem?"

He laughed softly and flipped the paper over. "Not if you have to ask."

"Sorry." She scrunched her lips. "Anyway, I found quite a folder on you in our files. Army records, notes about your time at Minidoka." She opened a manila folder. "I found these photos of Minidoka at the library.

Asakura did not lean in to look, nor did his expression change, although his jaw tightened a little.

"I did not arrest you, Eddy. You were brought to me as a suspect. But from what I've read, the Minidoka internment camp sits at the crux of a long-standing argument between you and a person recently deceased."

His chin came up, and he breathed in once and held it. She said, "The Snake River Plain must have been a bleak, dry desert after the gardens of Chehalis."

The young man said nothing. She crossed her legs and sipped her coffee. "It couldn't have been a lot of fun."

Asakura sat, then, on the wooden chair that had come with the table and stared at the white concrete wall beyond her head. "Thank you for the tea," he said. "It was very thoughtful."

"Your file says you were a troublemaker at the camp, a 'hot-head.' Is that true?"

He closed his eyes and cocked his head. "Those are the reports of a concentration camp warden."

"You were not a hothead?"

"I suppose I was. Although to this day I think I did not make enough trouble. There are some who can accept the sort of injustice imposed on us. I was never one of them. My father could accept it—at first. He was full of old-world wisdom, and he wasted many lectures on me."

"He was a leader of the community."

"It was not a community, Mrs. Reed, but a prison population. He used to tell a story to the children of the mighty oak and the willow. All about *Shouganai*, you know? He must have repeated that damned story in front of me a dozen times. I didn't listen. Perhaps I should have, but back then I thought, 'Look where we are! To hell with wisdom,' you know, 'what about honor?'" He had been looking at her as he talked, face to face, but he raised his eyes again to the wall behind her.

Ada said, "In the end, as I recall, the oak was destroyed."

"Yes, but only once."

"You felt you were done a great injustice . . ."

"We *were* done an injustice!" He slapped the table. "You cannot understand. You have never experienced oppression; to be scorned and dominated; not afforded the least dignity."

She put down her pen, closed the notebook, and stepped away from the bars. After a long moment she said, "I don't get to call it oppression." She closed her eyes and the last night's anger rose up in her for a moment. She turned to face him. "Maybe you should . . ." she began. "Never mind. It must have been terrible for you and your father."

"It was terrible for everyone."

She held her tongue for a few seconds more, then asked, "I wonder, did you ever ask your mother if she felt a difference in *her* situation?"

"What the hell does that mean?"

"Very little, if you have to ask." She moved to the far wall and stood for a full minute before returning to her chair, then waited a moment more to regain her calm. "You were treated unjustly at the internment camp, there's no argument, and yet you joined the army and fought for America."

Now Asakura stood. He paced to the end of the cell. "I did not consider at the time that I was fighting for America. The Nazis were even more unjust, let's be honest. And the army provided me a gun with which to fight them."

"And a knife, it seems. Your service file shows you were a master of *Ninjutsu*: concealment, assassination, daggers and poisons. It was in your Army records."

He scoffed. "The *shinobi*? The *ninja*? I just told them that so I could sound bad-ass, you know. So I wouldn't get picked on in boot camp."

"Yet, you worked outside the perimeter."

He appeared to have calmed and now stood impassively but for his eyes, which closed tightly, then looked past her to the wall behind. He said, "Murder takes no special training."

For a minute the jailhouse quieted as she jotted a lengthy note. There was the sound again of workers upstairs, and of delivery trucks at alley level. Asakura sighed. "My parents, by then, were gone, you know. The Army got around to informing me—with regrets, of course."

When Ada looked up from her notebook, Asakura had stiffened and was standing nearly at attention. She asked, "How do you win a Silver Star and a court martial in a single month?"

This time the wry smile did not vanish so quickly. "Silver Star for killing; court martial for not killing. Wouldn't you just know it."

Ada cocked her head and held the pen above the page. He shrugged and said, "An order was given that . . . I thought dishonorable. Nothing more than that." He sat again.

She made a quick note in her book then asked, "Why do you think it was Clifford Neagle who shot your father?"

"I don't think it was. It was shown in court someone else pulled the trigger; a stupid . . . a scared teenager. Neagle wasn't even a guard; he carried no gun." He locked his fingers behind his head, leaned back, and took a deep breath. "I had no valid complaint. The suit was dismissed. So, you see Mrs. Reed, the whole question is moot." He turned his eyes, finally, to her. "Moot—a useful term. I learned that, at least, in my encounters with American justice." He closed his eyes and quieted.

As she was leaving, Ada asked, "Are the amenities not to your liking? The sergeant-at-arms says you are not eating."

"The food is generous."

"Are you protesting your incarceration? A hunger strike—like Ghandi?"

He dropped his head and chuckled. "I am far too selfish for that. It's only that I have not eaten meat my whole life."

Update 11:30 a.m. – Lunch with Mr. Mayor

DOLLY'S CAFÉ CLATTERED WITH A MIDWEEK lunch crowd, and Ada was lucky to get a booth at all, let alone the one under the picture of Old Faithful. Mayor Applegate wasn't there yet and wouldn't be for another ten minutes, so she pulled out her notebook and pen. She was used to Ephraim's estimation of the importance of his time. Besides, he was paying and beggars can't be finger-snappers, she supposed, with her whole paycheck gone to buy food for the Redfish encampment.

Her stomach felt queasy, as it should after a whole bottle of champagne, and she'd not had a thing but coffee all morning. She ate a half dozen soda crackers while she waited. It helped a little.

When the mayor entered, it was with handkerchief mopping his hatless head. He left his linen coat on the hook by the door, preferring to be seen in suspenders and a loosened tie to sitting at lunch flushed and sweating.

"Pardon the suspenders," he said, stuffing the handkerchief

into his pocket and holding his tie so he could lean in for a kiss on the cheek.

"You weren't at the rally on Saturday," Ada said. "Chief Munson noticed; he was disappointed."

"I am sorry, sweet . . ."

"Kellen thinks a lot of you. A number of people mentioned your absence. I told them you would stop by later if you were sober enough."

"You did not!"

"And then you didn't show, and what were they supposed to think?"

"Is it fun, Ada?—teasing your old uncle like you do?"

She shrugged and twisted her lips. Applegate said, "I like Kellen Munson. It was nothing personal to him, or to you. I'm just not sure of the way things are going; whether the way things are changing is the right way right now."

A willowy girl of maybe twenty-two hurried to their table with glasses of water and menus. Ada smiled up at her. "How are you getting along, Debbie Lynn?" she asked.

"I'm real good, Mrs. Reed—I mean sheriff." She wore a bright smile and her red hair in an up-do. Applegate studied the menu, glancing up at the girl a couple of times.

When she'd gone, Applegate leaned forward and in a hushed voice said, "This is exactly what I'm talking about. That Greiner boy disappeared—hasn't been seen since June. And now Debbie Lynn is living in the house all by herself. She's not a schoolgirl anymore, Ada. She's a grown woman who men take notice of. It could be misconstrued."

"It's not being misconstrued."

"It's . . . not the way things ought to be."

"He didn't disappear, he caught a train to California and left Debbie Lynn behind." She turned her eyes back to the menu. "That may not be the way things ought to be, Uncle Eph, but it's how things are and always have been."

The girl returned with her order pad, and Ada asked for a chef salad with buttermilk dressing, thinking that would sit okay. The mayor ordered the meatloaf special. When she had gone, Applegate leaned back to dig out his handkerchief again and asked Ada about the Jap she was holding in her jail.

Her eyes darted to the nearby tables. "Japanese, Uncle Eph," she whispered.

"I know the proper conjugation, Ada. I'm not prejudiced." He mopped his forehead. "How did he kill those people? It's important you reason that out. When I was a prosecutor, I could sometimes get a conviction based on the circumstances . . ."

"Uncle Eph . . ." She leaned her elbows on the table and laid her chin in her hand.

"But a means of death would make it a lot quicker trial for you."

"There is still no direct evidence they were killed."

"They're dead."

The pounding in her head was faint but coming on fast. She put away her notebook and pen and, fighting to control her patience, said, "I mean, other than by the fire."

He buttered a cracker and waggled it at her. "Well, it's your business, sheriff. I would never look over your shoulder, but the Nipponese are an ancient culture. We're a much younger people; we can't begin to fathom all their ways. Remember, there was a reason the government moved them off the West Coast, and you know there was. They have ways and means of which we are yet innocent."

"Ephraim . . .!"

"Now don't look at me like that. There's not a prejudiced bone in my body. I'm just saying, they don't assimilate into our society. They think differently."

"Let's leave the enigmatic Mr. Asakura aside for a minute." She took a deep breath. "How well do you know Louis Boniface?"

Applegate cleaned butter from his thumb and stared for a moment at the geyser scene above them. "Well . . . I hardly know him at all. Why would you ask that?"

"Didn't you prosecute him at one time?"

"I see. No, not exactly; the charges were dropped." He dabbed his neck with the handkerchief. "There was some suggestion of . . . mishandled evidence."

Ada didn't dare look up. That sort of thing happened now and then, but Applegate's words and his hesitation brought back a creepy feeling she'd had since talking to Holland Riis-Moreau—since hearing of Montgomery's name on ledgers. She cleared her throat. "Mishandled by whom?" she asked.

"It doesn't matter." He twisted in his seat. "Where is that girl with our lunch, do you suppose?" To Ada he said, "The decision to drop hinged on complications regarding jury selection, in any case. Why do you ask about Boniface?"

"I found an object that once belonged to Boniface on the person of a young man, and I was wondering how he may have come upon it; whether it was a gift or a sticky-fingered acquisition."

"I see. Not one of the Neagles?"

She nodded. "The older boy, Dolf."

"Oh, no. It would not have been a gift to that boy. Boniface disliked him—they had a heck of a row on Main Street in Stanley. I did put him away for that, and for resisting arrest. This would have been earlier—five or six years back. I thought him a danger-ous man back then. He called thunder and hellfire down on me, as I recall the day; cursed and threatened me publicly, the unbalanced old eremite."

Debbie Lynn brought their orders in one well-balanced load, and she fussed for a minute with their napkins and flatware. Ada gave her time to finish and leave, then said, "I had to go out to the Obsidian Ranch the other day. The same young man had an item belonging to Riis-Moreau."

"Now, that sounds more like a gift, perhaps. But not from Holland—more likely from Mrs. Riis-Moreau."

Her stomach was a knot by then, and she wondered if her uncle knew more about Montgomery's business than she did.

"Why her?" she asked. It occurred to her the whole damned county might have known Montgomery's business while she was golfing, and lunching, and busying herself with Junior League and the Women's Auxiliary.

Applegate was saying, "I am hardly an authority on the larger or the smaller subject here, but my barber's brother-in-law delivers groceries and liquor to the ranch. And from what I'm told and can surmise, the Neagle boy might well have been attractive enough and of sufficiently low morals to have his attentions rewarded by the lady of that house."

"It makes me sick," Ada said, her mind racing beyond the mayor's meaning.

"It does me as well." Applegate tucked the napkin under his chin and dug into the meatloaf and mashed potatoes.

Between bites he said, "This is exactly why I hate to see you doing the sheriff work, sweetheart. These themes are unwholesome. What would Montgomery think of you going out to that den of iniquity?"

"I'm sure Montgomery would be very open-eyed about it." She stabbed at shreds of cheese, ham, and lettuce, force-feeding herself before her appetite faded completely.

She asked, "Did you uhm . . . . Did you know anything about Montgomery's poker nights?"

He didn't answer directly, but said, "I certainly see how an inappropriate dalliance at the Obsidian Ranch might raise doubts regarding the Japanese prisoner."

He spoke without looking up from his plate. "Holland Riis-Moreau is not one to mess with, either."

"When I was out there, Holland seemed uninterested in anyone's dalliances but his own."

"As you said, it's a disgusting line of inquiry and I can't believe I'm talking to my niece about this. I won't even tell Corrine. She won't hear a word about it!"

Ada offered Mayor Applegate a ride to the Town Hall, inasmuch as it was on her way to the clinic at 7th and Pleasant. Doctor Mink wanted to discuss some findings of the blood work he'd had done on the Neagle family members. On 4th Street, one block from the Town Hall, her political opponent had put up a campaign sign:

JEFF BANNING FOR SHERIFF
Honest – Competant

Ada pulled up to the stop sign. "Your man's getting his message out," she said.

Applegate sighed. "Politics isn't personal, Ada. Banning is a solid choice . . ."

"He's a solid he."

"He's got experience; he's got expertise."

"Yeah." She sat for a second with her head down and her lip between her teeth, then set the parking brake of the truck.

"Yeah," she said again, and reached across to fumble in the jockey box for a small metal tube.

"He may have all that, but he hasn't got lipstick." She waited for a car to pass on the crossing street, then got out of the truck and hustled over to the sign. She crossed out the 'a' in 'Competant' and drew an 'e' over it with the red lipstick, then hurried back into the truck. She said nothing, but released the brake and continued to the Town Hall.

As he stepped to the sidewalk, the mayor said, "You think that was clever, don't you?"

"Thanks for lunch, Mr. Mayor. Love to Aunt Corrie."

Update 1:45 p.m. – Salmon River Clinic:
reviewing additional Valley Creek evidence with Dr. Mink

"But that makes no goddamned sense, Dennis!" Ada took up the laboratory reports a third time and scanned the charts and tables as though the numbers might change. "Pardon my French," she allowed.

"Well, it's pretty clear," Dr. Mink answered. "They were alive as the fire came through. They could not have been dead beforehand." He'd shown her the blood workups done at the lab in Pocatello. In the samples from Mooch, Dolf, and Clifford Neagle the carbon-monoxide levels indicated the victims were breathing heavy smoke shortly before they died. The blood samples from Irma's body were less definitive because of the high degree of immolation, but they too showed elevated carbon-monoxide levels.

"They were all alive and breathing," Mink said again. He hung up his suit jacket and put on a white laboratory coat.

"Could they have been near death; barely hanging on?" Ada asked.

"From the high levels of C-O, they had to have been breathing deeply, and probably coughing violently for a couple of minutes before death."

"Unconscious?"

"Impossible to say how they started out, but they would eventually have lost consciousness—if they were lucky."

This was not good. Actually, it was good, but it wasn't. She had four victims who had let a fire overtake them without any noticeable effort—but for Dolf in the very last-minute—to save themselves. There was no sign they were drunk, and no sign they had been assaulted in any way. And she'd just spent over two hundred and sixty-four dollars of County funds to say they'd sat down and waited to burn to death.

"Have you transferred the bodies to the funeral home?" Ada asked.

"I had to. They're awaiting your instructions."

"Thanks, Dennis. I'll check with them later."

SHE'D DREADED MAKING THE CALL from the minute she read the carbon monoxide report. Now she sat with the blinds pulled and both her elbows planted on her desk. The phone squawked in her ear. She'd already been 'goddamned' half a dozen times.

She said, "Ken . . . Sergeant Blevins . . . I have to release him in the morning. It's the law." She banged the phone against her head. "Huh-uh . . . No. And that's just it," she said, "there's no evidence the Neagles were murdered. There was no physical assault, and no sign at all they were killed by anything but smoke and fire."

She held the receiver away when Blevins practically yelled, "People don't sit down and wait to burn!"

"Thank you for that insight, Sergeant." She leaned as far back in her chair as was safe. The state cop didn't actually call her a dumb broad, but the meaning was right there in the tone of his voice.

She said, "Because . . . I cannot . . . hold Mr. Asakura as a suspect in a murder when there is no evidence of a murder! If you want to go back to the scene and find more evidence, be my guest. Don't fall in the goddamned well."

Blevins knew the law as well as she did, but he was being a pissant. "Yes, but . . . Ken, it's called *habeas corpus!*"

She held the receiver away for a minute and rubbed her eyes. "No. No . . . No, you cannot hold him for evading arrest when there was no arrest warrant, and not for fleeing a crime inasmuch as there's no evidence of a stupid crime! That, I believe, is called wrongful imprisonment!"

"The man is dangerous," Blevins bawled over the phone. "He's always been a malcontent; a damned troublemaker!"

"He's a war hero. He won the Silver Star."

"For killing!"

"Well Ken, that's the thing about war, isn't it?"

"Do you have any other leads?"

"There's . . . There is some complication involving . . . well, some items that might have belonged to a Mr. Louis Boniface." She cleared her throat.

"Ada!" There was a pause and the sound of the phone receiver banging a hard object. "Madam Sheriff, no!"

"I have to get out to his farm, if I can find the place, and have a chat with him . . . tomorrow if possible."

"No, Ada! This is a rock-solid case, and there's no reason to drag in a drunken, washed-up cowboy moonshiner."

"Have you had dealings out there? Have you been to his place in Basin Creek?"

"It's on you! If you release that Nipponese son of a bitch and things go south, the whole county—hell, the whole damned state— is going to know you did it."

CHAPTER NINE

25 September 1951, 8:00 a.m.
Releasing Eddy Asakura today,
Then to Basin Creek to see a Mr. Louis Boniface.

EDDY ASAKURA WAITED FOR THE ACTING SHERIFF to work the key in the lock to open the cell door. His face remained unexpressive, and his posture dignified but relaxed. He said only 'thank you' when Ada handed him the envelope with his personal effects, then turned away to run his belt through the loops of his trousers and buckle it. He gathered up his papers, tossed his jacket over his arm, and followed quietly to the motor pool.

Her passenger did not speak during the drive, and she could think of nothing to say, so they rode quietly for thirty miles. A few minutes beyond Clayton, the packed gravel highway hugged in between the river and a high alluvial terrace on the south side of the canyon. There, Ada turned her pickup onto the dusty and washboarded Juniper Flat Road, which carried them up onto a small, half-mile-wide terrace. The land lay about fifty feet above the highway and the river and stayed flat for about a mile in length. It pinched at either end where the river cut back in against the steep forested hills.

Dust billowed from under the truck's wheels, although she drove slowly across the flats. A dozen or so farms scraped the rocky soil of the terrace, and bony cattle and mules grazed along fence lines and two-track driveways. They passed dead and stunted fruit trees planted in wide-spaced rows, and bounced and rattled between fields of alfalfa, potatoes, and what was probably barley. The farms of Juniper Flat were mostly settled with trailer homes and tarpaper shacks baking in the sun. A few scattered locust trees shaded some of the homes, and she noted lilac bushes and hollyhocks amidst the general misfortune of the place. The flat land was bisected by the deep and straight Juniper Gulch, which was dry where the road dropped into it and climbed back out of it.

Asakura guided her with hand signals through turns, across gullies, and past mule and chicken sheds to an open gate that let them into an unexpectedly cool and shaded property. She parked under a stand of elms before a neat cottage that reminded her of Maggie Li's small house with the mossy roof in the town of Custer.

"Thank you for the ride, Sheriff," Asakura said as Ada pulled on the brake handle. They were his first words since his mumbled 'thank you' back in Camas. He opened the door of the truck, paused, and asked, "May I offer you a drink of water before you go?"

"Thank you, if you don't mind. It's ridiculously hot, isn't it?"

"I've not seen such weather."

She stepped out of the pickup and put on her Stetson, but then took it off again at the front gate. She said, "I'm sorry, Eddy. I'm sorry you had to go through all that."

"All that." He turned and with hands on hips examined the sage-studded hills across the canyon. "It was not such a tribulation. Our imprisonment at Minidoka inured us, perhaps, to these smaller ordeals." He put on his hat and started toward the house. "At least this time you dignified me with a charge of murder and not just one of brown skin and narrow eyes."

Ada drew in a breath, which Asakura must have heard even above the rustle of the elms. He turned with a thin smile and added, "I didn't mean you, Mrs. Reed. You did not accuse me." He gave a shallow bow and stepped through the door, leaving her to wonder if his bow had been meant ironically—or even mockingly.

She stretched one way and the other, then waited a step inside the gate. In the dappled light the air was comfortable, and smelled of dust and manure, and of sunbaked fields. After a minute and because the shade was fine and birds were singing in the trees, she strolled as she waited into the well-tended yard and to the back of the house, to where she could see over the edge of the gravel bench through thick birch and pine to the shining river below. The highway was not visible through the foliage, but she could hear cars rolling by in both directions.

"Mr. Asakura is not here," a woman's voice called above the sound of the wheels and the birds. "Is there something I can help you with?" Beyond a lilac hedge, hidden from where she'd parked, a clearing opened up and there a woman with water can and trowel stood amid rows of corn, tomatoes, and root vegetables.

Ada started toward her. "Yes, I know, but he's home now," she called back. The woman was short, maybe five-five or so, but not stout—or not yet stout. She wore her yellow hair in braids and waited, a little uneasily perhaps, in many-pocketed khaki trousers and a long-sleeve cotton print blouse. She must have been younger than Ada, although her face was more deeply lined, and her eyes a little more sunken than . . . than when Ada had known her well.

"Inga Nilsen, is that you? Why, it is you!" Ada hurried through the hedge row and into the furrowed field.

"Well, bar the gates of Hades. I thought it might be you, Ada Reed."

"How long has it been? Inga, where in the world have you been?"

The woman wiped her arm over her face, leaving a small smudge above the eye. She seemed not quite pleased by Ada's question, though not fully put out by it either.

"I heard you'd stepped out of your tea dresses and heels," she said. "It's been six years, and I have been easy enough to find right here in Juniper Flat. I've gone nowhere."

Ada stepped forward to give Inga Nilsen a hug, but when the other woman stayed put and glanced aside, she offered her hand instead.

"It's good to see you," she said. "How have you been?" They'd known each other during the war, the last war. Although never close friends—Ada assumed it was the nearly ten years that separated them—they had waited out the war and worried for their husbands together. Mont served in Europe as an Army major, while Lars Nilsen swabbed the decks of a Navy cruiser in the Pacific. Ada and Inga had sewed together and collected for this and that together; and of course there was the Women's Land Army where Ada, by virtue of her college years, had served as a local officer. Montgomery had already returned from Europe when they learned Inga's husband had died at Leyte Gulf. The Japanese— those damned kamikaze fanatics had . . .

"There you are." Eddy Asakura approached from the lilac bushes with two glasses of water. He joined the women and they all stood together among the carrots and radishes for a long moment. Nilsen had to stick the trowel in her pocket in order to take the water offered but thanked him with a smile.

He said, "Mrs. Nilsen, I am most grateful to you for looking after the garden in my absence." He turned and smiled at the two acres or so of lush vegetables. "I had lost hope someone would."

"It was the least I could do." She glanced sideways at Ada.

Ada said, "Well, I'm pleased things worked out as well as they did." When no one answered, she said, "Anyway, Inga, I had thought you'd gone back to Boise. Your family is from there, as I recall?"

"Nampa. But no, I stayed on here, on my husband's land." She nodded toward a clapboard house and a patched and weathered barn a hundred yards beyond a weed-tangled fence.

"So, you're taking up where Montgomery left off, are you?" she asked.

"I'm not sure what you mean. It was a temporary appointment, but it doesn't look like things will be settled in Korea any time soon. The voters will decide in a few weeks."

Again there was silence until Asakura said, "But the garden looks fine, Inga. You have been busy, it's easy to see." He turned to Ada. "Isn't the garden doing well? You must take some fresh vegetables home with you. I'll have more than I can harvest, thanks to the help of my neighbors."

"You must," Inga said. Then slightly embarrassed, "I'll fetch a basket."

While they waited for her to return, Asakura pulled carrots and radishes, and dug up a potato hill for her. He kept quiet as he worked, and Ada wasn't sure what else she could say to him in apology. She found a raised bed planted with herbs and spice bushes and asked if she could take some cuttings to her friend in Custer.

"Do you know Margaret Li? She's quite a gardener herself, although much of her plot has sunk into the dredge pond."

"I know her by reputation, but we have not met. Yes, please take whatever you think she might like."

The woman in the combat trousers returned from the garden shed with a cane basket, and she and Asakura filled it with root vegetables and cabbage, tomatoes, and a half dozen ears of sweet corn. Ada thanked them, and then thanked them again because there was little else to say. She drove back through the gate, past the chicken coops and up and down across the gullies as the two gardeners watched from the furrowed plot under the unseasonal sun.

Update 1:45 p.m. – Continuing on to Basin Creek
to see Louis Boniface, if I can find the old Québécois.

Louis "Frenchy" Boniface was known to be a rodeo star in bygone years, and a fighter and a lothario, also in bygone years.

It was whispered he was a moonshiner and a trader of items of undocumented provenance. Ada's current interest, however, was his alleged disagreement with a young man who happened to be wearing Louie's belt buckle when he died. It was the best lead she had. If the two had indeed fought, even years ago, it was the place to start. From Juniper Flat, therefore, she continued west up Highway 75, past Sunbeam Junction, to Basin Creek for a chat.

The road north up Basin Creek was narrow and washboarded, and flanked on both sides by thick pine forest and by undergrowth so dry it gave off dusty chaff whenever a breeze stirred it. She started up in early afternoon with a plume of dust rising in her rear-view mirror. As the road twisted and turned, glimpses of smoke spread across the northern sky in stratospheric layers. The middle distance in all directions was hazy and gray, and she would not ordinarily have continued on the drive, especially alone, but Ben's—Ranger McGann's—deputy ranger had told her the Loon Creek fire was a full day from the Crags and unlikely to jump that rocky ground. She passed no one coming out of the sparsely peopled valley and saw no wood gatherers or sportsmen along the way.

The road clung mostly to the east side of the creek but splashed over to the other side half a dozen times across gravelly fords where the water reached to her axles. The road would be impassable in the spring by any vehicle, she guessed, and by hers after any kind of a rain. Seven miles in from the highway the road narrowed to a sandy two track, and there Boniface's road, according to the map she'd found in the files, took off to the east through a narrow cleft between red cliffs. It was barely a dusty trail through the trees when she found it.

She followed the trail and soon came to a heavy chain stretched between two ponderosa pines, which effectively blocked further ingress. Ada honked her horn then turned off her engine and waited. For twenty minutes she waited. She tried her AM radio and then her police band radio, but there was no reception of any kind down in the canyon. Deer and even bear crossed the trail in front of her—nervous creatures smelling but not seeing a fire in their hills. She waited ten minutes more, then cut one of the links from the chain and drove through.

Boniface's ravine opened up beyond the cliffs and the stand of ponderosa to a flat meadow a quarter mile wide and twice as long. Farm buildings stood near the top of the meadow and included a log house with a broad covered porch. Stables, a paddock, and a badly weathered barn stood to the left of the house, but there were no horses, nor did the air smell of livestock when Ada stepped from the truck. The barn was hung with tack, but it was otherwise empty except for a swarm of cats. Behind the barn, three acres of corn rustled in a light breeze, harvested of ears but with stalks standing in the ground. The place was quiet but for the rustling of the corn and the cries of blue jays.

Ada called out but heard nothing in answer. Neither was there an answer to her knock at the front door of the house. She smelled smoke in the air, though. She'd been driving through the smoke of burning pine forest all day, but this smell was sharper, like burning hardwood, and when she stepped around the house she saw a thin column of black smoke rising from the trees a few hundred yards up the hill. She trotted back and retrieved her service revolver from the glove box, slung a canteen over her shoulder, and headed through the cornfield toward the smoke.

A wire fence had to be crossed, and then another, to get to a jeep trail that wound into the dense spruce wood. The trail rose steeply; her lungs burned with the smoke, and her boots scraped in the loose gravel as she followed the trail up and around a tall outcropping of rhyolite. In a patch of sunlight, she mopped her face and was drinking from her canteen when the rock above her head smacked loudly. A split second later, a rifle crack reverberated over the gulch.

Ada dove into the brush beside the track and from her belly shouted, "Boniface? Is that you, Louis Boniface? Hold your damned fire. Don't make me pull my gun!"

"You're a woman?" a man shouted back.

"Jesus! You didn't figure that much out before you took a shot? I'm Sheriff Ada Reed."

"What the hell do you want?" He was hunkered on top of a rocky knob some forty yards ahead. There was little cover between him and her.

"I want to talk to you about Dolf Neagle!"

"Is the son of a whore dead?"

"Yes."

"Guard his soul."

She rose to her knee. "Can we talk?"

"I don't see the need, but if you think it's important, you leave your gun there on the rock and keep your hands out front for a time longer."

"I'd rather not do that."

"If I was going to shoot you, we wouldn't be talking."

It was a fair point. She unbelted her holster and left it and the canteen on a flat rock as requested, then walked forward with her hands out to her sides. The trail carried her up and around the rocky knob, but when she got there Boniface was not to be seen. She followed the trail another twenty yards between rhyolite hoodoos that guarded a sandy flat surrounded by tall pines. A rough timber lean-to stood to the back of the flat flanked by a cord of willow wood. Water splashed from a steel pipe extending out of the trees in back, and smoke spilled out from the front edge of the lean-to and rose in a Coriolis twist. A copper tank and pipes were situated under the roof, and a fire burned under the tank.

"What are you cooking?" Ada asked the man lurking behind the tank.

He stepped out, took a seat on a worn stump, and indicated to Ada to find a like seat. He laid down his rifle, but near to him. "I'm preserving some corn for the winter months," he answered.

"I'm Sheriff Ada Reed."

"Come to ask for my vote?"

"Not today. Are you Louis Boniface?"

"That is what *maman* told me many years ago." The man spoke with a heavy accent, but one as much Canadian backwoods as French.

"Distilling alcohol without a license is against the law."

"Yes, I've heard something about that. Letting good corn go to waste is against God's law. Do you come to arrest me?"

"Not today."

His hair was mostly black on the top of his head, but nearly white on the sides. He was dark-eyed and heavy-browed with a prominent nose but soft lips. His face was deeply weathered but taut, and Ada could not guess his age within a decade.

"How did the Neagle boy die?" he asked.

"He and his folks, his brother too, were caught up in the forest fire that swept through west of here."

"Caught up? They couldn't outrun it?"

"Didn't try to. It appeared they just sat down and waited for it."

The man inched forward on the stump and tilted his head. His flesh seemed loosely draped over the frame of a man once powerful who'd gotten soft. "But they were dead before it got to them?" he asked.

"Hard to say. A couple of them appeared to be moving around."

"What about Dolf, how did he buy it?"

"You fought with Dolf Neagle a few years ago; did some jail time. Want to explain what that was about?"

"You want to explain where's your old man?"

"Korea."

"Oh. Makes sense. Montgomery never bothered me out here in the woods. He always took care of legal matters in an equitable fashion. Are you like him?"

"Generally, no."

"Too bad." The man cleared his throat and turned to spit. "Three weeks I sat in jail. It wasn't Montgomery Reed who locked me up but the gentleman who held the job before him. Lance Harding, keep his black soul."

Ada was only half listening, and wondering what he'd meant by 'an equitable fashion.' She started to ask, "What did you mean . . ."

But Boniface's head had slumped, and he was saying something, mumbling, as much to himself as to her: ". . . But you'll say, 'Harding was only doing his job as any lawman must.'" He squinted up at Ada who had sat with the hazy sun behind her, and he turned his lips and his eyes into a disarmingly pleasant smile. "And the prosecuting attorney, too—am I right?—just doing his very important job."

His face changed back quickly. "Dolf Neagle was a rutting pig, but I wasn't trying to kill him, it was merely a miscarriage of communication. Besides, all them bilious thoughts are behind me. I have said to all that hatred and reprisal 'get thee behind me!'" He coughed, then needed a couple tries to refill his lungs. "Yes, behind me along with the devil his self."

Ada had taken out her notebook when the moonshiner began to speak but didn't put pen to paper. She leaned forward with elbows on knees, surprised to be enjoying the man's accent and the rhythm of his speech.

He said, "I've been making amends for those shameful affairs of my past."

She smiled without meaning to. "You get religion?"

"I had religion. I got cancer." He coughed again, and Ada noticed he'd been holding his right abdomen, and it was distended out of sorts.

He said, "The doctors say it's going to kill me, and recently it feels the old quacks may be on to something." He took a drink from a Mason jar, gulping the clear liquid. "They'll always be right in the end." He winked at her, again disarmingly.

Ada sat back on the stump, crossing her leg over her knee. She clicked her pen. "Making amends how?" she asked.

"I been sending offerings of peace to the folks with whom I have quarreled, the folks whom I have accused and thought ill of; to those who may have gotten a short measure of truth and justice. Won't you have some?" He extended the jar to Ada, who shook her head.

He said, "I haven't the time for quarrels no more, you see. I'm making things right before that cold wind comes to scatter my dust."

He paused and went through another coughing ordeal, catching his breath and squeezing his arm to his side. "I sent a fine gift to Dolf Neagle in hopes of burying the hatchet. My desire was for righteous understanding between us; for nothing less than to abort . . ."—he coughed—"to purge all those heinous passions and iniquities."

"The gift you sent—that would be the trophy buckle, then?" Ada asked.

"To abort the very . . ." The old man slumped down and popped his neck one way and then another. "He was wearing a trophy buckle?"

"It had your name engraved on the back. *L. Boniface, 1946.*"

The man had been sitting with elbows on knees, and now he dropped his head low and brought his hands up to cradle it.

When he raised his head, he stared a long moment directly into the declining sun. "He was wearing it when he died?"

"He was, yes."

Boniface took a deep drink from the jar, then had to catch his breath again. "Blessed Lord, my peace offering was not wasted. Dolf Neagle died knowing my heart."

He jerked his elbow in and his whole body racked with a cough. "Redemption came in heaven's time, carried on the wings of angels." He wheezed. "Sweet Jesus!"

THE SUN HAD ALREADY SET BEHIND distant Basin Butte by the time Ada retreated down the trail. The sun was gone but there was still good light, and she walked hastily but upright. All the way down she could hear the man coughing and cussing her and making all manner of threats and curses. She stopped for her holstered gun, leaving Boniface's *30-30* on the flat rock in its place. She'd taken the rifle even though she knew he would not have shot her—probably not, anyway. She was his witness; as much as he cussed her, she carried his testament. But she'd taken the rifle anyway, because he'd been so drunk she thought it irresponsible to leave it with him.

She buckled on the holster and crossed over the wire fences, made her way back through the cornfield, and started up her truck under a frightful orange sky. Night had all but fallen as she crossed back over the chain barrier she'd cut on the way in and wound her way back out to the Forest Service road.

She found herself hurrying down the road, skidding through the tighter turns, and in the straight stretches throwing up rocks that knocked and banged against the undercarriage. The interview with Louis Boniface had gone astray and she'd left there almost ill with apprehension. It wasn't only having been shot at; it wasn't the forest fire vaguely threatening in the north, nor the willow wood fire she'd doused, nor even the smell of sour corn rot suffusing the clearing where they'd sat. He'd wanted to talk, and he had rambled, had admitted to years of infractions, sins, and regrets. She hadn't wanted to hear it, but she didn't want not to hear it either, so she'd let him go on for what seemed hours. He'd boasted and cried over crimes and loves, and even over the family he'd once had and lost; the wife who'd run off, and his darling girl, defiled and betrayed.

Ada would not taste his liquor, and he'd been furious at her refusal; had cursed her in the most vulgar ways; threatened her.

In the end, he'd said it was just as well. "Go on your way, then, Ada Reed," he told her. "This is no place for your kind—this mountain of whiskey and romance. You'll find nothing here to solve your riddles nor to cure what ails you."

He could barely sit but had gone on drinking. "Oh, the purification of fire," he'd shouted. "How I envy Neagle for knowing such purity!" He'd poured the jar of liquor over his head and laughed stupidly. "Lord, I could drown in it!"

She'd jumped up, filled a bucket at the pipe, and doused the fire so the fool wouldn't catch himself ablaze.

"*Connasse!*" He screamed. "Self-righteous whore!" But he'd stumbled going for the rifle and sprawled in the mud and corn mash.

She'd dropped the bucket and taken the rifle, then, and walked disgusted from the puking, urinating drunk. But even in the depth of debasement there had been dread about the man, and she could feel it yet: an awful apprehension, as with a candle that flickers at the breath of a storm.

Ada hit the first ford of Basin Creek at high speed, and the water splashed up over her hood and nearly drowned out her engine. It took a quarter of a mile to get all of the cylinders firing again. She slowed her truck, but her breathing and her heartbeat took a while longer to control. In the next crossing of the stream, she let the dark waters bounce her sideways as she crawled the truck over the creek bed. Her headlights slashed through aspen and pine climbing out of the stream and with every turn of the road. She followed more gently now, but the damage had already been done: a tire went flat not halfway out to the highway.

In an open stretch of road, she stepped out into a moonless night with a strong wind blowing down from the north. As she stood in the road with the tire iron in hand, a bear trotted out of the darkness, looked her over and sniffed, then hurried on its way southward. The skyline in the direction from where the bear had come glowed orange, and the north wind was heavy with smoke and ash. Ada tightened the lug nuts, wrestled the broken tire into the bed of her truck, and continued on toward town.

'A mountain of whiskey and romance,'—Sybil Riis-Moreau had used the same words. She had to know Boniface. But did Holland know him too, or would this be another . . . private affair? Sybil knew Boniface, Boniface knew Dolf Neagle, and Dolf knew Sybil—knew her well enough to be rewarded for his attentions. Was it coincidence, Ada wondered? Was it merely the way things go in a small county, or was there more to it?

CHAPTER TEN

Wednesday, 26 September.
Making the rounds today
Custer jailhouse with Chief Munson

ADA HADN'T FELT COMFORTABLE AT THE Custer jailhouse since the tragic events of July. Nevertheless, she jammed the Stetson on her head as she stepped out of the truck, straightened her tie, and walked head up across the street. She hopped up onto the board-walk, allowed herself a deep breath, and eased through the door.

She said, "Morning, Chief. I stopped by to tell you I drove Eddy Asakura home yesterday. I didn't want you to hear it from the rumor mill."

"Already heard it." Munson set down his coffee and pushed back in his chair. "And good morning, Sheriff. I hope it's a good thing, releasing him. The State agreed to it?"

"There was nothing to hold him on."

"Means, motive, and oppor . . ." The Custer police chief liked Ada Reed, but he knew her well enough to recognize the beginnings of a lengthy discussion. "Never mind," he said. "Do you have any other suspects?"

"I still have no direct evidence a crime was committed. But yes, if it came to that, I'd be interested in Holland Riis-Moreau and maybe Louis Boniface."

"There's a pair to draw to."

"Dolf Neagle knew them both—in not the best of ways." Ada poured herself a coffee, smelled it was burned, and added two heaping spoons of sugar.

"How well did you know the victims—the Neagle family?" she asked, sitting in the chair opposite his at the desk. "How did they get on in the valley?"

He took his feet down from the desk and turned his head to remove a chew from his cheek. "Oh gosh, Clifford Neagle moved to Valley Creek some twenty-five years ago after his uncle died. William, I think, or Wilson Neagle; he had the original homestead from the 1800's. Clifford's boys were both born on the place."

"Were they any trouble?"

"Clifford himself was an okay citizen, if somewhat improvident. He'd been on the relief roles twice in the last five years."

The coffee was awful, and she struggled not to make a face. "What about Dolf?" she asked. "I didn't find much in the sheriff's files, but everyone seems to know him."

"Dropped out of school at sixteen. A real piece of work." Munson talked as he fetched himself another coffee, but then smelled it, and poured out the pot.

He said, "Dolf worked at the Obsidian Ranch. Pool boy or errand boy—Don't drink that, Ada, I'll make a new pot—but then he got let go for reasons unknown. That was three years ago, but last winter he's rumored to have caught Sybil's eye."

"I heard . . ." she spoke up because Munson had ducked into the bathroom to fill the coffee pot. ". . . well, some loose talk that he has a history of . . . being with the wrong girl."

"A first-class philanderer, although I don't mean to speak ill of the departed." Munson set the full pot on the electric plate and dumped in a handful of Folgers. "Got him a beer bottle across the noggin a couple years ago. Got him shot at a few years before that."

"Shot at?"

"Uh-huh. There are some stupid things you can do in Yellowpine County. Messing with Frenchy's daughter has to be high on the list."

"Louis Boniface tried to kill Dolf Neagle?"

Munson sat again behind his desk. "Ah, hell, he took a couple of pot shots. No serious attempt at mur . . . Never mind."

She looked at him sideways. "Anyway," she said, "Boniface's got cancer and he's dying. Dr. Mink confirms it, sort of. He's making amends for all of his mistakes of the past."

"Mink is?"

"No, Boniface. He's making amends with everyone before he dies. He sent Dolf Neagle a peace offering." She opened her notebook and showed Munson the sketch she'd made of the trophy buckle.

Munson whistled. "Nice gift. Those things are worth hundreds of dollars." He stood abruptly, though, and looking flustered, took his revolver from the drawer and said, "Now Riis-Moreau—there's a bigger fish to fry."

He belted on the gun as he side-stepped around the desk, grabbed his hat from a peg on the wall, then side-stepped somewhat embarrassedly to the hot plate and turned it off although the coffee hadn't yet started to perc.

He held his hat in both hands and said, "Ada, I cannot offer you another cup of coffee at this point in time. I got rounds need doing."

At the door he asked, "How was Blevins convinced to release the Jap?" He cleared his throat and rolled his eyes. "I didn't mean Jap, Ada, I meant Japanese gentleman."

Ada stood too. "He's not Japanese, he was born in Chehalis. He's an American."

"I meant . . . heck, you know what I meant. But as far as the Neagle case, sure there was no signs of trauma, besides the flames, but those folks could have been poisoned, or electrocuted, or suffocated, or killed any number of ways without there being signs of trauma."

"But they weren't killed." She stepped through the door as he held it open. "That's the point," she said. "The carbon-monoxide levels in their blood show they were alive and breathing deeply when the fire came through. All four of them. Mooch and Dolf were up and moving around. Irma lay in her bed, as you saw, but the old man was settled into his rocker. They couldn't have been killed beforehand."

With the sun hanging directly overhead, the boardwalk out front baked like an oven. Munson said, "So they sat down and let the fire come and kill them? Heck, even if the car was broken down, they'd have hoofed it down towards the creek."

"Beats me."

"A mass suicide?"

"Mass insanity," she said.

A QUARTER MILE WEST OUT OF CUSTER, the county road swung south to cross over the Yankee Fork. Ada's route, though, took her straight ahead at the bend, through a tangle of felled trees, trenches, and torn-down houses, toward Maggie Li's cottage. It was the last house standing in what folks had called Chinatown. Maggie didn't care for the name 'Chinatown,' but she disliked 'the Bottoms' even more. The neighborhood had been cleared to make way for gold dredging, but for two months the Mansfield and Midlands dredge had floated rusty and lifeless in its pond. Ada eased her truck through the maze.

The pond banks were crumbling away, so she parked back a ways and walked the last twenty yards to Li's house. Ripples slapped the iron hull of the dredge as she neared, whipped up by a sudden afternoon breeze, and the sound echoed like a kettle drum over the water. The bow gantry towered over her, and the line of buckets, big as bathtubs, jutted down into the water where the last shift had ended—where she had leapt the water onto the bucket line that night and climbed into the guts of the machine.

The ground in front of Maggie Li's house had finally sluffed in ahead of the last cut of the dredge, and Ada had to cross a rickety wooden foot bridge to reach the front porch.

"Are you here to ask for my vote?" Margaret Li asked at the open front door. She greeted Ada with a broad, closed-lip smile; her white que hanging over her shoulder nearly to her knee.

Ada said, "I'm here to buy your vote." She held up the basket of garden vegetables in triumph, then carried it to the kitchen, where the two women set about washing the vegetables.

Li put a kettle on for tea. "Please remember to thank Mr. Asakura for me," she said. "Although you will have to take the corn home with you. My teeth, I'm afraid, could not do battle against a corn cob.

"Assuming the same, I already pinched two ears of corn for dinner last night."

"You may have the remaining ears as well. My teeth are sore, and I fear they may start to blacken."

"The lead poisoning?" Ada asked. Margaret Li had worked for fifty years as a geochemist in the assay labs of mining companies and had breathed in the fumes from heated ore samples. The lead had accumulated in her blood and bones.

"Yes," Li said, "and silver, as well, which can cause discoloration. But it is the same diagnosis; it all goes hand in hand." She handed Ada a lacquered tray with the hot water and tea leaves, then led the way shuffling to the parlor.

Two months earlier, the clamor of the working dredge had made it impossible to open the window to air the small room. But this day, birds sang through the lace curtains, and although the ground outside lay defiled, a few asters and marigolds hung on here and there.

Ada jumped up and pulled from her pocket the bandana filled with herbs she'd brought from Asakura's garden. "Let's try an herbal tea," she said. "Compliments of the young Mr. Asakura." She laid the bandana open on the coffee table.

"Oh, lovely!" Li tried each herb, pinching a leaf and smelling, and setting certain ones aside for the tea. She picked out a few dry, spikey seed pods and sniffed. "Star anise?" she asked. "This was in Asakura's garden?"

"Yes. It was a small, woody bush. I found it growing to the side of the herbs."

Li considered the pods, even getting a magnifying glass from the drawer in order to examine them closely. "It is *illicium*, of course," she said. But is it Japanese star anise or Chinese star anise?"

"Does it matter?"

"Oh, very much. One can kill you, and they are almost impossible to distinguish except by smell." She placed a seed pod onto the lacquered tray and crushed it with the back of a spoon. "Ada, I'm afraid my sense of smell has been compromised by my medicine . . ."

"Your cannabis."

"Yes, Ada, my dàmá." She held the tray to the younger woman. "Forget that, and smell this. Is it richly like licorice, or only weakly like licorice?"

Ada bent in, holding her hair back, and sniffed. "Weakly, I think. More like cardamom than anise."

"Oh dear. I think we shall not use it, then. If it is indeed Japanese star anise, it will contain *anisatin*, which is highly toxic. It can cause hallucinations and even epileptic fits. It will kill your kidneys in larger doses—as though mine need much to kill them now."

Li crushed the selected herbs in a mortar and added them to the teapot, then crushed a small handful of tea leaves in the same way. The making of the tea always charmed Ada, and as Li worked methodically, she admired, too, the fine lace laid over the arms of the chairs and the small silk paintings on the walls. But the old woman's words echoed in her head, and she jumped to her feet, bumping the coffee table and nearly upsetting the teapot.

"Hallucinations?" she cried. "Are you sure?"

"And epileptic fits. *Anisatin* poisoning can make you mad as a hatter, and you may die eventually."

Update 12:20 p.m. – Back to Juniper Flat and Asakura's farm. Revisiting yesterday's possibly hasty decision.

THE TRUCK SLID THROUGH THE CURVES, kicking up rocks that knocked under the floorboard. The windows and the jockey box rattled, and the tailgate chains slapped and banged with every chuckhole. Damn her anyway, she'd let him go! She had him in her jail and she'd just let him walk . . . Christ, he didn't even have to walk away. She drove him home!

Asakura had a perfect opportunity, a motive, and now a means to commit the crime. Epileptic states could explain why the Neagles were all just sitting there waiting. And Dolf lowering himself down the well—he was hallucinating, the poor fool!

She'd been so taken in by Asakura; swayed by his civility and his articulate manner. It was a breath of fresh air, after all, to talk with someone so polite and respectful. He was educated; well-read to be sure, but civility can be sneaky. It can mask dislike, even disdain and . . . his damned oriental superiority! And she'd also been focused on Montgomery and his "equitable" ways, and then from him on to Boniface and Riis-Moreau. She'd let her personal concerns distract her from the evidence in front of her face.

The truck rocked and clattered down the Yankee Fork valley, splashing through the swales and lifting at the tops of knolls till she thought she'd lose her stomach. Deer bolted from the road into the woods, and crows scattered on the wing. The washboards and chuckholes eventually jarred her kidneys and caused her to slow a little, and she got her breathing under control as well. Eddy Asakura, damn him, was a war veteran—she'd let that sway her too. An Asian in a less-than-tolerant country, and Ada knew well enough how it felt to be looked down on and powerless. Her sympathy had clouded her common sense. The man was obsessed with his internment six years earlier and could not forget some injustice done him by Clifford Neagle. Damn her for dismissing it so easily!

A grocery truck passed her in the canyon above Sunbeam, blinding her in the sun and dust so she had to slow further and finally pull to a stop on the wide, cobble-strewn shoulder. She sat there for a minute with her head down, catching her breath.

Asakura grew a poison in his garden. He was an expert at—what the hell was it?—the *ninjutsu*: trained in the art of poisons and assassination. She had so been taken in!

Update 1:05 p.m. – Follow-up interview at Mr. Asakura's residence.

THE JUNIPER FLAT ROAD WAS NO DUSTIER than the day before, but her sheriff's rig kicked up a tall rooster tail to settle out over the misfortunate farms and trailer homes. She slowed only at the gate to Asakura's shaded farmyard. The garden was not being worked as she drove in, and the place was quiet but for birds chattering in the elms above.

She climbed out of the truck, tense from the drive, and stuck on her badge and jammed on her hat. She considered for a long moment her gun, but left it rolled in its holster in the jockey box.

Inga Nilsen walked among apple trees in the field bordering on the south. Ada was sorry to see her, given what she had to do. Neither woman waved.

Eddy Asakura met her at the front door. He greeted her politely, although he appeared embarrassed to be caught in slippers and with the tails of his shirt untucked—and perhaps a little annoyed, although he hid it. "An honor to see you again so soon, Sheriff. Is this an official visit?"

"I was in Custer and remembered I had your garden basket." She set the cane basket on the step, stood tall, and looked around. "I was hoping perhaps we could talk. We didn't get much of an opportunity, and I've been wondering about some of what I've read about Minidoka."

"I'm just a little . . ." He sighed. "Of course, Mrs. Reed. I'll put on the kettle."

"That would be lovely. I wonder if I can visit your garden, in that case. An herbal tea sounds just right, this hot afternoon."

From the raised herb garden, Ada selected a handful of leaves and buds, then waited again on the porch, where a small table and two chairs had been set up. Inga had put up a step ladder in her orchard and was picking apples into a basket. The farm to the east stirred as well, and though a five-acre field lay between them, a woman watched intently as she beat the dust from a large rug.

Asakura returned to the porch with a lacquered tray holding two handle-less cups and a small teapot. He asked what herbs she had selected and brought out a green serpentinite mortar and pestle for their preparation. He sat.

A rhythmic thumping drifted over the field as the neighbor lady started in on her rug. Ada said, "I was surprised by the pictures of ballfields and the large recreation hall at Minidoka. The article described barber shops and grocery stores. Much like a village." She smiled and tore mint leaves and lemon balm into the mortar, crushing them with the stone pestle.

Like a Potemkin village, perhaps," he said. "A false front to make happy over a prison camp." To Ada's raised brows he said, "That's what it was, after all. You can say relocation center, or internment camp, or whatever you please. Did the magazine show the electrified barbed wire? The place was made fundamentally to imprison, and it fulfilled its mission."

"It looked as if an effort was made, anyway, to make it . . . livable." She scraped the crushed leaves into the hot water, and added a teaspoon of black tea, then selected buds of echinacea and chamomile to crush in the mortar.

Asakura had twisted in his seat and was staring across his garden. "I'm not suggesting it wasn't unjust," Ada offered.

"Unjust!" He stood and walked to the edge of the porch. "We were given six days to sell everything we had built in our lifetimes, keeping only what we could carry. My father refused to sell, preferring nothing to the pennies offered him for our home. We were taken to the fairgrounds for assembly, and for a week we slept under guard in stables meant for animals."

"I did not know that part." She added the crushed buds to the pot of water.

She had passed a small brown church on her way in and thought then that someone had taken notice of her passing—perhaps of the sheriff markings on her truck. Now a tall man in black stood in the doorway of the church watching them, she thought, although it was nearly a quarter mile away.

She dropped into the mortar four or five of the star anise clusters. A strong aroma like cardamom swirled around the porch as she began to crush the pods. As she did, though, Asakura took hold of her shoulder from behind.

"Did you get this from my garden?" he asked.

She turned. "Yes, I thought the anise would add a spicy flavor."

"It is not anise, I'm afraid, but *shikimi*. You did not take this seed to Mrs. Li did you?"

"No. Is there a problem?"

"*Shikimi* must not be eaten."

"Why would you grow a spice not to be eaten?" she asked.

"It is not grown as a spice at all." With a sigh and a slight bow, he stepped off the porch and walked back to the herb garden. The three interested neighbors, Ada noticed, watched him go and return. He brought back a small handful of dry leaves.

"We grow *shikimi* for the leaves of the plant." He sat again and crushed the leaves in the palms of his hands, rolling them patiently into a tight rope. As Ada watched, he held the rope of leaves over a match until it began to smoke, blew on it to make it glow, then dropped it into a small brass tray.

The leaves gave off a burnt, dusty aroma somewhere between licorice and eucalyptus. It reminded Ada of making spice cookies as a child—and burning them. The aroma was pleasant enough, though, and calming as she sat and collected her thoughts. "The anise . . . the *shikimi*, it is a traditional incense?"

"It is not easy to grow in this climate, but it is a connection to the old ways, and worth the effort."

Ada poured the herbal tea, minus the star anise, into the cups as Asakura continued to gaze over his garden. The neighbor to the east kept up her thunking of the carpet, and Inga glanced from time to time from her step ladder. The preacher had gone inside.

The tea sat waiting. Asakura breathed deeply, smiled, and said, "Please, after you." They both sipped, and he nodded politely.

After a pause, he said, "You were right, Sheriff, in your questioning the other day. I never asked my mother what she thought of her changed circumstances. My parents' marriage was traditional in the sense you imply—in every sense, I suppose. But you see, my mother made a home where we lived in Chehalis, and if her position there was subservient, at least it afforded her some small dignity. She kept her own kitchen and set her own table; the rules of the house were her rules. At Minidoka she had none of those things to call her own. We ate in a communal mess hall with scores of others. I could play ball or get into trouble as I chose. My father could work; he helped to maintain the camp electricity. But my mother had no home to oversee at Minidoka."

Ada said, "I was wrong to imply it might not have mattered to her." She'd been wrong about a number of things and was, once again, confused. She had come ready to clap Eddy in cuffs, but now, again, his guilt seemed unlikely.

She gave it another moment, then asked, "The courts threw out your first suit against Clifford Neagle three years ago. Why did you re-file?"

His face did not change as he sipped his tea. "Why are you running for sheriff?" he asked.

"Did you know Neagle in the time you were at the camp?"

He dropped his head. "I see. I am still a suspect, then?"

He was her number-one suspect. But his answers were not evasive; they were not those of a cold-blooded killer. She said, "Everyone is a suspect until the case is closed."

He nodded. "There were a hundred Caucasian guards. I'm sorry, but they all looked alike to me." He drank slowly from the tea, but then let show a small grin. "Forgive me, I should not tease. It is fine, your choice of herbs, by the way. Thank you."

After a moment, he said, "I was not there when it happened. I was at war in the uniform of my jailers, so I could not go in my father's place. You see, it should have been me that night. It would not have been my first time in the shadows after curfew, and I might have succeeded. If not, then I should have been the one to take the bullet."

He drank his tea until it was gone, then wiped the rim of the cup with a napkin. "No, Sheriff, I was not there to see Clifford Neagle kill anyone. But neither have I seen a virus kill, nor an atomic radiation."

He stood. "I will not lie to you and say I am sorry he is dead. I wish I were a better person. I wish I could be content and find the ancient harmony, the *wa*, as my father could, to rise above as he could. But it is not in me."

Asakura accompanied her to her pickup truck. Ada noted Inga had descended the ladder, but the rug beater remained at her station. "Eddy where were you on the day before Clifford Neagle was . . . before Neagle died?" she asked from the open door of the truck.

"As I told you, I was fishing."

"Fishing, but with no one to confirm your story."

"Sometimes it is a relief to get out from under prying eyes." He nodded to the neighbor lady, and to the brown church on the rise.

"And the day before that?"

"The day before that and the day before as well, I was here in my garden, as my neighbors can corroborate. It is not easy to lose track of someone like me."

She turned again but hesitated with the truck door open. "Mr. Asakura, your pickup truck should be returned to you later today, but you should not try to leave the County. That isn't an order, but not everyone is in agreement with regard to your release. Sergeant Blevins of the Highway Patrol, whom you met . . ."

"Thank you. I have no immediate plans to travel."

She turned the truck around in the driveway and exited as she had come. But where the road dipped down to cross the first gulley at the edge of Asakura's property, where sage and alder grew thick, Inga Nilsen waited and motioned to her. She pulled to a stop.

Inga put a foot on the running board and her hands on the open passenger window. "You think he's guilty," she said.

"I can't really discuss the case, Inga. It's . . ."

But the woman laid her arms on the window frame and her forehead on her arms. "Suppose he was up at the lake all that weekend like he told you, that's why his truck was seen up at the pass. But suppose he was with someone."

"With whom?"

The young woman raised her head but turned to look across the field. "Maybe someone he can't be seen with. And of course, he would never say so."

Inga's neck, turned in the dappled light, was slender, and the flesh fair and smooth. Ada had only known her as a young wife waiting for her soldier, and then as a widow in tears.

Ada started to speak but hesitated. She said, "The witness said nothing of a passenger when he stopped at the filling station in Stanley."

The young woman's chin came forward and her blue eyes would not look at Ada. "Suppose she was down on the floorboard."

The idea, just picturing it, was so shameful Ada had to fight to steady her voice. "Why would she do that?" she asked.

"Why do you suppose?" Inga stepped down and disappeared into the brush and tangle, following a narrow path worn in the sandy soil.

Update 4:00 p.m. – Leaving Juniper Flat. Alone. Back to the office

Ada took it more slowly leaving the rocky bench, keeping the dust low and sparing her nerves and her kidneys the larger chuckholes. She stopped a couple of times on the way out to sit in the sun among the ruined orchards and wonder if she was doing the right thing, again letting Eddy Asakura off the hook. But between his explanations, Inga's veiled revelations, and her own feelings, she could not put him back in jail—at least not yet.

Once onto the smooth, graded surface of the highway, however, she was able to think more objectively . . . and damned if the star anise wasn't the toxic variety after all. Asakura hadn't let Ada drink poison tea, but he knew what it could do, and if his army record was accurate, he knew damn good and well how to apply it. She wasn't sure if Mink's blood workups included testing for—what was it?—*anisatin*. She made a mental note to have him check for it.

And that would be all they needed to hang Eddy Asakura, she thought regretfully. That would be the 'means.' They had a witnessed opportunity, a means now to commit the crime, and a motive that would not go away. He said his case was moot because someone else shot his father, but for some reason he still hated Neagle. "A virus," he'd called him.

It was all neatly laid out for her. The problem was—problems were—Asakura more than ever did not seem like a killer, and now he had a 'maybe, just suppose' kind of alibi, and one Ada could believe to her bones. If Inga Nilsen was with him at the lake, a white woman with an Asian man, then no, he would not say anything about it. His sense of honor would preclude such a defense even if it put a rope around his neck. And if Inga was there with him, then a reasonable opportunity to commit the crime was taken away—probably. And the 'probably' part would not stand in the way of Patrol Sergeant Blevins' push to arrest the man again.

Her arms ached from the heavy steering, and her leg from the clutching and shifting through the tight curves. Inga's belated alibi notwithstanding, it did not look good for Eddy Asakura—not with a hallucinogen growing in his garden. But at the very least, she had to check all leads and evidence before arresting him again—and that meant looking into what actually happened at the Minidoka internment camp.

IT WAS PAST 5:30 P.M. WHEN ADA ROLLED UP in front of her house—Montgomery's damned house—but she was done-in and done for the day. Her eyes burned from the smoke, and her heart ached from her marriage woes, neither of which ever seemed to clear up. And now she had Inga Nilsen to fret over too, because life was getting too easy, she supposed, so why not take on a little more. She brought in the newspaper and kicked the door closed behind her.

After hosing out the garage and getting the dogs fed in the back yard, she set about dinner for herself. A piece of her campaign-rally chicken had somehow survived in the Frigidaire, and she made a salad of it with a stalk of celery and a cucumber from Asakura's garden. A last slice of bread smelled suspicious, but not once it was toasted, so she buttered it and sat at the kitchen table to dine. The dogs came in through the open door and crowded around her feet, and they, too, needed her attention. The poor things had lost the one person who loved them and took care of them, and they'd ended up in a strange place with strange new rules. Everything they'd counted on was changed or gone. She kind of knew how that felt.

She scratched the ear of the closest one. "It isn't fair, is it?" she said.

The Camas Courier had nothing new to report on pages one or two, and only grocery specials lyon pages three and four—although she studied those hungrily. Much of the back page, however, was given to Jeff Banning and his opinion of the job she, *"Our so-called sheriff Ada Reed,"* was doing.

She rose, reached far back in her pantry for the bottle of Christian Brothers, and poured herself a small glass before reading on. Banning apparently had discovered the 'terrible human cost' of the forest fires, and he waxed on about the families chased from their homes and farms. Refugees, he called them. "*. . . No better off than refugees displaced by an act of war, and what in the name of heaven is our sheriff doing about it?*"

She took a long sip of the brandy, breathed deeply, and kept reading: "*. . . But Mrs. Reed appears not to care a fig,*" Banning was quoted as saying. "*She's out day and night holding the hands of Japanese troublemakers. Maybe there's not enough publicity in caring for American families.*"

"I don't care a fig?" she shouted at the paper. "I got some food in their bellies, which is a damn sight more than that ass Banning . . ." She stood a moment to calm herself, but then shouted, "I'd find them homes, too, goddamn it, if the county would let me!" Her shouting scared the dogs, who slinked under the table.

With a second glass of brandy in hand, she retired to the living room where she put a stack of Sinatras on the Magnavox. "My life is a bit of a mess right now," she explained to the dogs when they'd curled up by the sofa.

CHAPTER ELEVEN

Thursday, 27 September, 4:00 a.m.
Long Drive south today
Minidoka War Relocation Center, Jerome, Idaho

THE MOON WAS LONG SET AT FOUR O'CLOCK the next morning when Ada backed her Buick Roadmaster out of the garage and rolled it quietly through her neighborhood. The sun was still hours away. It was an ungodly hour to get going, but she was headed that morning for Minidoka County, two hundred miles to the south.

There was no real evidence the Neagles were victims of murder, but it was possible she might have been looking too hard. The Japanese star anise—the *anisatin*—could have left the Neagles incapacitated so it didn't look like murder. She felt a twinge again that she might have released a cold-blooded killer. The editors of the Canyon Courier certainly thought so, and they'd spared no ink making their point. In any case, the long-term enmity between Asakura and Clifford Neagle arose from their shared time at the Minidoka internment camp. Eddy claimed the argument was moot because someone else pulled the trigger, but that was just his word. She hoped to find answers at Minidoka.

She left the sheriff's pickup on the curb this time and took her own car, because Mike at the Service Center had been telling her the Buick had to be driven or the seals would start to dry and leak oil. Hence, the non-official-looking transportation, and hence the smile on her face, because, after five months wrestling with the Ford half-ton pickup, the Buick's power steering and Dynaflow transmission felt like driving a cloud.

She floated down Main Street and turned south onto the highway with her two orphan dogs in the backseat pressing their noses to the cracked-open windows. It would have been easier to drive straight south on the paved Highway 93, to Arco and then west to Jerome, but she had the darned dogs, and therefore had to swing through Custer on her way. She dropped Mutt and Jeff with Chief Kellen Munson at 5:30 a.m., then headed back to the highway and to Stanley. From there she continued south, up and over Galena Summit. A few families were leaving Redfish Lake campground as she passed, heading back to their burned-out farms, but otherwise the road was nearly deserted all the way to Ketchum.

She gassed up in Ketchum, taking special care to get a receipt, and once south of town found some pavement at last. Beyond Hailey, she slowed and had to dodge around tractors and loads of baled hay taking up nearly both lanes of the road.

Dropping down to the broad Snake River plain at Shoshone, the highway flattened and straightened but for the wide bends around farmlands, rocky badlands, and scoriaceous volcanic flows. She checked her map, and ten miles north of Jerome turned onto a rough county road. The Roadmaster threw up a plume of dust for another ten miles through the heart of cheat grass and sagebrush country. Around eleven a.m., she drove between twin watchtowers and through the unguarded gate to the Minidoka War Relocation Center.

Her tires crunched in gravel rolling up to what she assumed to be, by the presence of the only other two cars within twenty miles, the administration building. It was a one-story board and batten structure about forty feet wide and maybe a hundred feet long. It had twelve louvered windows down each side, only one of which, near the front, was swung open.

Behind the building and beyond what must have been ware-houses, tarpaper barracks, row on row, stretched into a gray-brown haze. There was not a tree in any direction, but a wooden water tower stood about two hundred yards from the edge of the camp, and watchtowers, perhaps a dozen poking through the haze, marked the distant boundaries of the thousand-acre site.

A stiff wind and a dry heat hit her as she stepped from the car, reminding her what a different world the Snake River Plain of southern Idaho was compared to her part of the state. The wind swirled chaff and piled tumbleweeds against the barbed wire fences, and the place smelled of abandonment: of old tarpaper, sage, and sunbaked lumber.

She had in fact found the administration building, she was informed by the square-shouldered and square-jawed Miss Jeanie Lamoille, who sat behind the front desk. The building had been used as the arrival and departure center back in the confinement days. Since the internment of Japanese Americans ended in 1945, however, the whole place had been put to a more constructive use: the housing of returning veterans. Of course, that was all done with now, too, and neither Miss Lamoille nor her suspendered boss, a Mr. Carl at the corner desk, could quite explain the current mission of the facility. "But how can we help you, uh . . . Sheriff?" Carl asked.

"I'm working on a case." She brought out her notebook. "It's an open case, and there may be no connection at all, but I was hoping to get some information on a family who were interned here dur-ing the war. The Asakuras; I believe the father was Hideo Asakura; from the Chehalis Washington area . . ."

"I have their numbers right here." Lamoille said. "There has been a lot of interest in the family. Lawyers, you know."

"I'm sorry, what do you mean 'their numbers?'"

"The family members' identification numbers."

Ada had never heard of such a thing, but she took the numbers down on a scrap of paper: MD-4172, 4173, and 4174. The files,

Ada was told, were kept in the dancehall-sized room behind the plywood wall behind Miss Lamoille. She was keyed in and told to knock when she was ready to leave.

Behind the wall, army-green file cabinets, rank on rank, filled half the room, while dust-covered trunks, suitcases, and boxes were stacked in the other half. There was no electricity, but the many windows provided sufficient light, if somewhat smudged, for her to do her work. The same windows rattled now and then as the breeze swirled outside, and they let in a fine dust to settle in the shafts of light.

The filing system was fairly straightforward, and Ada had no problem finding the right green cabinet. The Asakuras had arrived, all three together, on the fourteenth of October 1942. Their embarkation point was recorded as Kelso Station in Washington. They'd disembarked in Jerome, and rode the last twenty-five miles in a hot, crowded bus. The three of them and their one hundred and eight pounds of belongings had been searched, and they were processed in at 6:15 p.m. Hideo was classified as "skilled: electrician;" Shirley was "wife." Edwin was listed as "male dependent, seventeen years of age." The family was assigned to H Block, rowhouse five.

By half-past noon, barely an hour into her review, the room began to warm, and the rafters creaked and popped. The files held little information on the parents until both died in December of 1943. Mrs. Asakura, No. 4173—Shirley—died in the camp hospital, just as Eddy had said. She died on the fourth of December, the thirteenth patient of an eventual twenty-four internees to die of whooping cough that winter. Mr. Asakura, No. 4172, was shot— apparently while trying to escape, although parts of the report on Hideo's death were redacted. He was killed leaving the camp on December second, two days before his wife died.

There was a file on Number MD4174 as well; a thick one, and the papers inside dove-tailed with the 'hothead' notes she'd found in her own files. Edwin Ayuma Asakura had refused to fill out official questionnaires and had refused to sign a loyalty oath. That had gotten him weeks in confinement. Fighting with the guards had earned him a trip to the infirmary, more weeks in confinement, and nearly got him transferred to the high-security segregation center at Tule Lake, California. Instead, 4174 had been allowed to enlist in the Army in July of '43. A board of elders vouched for him. Their numbers were listed as well.

By two o'clock the file room was an oven, and the wind had picked up outside until the windowpanes rattled. Her eyes smarted from the fine swirling dust and from the glare through the filthy windows as the afternoon sun swung around. The filing cabinets themselves began to ping as they warmed.

She'd found no mention whatever of a guard named Neagle, although some items had been temporarily removed from the files according to faded, paper-clipped notes. Jeanie Lamoille came to her rescue at a quarter past two with several additional manila folders. "You'll probably want to see these too," she said. "I haven't had a chance to re-file them since the last bunch of lawyers left."

Ada had neglected to bring lunch, and that was fine, because by mid-afternoon she was too sick from the heat to eat anything. She sipped from her canteen. The files Lamoille gave her contained much of the redacted and temporarily removed materials, and they showed the elder Asakura had been shot by a guard named Beterman, Private First Class, on the kid's first night of duty. So, Eddy had told the truth about that, as well. The killing happened not at the wire, but near, or just outside, or maybe just inside a warehouse building—even this report was confused. Beterman was subsequently transferred to Camp Amache in Colorado. There was no mention of Neagle.

By four in the afternoon she'd loosened her tie, undone the top two buttons of her duty shirt, and rolled the sleeves up to her elbows. Beads of sweat rolled down the small of her back. She could barely breathe by 4:35 p.m., so she wrapped up her notes, got her uniform back to code, and said goodbye to Mr. Carl and Miss Lamoille.

THE TIE WAS OFF AND THE BUTTONS LOOSENED again before she hit the highway, and she bee-lined for Shoshone, where she stopped for a hamburger and an extra-large root beer at the Frostop. On the road again, she lowered the Roadmaster's window with a light touch of a button, and smoked a cigarette with her hair swirling in the wind.

Signs of the long summer drought were nowhere to be seen on Ada's return drive up the Big Wood River. Autumn-painted aspen and cottonwoods weaved and snaked along the water courses or bordered fields in straight rows, glowing like fire under the late afternoon sun. Geese and sandhill cranes honked and trilled in such numbers it nearly drowned out the rush of wind and the whine of her tires. The air was sweet with the heady aroma of fresh-mown hay and it made her homesick for the farm. But the long trip to Minidoka had been worth every mile; she'd found her answer. Clifford Neagle had had nothing to do with the deaths of Eddy Asakura's parents. It was some kid named Beterman. Learning that, in the last court proceedings, Eddy Asakura would have seen his cause was moot, just as he said. He had no motive whatever to take revenge on the man.

A clanking combine held her up for a couple of miles, but she managed to pass the thing before she got to Hailey, where traffic thinned for the dinner hour. Gassing up again in Ketchum, she continued another twenty miles along the forested river bottom before starting the tight switchback climb toward Galena Summit. The sun was setting beyond the Salmon River headwaters by the time she reached the pass, but she caught glimpses of gold glowing on the White Cloud Peaks far to the northeast.

It was 7:15 when Ada started down the north side of the pass into the deeply shadowed Sawtooth Valley, and the late hour presented a problem. It would be dark by the time she got there, but she would be passing by the Obsidian Ranch. Holland Riis-Moreau had moved up on her list of suspects in the Neagle deaths after what she'd found and not found in the Minidoka files, and she really wished to question him again. But there was more to ask about than the Neagle case. The comments he'd made about poker playing hadn't sat well with her after the first interview, especially after finding her husband's name on lists and in ledgers that had belonged to a crook. She hadn't let herself think about it until now; but since talking with Riis-Moreau and then with Boniface, it made her sick to her stomach. So, buoyed by her success at Minidoka, she determined to stop in and demand answers.

Update 8:10 p.m. – Follow-up interview with
Holland Riis-Moreau: person of renewed interest.

OF COURSE, SHE WOULD HAVE TO SEE SYBIL, as well. Ada promised herself, as she ignored the "No Trespassing" sign, crossed over the iron-rail cattle guard, and headed up the road between split-rail fences, that she would not shoot the woman.

The honking of her horn at the upper gate brought to her the deceptively intelligent-looking cowboy, who swung the turnstile and nodded her forward.

Holland himself answered her front-door bell ringing. He was fully clothed this time, in what he must have supposed to be ranch wear, but swarthy complexion and crooked nose notwithstanding, a piped and pearl-snapped blouse and embroidered bandana made him look more like Roy Rogers than any honest rancher. He led her through the foyer and the living room and into the lounge, all the while apologizing for the goddamned mess no man of his means should ever have to live in. They couldn't keep a fucking maid around, he explained, and Sybil might break a nail if she ever bent her precious ass to a broom.

They found Sybil in the lounge, propped upon a chaise at the far end of the room. Her head was turned away and she did not look up, but offered a soft "Evening, sugar," when Ada entered. Holland stepped around behind the bar, and set to work with bottles, highball glasses, and ice cubes. Sybil remained on the chaise with her head leaned askew on the high back, and that was fine with Ada; the less she had to interact with Sybil, the easier the evening would go.

She'd been led quickly through the lounge on her first visit. This time she noticed the room was done in rich mahogany paneling with dark leather furnishings. Brass sconces lit the walls, and higher up, a herd of big-game animals thrust their heads out from the paneling. The Riis-Moreau crest—that of dubious validity, according to Ethel—hung above the bar.

"There are a few things I was hoping to get clarification on," Ada said to Holland.

Holland laughed. "Of course, there are." He carried an acid-blue cocktail to his wife, who took it without looking up, then returned and handed Ada a glass containing an inch of amber liquor. He said, "You're a brandy girl, I understand."

For a couple of seconds, she didn't answer but tried to think how in hell and from whom he could have learned that information. It unsettled her a bit. She said, "Thanks, but I still have a long drive tonight." She set the drink on the bar.

"But it's just the one, Ada, and I think you'll like this brand more than that Christian Brothers you pour at home." He showed a practiced skill with the bottles as he mixed a cocktail for himself.

Ada said, "Okay. If it's just the one, let's try something special. Maybe something from—what was it Sybil called it?—this 'mountain of whiskey and romance.'" Sybil sat up at her words but didn't turn to face them.

"If you'd like." Holland smiled and put down his drink, "Yes, let's do give it a try." He reached far back in the cupboard for a Mason jar half filled with a clear liquor and poured a bit into two glasses.

Ada accepted the new drink, and they clinked glasses. She took a small sip and had to catch her breath before saying, "I was talking to a Mr. Louis Boniface the other day. He used the same phrase, of all things, 'a mountain of whiskey and romance.' He, too, offered me a clear liquor like this."

"Was it any good?"

"I declined."

"Well, then, I am especially honored."

Holland's wife had twisted on the chaise to listen. Ada started to say something about how small of a county it was, but just then Sybil leaned from shadow into the light of a wall sconce. The woman was holding her chin high; her lips were closed. Her brows were raised, although her eyes were cast down. Ada forgot what she was going to say. She knew the look on Sybil's face and knew it in spades: part pride, part submission, a little fear; and, of course, the heartbreak. Even from across the room and even under expertly applied makeup she discerned the shadows of bruises on Sybil's jaw and cheekbone.

They were waiting. It took a moment to get her head back into her questioning. "How well do you know Louis Boniface?" she asked.

Holland downed his drink and rattled the ice for a moment. "Louis, Louis, what you do to us!" he said. "Frenchy with a penchy for the wenchy."

He laughed, but the hollowness of it echoed in the room, and Sybil turned again to face the wall. Holland said, "We know him well, *Cherie*."

It was too flippant, with his wife lying bruised and cowed across the room. His answer and Sybil's condition disgusted her, and as a result, her voice rose and her next question came out brusque, "What business arrangements do you have with Boniface?"

Holland noticed the tone and answered in kind. "What's it to you? Are you going to run me in for an old jar of moonshine?"

"Mostly I'm concerned that you and Boniface had a mutual friend—or perhaps not so much a friend. Someone both of you might have had reason to turn on, and one who is now dead as a piece of toast."

Holland wiped the bar down. "Look, I have no idea what you're ragging on about. But me and Frenchy get along fine, and we get along with others fine. Live and let live, don't you agree?" He threw the bar towel into an over-filled laundry bag. "Because Monty always agreed with that philosophy. Live and let live."

"What does Montgomery have to do with . . . what arrangement did you have with Montgomery?"

"Arrangement?" He laughed. "We were poker buddies, like I told you."

She'd set down her drink, and now she backed a step from the bar and crossed her arms. She uncrossed them and stuck her hands in her pockets. "Did he . . . Did Montgomery do favors for you?"

Holland scoffed. "Montgomery believed the badge comes with a certain responsibility to protect his constituents and their interests. And he did protect us, so we could lead peaceful and prosperous lives."

Sybil had turned again and was watching. Ada said, "Not everyone finds it so peaceful." Her hands came out of her pockets, and she took up her pen and notebook. "Where were you Sunday, the sixteenth?" she asked. She'd gotten her voice under control.

He thought a moment and grinned. "Humping our last maid, the homely cow. Hence the dump I have to live in."

His words, the meanness of them, took the breath from her. She stood open-mouthed for a second, then sputtered, "On the sixteenth, Dolf Neagle . . ."

"You're still on about that chump?" Holland shook his head, perplexed. "You think a little dicking around is enough for me to kill the guy?"

Sybil was sitting on the edge of the chaise favoring her right side, quietly sipping her blue cocktail. The bruises on her face were already shading green, a week old by Ada's experience, so the abuse might have been brought on by her previous visit. It could have been about Dolf Neagle, but then again, it could have been about the messy house, or about a locked bedroom door when he was in the mood, or just a joke when she didn't notice his temper in time. Or it could have been about Ada's questions regarding Dolf Neagle.

She turned back to Holland. "Well, it does appear the news of him last week was received with some violence."

"That's none of your fucking business." He leered. "Unless you're the kind of girl who enjoys that sort of thing."

She looked around for a pool cue or an ash tray she could throw. She said, "You're lucky I'm not wearing a gun." And she meant it, although it was a stupid thing to say.

He slammed his drink down on the bar. "You skinny bitch, I chew up tinhorn cops like you and spit them out."

Ada didn't flinch, and this time she held her tongue, but she'd shot lesser assholes than Holland Riis-Moreau. She put her notebook away and stood with hands on hips. "I have to talk to Sybil alone."

"You have to go." He leaned forward with his hands on the bar, his dark eyes and clenched jaw leaving no doubt he was giving an order.

But instead of intimidating, his menacing look in conjunction with his Roy Rogers outfit was just creepy. Ada was lucky not to scoff. She said, "Sybil is a material witness and possibly the last person to see Dolf Neagle alive. It is a murder investigation, Mr. Riis-Moreau, and we take that as seriously here in Idaho as they do in New Jersey. I need to talk to her alone—here or at the office. And if at the office, I can't stop it from getting noisy."

Holland said, "Noisy? My name won't be the only name printed in the papers. And if you're so curious about your old man, maybe it is time we read some things in the papers and the magazines. The famous lady sheriff and her shyster husband."

Hard as it was, she held her tongue again, but she thought, *Goddamn Montgomery all to hell!* He'd given Holland an edge, and she knew the man knew how to use an edge; it was his business to know.

She gave it a moment and a couple of breaths, then smiled nicely and said, "I'm sure we can come to an easy and convenient compromise, Holland. I won't question your wife after all. I'll simply chat with her." She cocked her head and grinned. "You don't want to be around for the girl talk, do you?"

He grinned, too. He grinned broadly the whole time fixing another drink. Grabbing a couple of cigarettes from the tray, he excused himself to the front porch.

Ada waited until the door had closed before turning to Sybil. "Your husband hit you?" she asked. "Was it over Dolf Neagle?"

Sybil swirled her ice cubes. She said, "Did you come here just to check on my well-being, sugar?"

"As a matter of fact, I came thinking I might shoot you."

Sybil laughed but cut it short with a wince. "Oh, dear. Yes, I suppose you'd be the type who might want to. Little Red Riding Hood."

She struggled to get up. "Well, stand in line if that's what's on your mind." She took small steps over to the bar, found a cigarette, and lit it with a silver lighter.

Ada asked. "Was it over Dolf?"

"Yes. No. Who knows? It was about the smoke and haze, the heat. About the mess in the living room; about the mess I've made of my bedroom. What does it matter?"

Ada reached out and touched Sybil, gently, below her breast. The woman flinched. "You have a broken rib," she said.

"I know. It only hurts when I laugh, which isn't as often as you might suppose."

"Do you want to come out with me. We can find a safe place for you."

"I don't need you, Miss Riding Hood, feeling sorry for me."

"It's part of my job, and I know . . ." She stared over Sybil's head at the hunting trophies. "I know what it's like, is all."

Sybil had been looking away or at the floor since stepping over, speaking bravely but not meeting Ada face to face. She looked up, and Ada could see in her green eyes the beautiful girl she once must have been. There had been hard years. Ada said, "He's not going to change."

Sybil breathed in as deeply as her injury allowed. "I know," she said.

"Why Riding Hood?"

"Don't you have a tall, strong woodsman to come rescue you? Or have I heard wrong?"

"What do you mean? No, you've . . . you've heard wrong." She stared for a moment, wondering who else might have heard wrong, or thought wrong, or assumed the wrong thing about her and Ben McGann.

Sybil said, "Never mind, then. I am sorry about Montgomery—you know, about him and me."

"It wasn't you who cheated on me." She found a cigarette in the tray and held her hair back for a light. But Sybil couldn't get the lighter to strike again, though she worked it with her thumb until tears started in her eyes.

"Let me," Ada said. She took the cigarette from Sybil's lips and lit her own from the glowing tip. She offered it back, and Sybil, clutching her side, didn't reach for it but glanced down and parted her lips. Ada gave the cigarette back gently, avoiding the swollen side of the lower lip.

"Do you want to come with me?" she asked again. "I can give you a ride tonight." But Sybil only scoffed. Ada said, "Really, I'm just doing my job."

"Well, do your job somewhere else!" She eased herself down on the arm of a stuffed leather chair. "What do you suppose I would do without my Holland? Wait tables? Clean rooms, for Christ's sake? I'm a rich man's wife." She took a shallow breath. "Do you know the difference between a rich man's wife and a cheap whore?"

"No."

"Well, I do." She turned and covered her face, and her breathing came in short, labored gulps. But she looked up after a moment, smiled like a trooper, and said, "First thing, honey, you shouldn't ask so many questions about Montgomery."

"Of you or of Holland?"

"And second, you don't have to get your panties in a knot over any of this. No one committed murder here. Dolf wasn't Holland's doing. I would be happy to tell you if he did it, but he didn't. And

Montgomery . . .? Sweetie, you're driving a big, blue Buick – I watched you drive up, all gleaming in the porch light; white-wall tires. My God, girl, on a sheriff's pay?"

Sybil finished what she wanted to say, or she ran out of strength. She turned away again, and again her breathing came in shallow gulps. Ada stood a long while staring at the buffalo heads and antelope heads lining the walls, wondering if they were shot by Holland or if he paid someone else to do his hunting.

She snuffed out her cigarette, then stepped over and went to one knee so she could talk to Sybil face to face. "Do you know where I live? Montgomery's house?" she asked.

"I've driven by. I've never been in your bed. I'm not that cheap."

"I didn't mean it like that. If you need to . . ." She looked down for a moment, then said very quietly, "I never lock the kitchen door. If you need to, or even if you just want to, you come over and let yourself in. I mean it, any time day or night. I don't have to be there for you to stay."

Sybil shrugged, and the room quieted for a minute. She sighed and said, "You should go."

Update 10:00 p.m. – It's gotten late.
Stopping in Stanley for the night

HOLLAND RIIS-MOREAU HAD A CIGARETTE GOING, leaning with his shoulder against the stone column of the porch, his legs splayed out on the steps. His highball glass was empty. He didn't look up, but said as she passed, "It's a shame, Ada. You'd be good at poker, I think."

She slid behind the wheel without answering and at the end of the long driveway turned her expensive blue Buick north toward Stanley. The night was clear but dark; there wasn't enough of the old moon left to light the way, and no other headlights but hers swept the highway. As she passed the turnoff to the Redfish campground, she glanced but did not slow for any kind of sentimental look up the road. There was nothing of the honeymoon memories anymore she gave a damn about. And the rest of it . . . she was too upset after seeing Sybil to even think about the cold nights she'd spent there alone. She was not the same woman she was five years ago, and that was enough for her right then.

Her front tire blew on an outside curve half a mile short of the village and, fishtailing on the packed gravel surface, she nearly put the Roadmaster in the river. She sat for a full minute catching her breath with the engine running and the headlights shining all akimbo over the water and into the trees on the far bank.

She backed away and straightened the car on the shoulder, got out, and on her knees with her flashlight felt the hot rubber of the tire. The whitewall had been sliced. A clean, straight, six-inch cut, just down to the threads, had weakened the sidewall of the tire enough that it broke open coming around the curve.

The tire was shot, and although she had a spare in the trunk, she was too worn-out and a little too shaken to change it on the side of the road. She limped the Buick into Stanley with the ruined tire flip-flopping in the gravel. She parked at Lettie Nance's grocery.

It was late on a Thursday night, and the Rod and Gun Club was doing a light business. The rest of the town was dark and quiet, without even an anxious dog to break the silence. Nance answered her knock wearing a pullover jersey and pajama bottoms and carrying a baseball bat. She hustled Ada into the house without a word and glanced around outside as though someone might be lurking in the shadows.

"I'm fine, Lettie, no one is chasing me. At least not the usual suspects."

"You blew a tire, I see." The woman closed the door and locked it.

"Someone helped me blow it, I'm afraid."

"Oh, Ada!"

"I'm okay, Lettie, really."

Lettie Nance wore a scarf over her hair and shuffled around in thick, woolen socks. She put down the ball bat and took Ada to the kitchen, where she started a kettle to boil. Ada sat quietly at the table with her face braced in her spread fingers.

The two had met by accident five years earlier. Lettie had been walking the shore of Redfish, scavenging and treasure hunting, when she'd found Ada there camping alone. Hiding alone, truthfully—she'd been there a couple of nights. Lettie brought the young Mrs. Reed home and fed her and let her stay in an attached room back by the alley. That had not been Ada's first time hiding at the lake, and it would not be her last time staying with Lettie.

When the kettle whistled, they made mint tea, and Lettie found a plate of cookies. They talked of Montgomery a little, across whose head and shoulders Lettie would love, someday, to lay the baseball bat, but Ada said nothing about Sybil. And they talked of Kellen Munson, and both laughed—but kindly. It was late, and Ada's stopping was nothing new, and they both had work in the morning, so they had just the one cup of tea before turning in.

It was a cozy room with a single bed and a tiny bathroom attached by the alley, and the heat was on as though she'd been expected. Walls were hung with paintings of deserts and French gardens—not so good, the art, but all familiar to her, and sweet. Tables were stacked and the shelves stuffed with National Geographic magazines going back decades. Ada had managed to read most of them through her several visits, sitting in a worn wing chair too big for the room, under a dim lamp.

She settled down with a newer issue and thumbed through an article all about dragonflies. But after a few minutes she put the magazine down and undressed for bed, taking the badge off first and laying it on the nightstand atop more magazines. But taking the badge off didn't help a lot. Even between the warm flannel sheets Ada worried about Sybil. She worried about the refugees at the lake stuck without enough of anything to get by on. And she worried about what she'd found and not found in Minidoka, and whether it would be enough to clear Eddy Asakura. She didn't have time to worry about her near miss with the river before falling asleep.

CHAPTER TWELVE

Friday, 28 September
Back to Camas.
More questions re the Valley Creek case

LETTIE HAD ADA'S TIRE CHANGED, a pot of coffee perking, and bacon and eggs fried up by 6:00 a.m. By 6:30, Ada was rolling through the canyon, singing a Roy Rogers tune about tumbling tumbleweeds, and watching for deer in the morning mist. She completely forgot she'd entrusted the dogs to Kellen Munson and arrived home at 8:00 a.m. The Buick was pulled into the garage and a bath was drawn. By 8:45 she was at Dr. Mink's office in a clean uniform with a few more questions about the blood work-ups for the victims. Not long after receiving Mink's answers, she was on the road again.

Update 9:30 a.m. – Why don't I just build a small cabin
in the back of this pickup truck and live in the thing?
Back into Basin Creek today; follow-up with Mr. Boniface

IF THERE EVEN WAS A CRIME! She slapped the steering wheel a second time. The Neagles burned in a fire; that was the only fact she had, although there was plenty to conjecture about. She had a trained assassin with a grudge—albeit moot—who grew hallucinogenic poisons in his garden; a mentally, physically, and spiritually unstable moonshiner with a grudge and a history of attempted homicide; and a New Jersey gangster with demonstrably violent tendencies.

Now she owed it to Inga Nilsen and to Eddy himself to check remaining leads. *Remaining* leads, because she'd forgotten to check with Mink about the *anisatin* test until that morning, and of course he'd had no reason to do one. Remaining leads because the blood samples had been destroyed by the Pocatello lab, and she'd let the bodies be frigging embalmed at the mortuary! She slapped the wheel again.

Eddy Asakura had no reason to murder Clifford Neagle. He had recently learned someone else had shot his father; he had no reason to take the dispute further. Now she had to check remaining leads because Eddy's name would never be cleared unless and until the case was definitively closed—simple as that.

HOPING TO MISS THE HOTTEST PART OF THE DAY, she had left straight from Mink's office and was at the Basin Creek turnoff by 10:45. Even at that hour her shirt stuck to the back of the seat and sweat beaded at her temples. And no, her kidneys did not need another trip all the way up the Basin Creek road, and her arms did not need to wrestle the steering wheel around a hundred more curves; but there was no question she had to get more information from Louis Boniface. He had at one time had it in for Dolf Neagle, and he was connected somehow to Riis-Moreau who also must have at least resented the "chump," regardless his denials.

Basin Creek itself was running lower than the week before. The fords were shallower, and algae slickened the cobbles in the stream. Ada drove almost dreamily along, trying to think her way through the evidence; but the canyon was already suffocatingly hot, and too much time dwelling on facts that wouldn't budge left her mind wandering. An illegal whiskey scheme made the most sense. Boniface, Dolf Neagle, and Holland Riis-Moreau could certainly have been entangled in something of the sort. If so, there might well have been a double-cross; someone thought he'd be a 'wise guy.'

So, was it whiskey, romance, or revenge? Maybe Dolf's fate wasn't sealed between the sheets, but when he came between the moonshiner and the racketeer. Others might have been involved, as well. If a business arrangement had gone bad and the killing was some kind of retribution, would that leave Boniface—or Holland himself—a suspect or a potential next victim?

The road bounced, and the rabbit's foot jolted on its string. Ada shifted between granny and second gear till her clutch foot ached. She choked on the dust. The sun stayed beneath the crest of the ridge all the way in, but the canyon bottom was still hot from the baking it had gotten the day before, and the air sat stagnant and heavy with the stench of a whole summer of fires. The pine trees climbing the hills were rusted, and the bottom brush was dry and brittle and scraped down the sides of her truck as she made her way into the heart of the basin. She was driving into a tinder box.

Seven miles up the rough, rocky road she turned east into Frenchy's draw, and there the mid-morning sun hit her square in the face. Grass and brush crunched under her wheels as she made her way through the stand of pines and up the long meadow. She parked back by the barn where she had a full view of the cornfield and beyond to the wooded hill where she'd last seen the drunken Mr. Boniface. A bullet buzzed over her head while she was buckling on her holster.

The crack of the rifle sounded nearly at the same instant. She dove behind a pile of fence poles and tucked up tight as two more rounds splintered the wood. "Hold your damned fire!" she yelled.

A cat-like howl rose from the porch of the main house, and "Sheriff Ada, darling? Are you here to take me in this time? You got a case, or do you change your mind about some refreshment?"

She raised up enough to peek over the poles. The man was on the porch of the house, but she could barely see him with the sun in her eyes. Her wooden cover stank of creosote, and there were spiders nesting between the posts. She backed off a little and rose to one knee.

"I didn't come to take anyone in . . ." Boniface wheeled and fired—that was four shots—and Ada dove in with the spiders.

"Who is it?" he called. "Who are you here concerning?" He paced from one end of the porch to the other, searching, almost sniffing the air. "Tell me, *connasse!*"

"I just want to talk to you . . . about Holland Riis-Moreau. Did the two of you have business dealings? Were you supplying him with . . .?"

"Who?"

"Riis-Moreau."

"Holland? How'd he die?"

"He's not dead."

"Well, that's a surprise, the cheating son of a bitch! I haven't seen him all year."

"But you know his wife pretty well?"

He swung the rifle barrel left and right. "What is it you want Ada Reed? Why'd you come back?"

She rose up on her knees to talk better, but remained low, as he was obviously no more stable than on her last visit. "Have you had business dealings with Riis-Moreau?"

"That was years ago." He had zeroed in on Ada's voice and raised the rifle to his shoulder. "We both know that ain't why you're here."

He was crazy as a loon, in fact, and it dawned on her . . . "I don't give a damn about your still, for God's sake! I'm here to talk."

The rifle cracked—five—but the shot was wide and she didn't duck this time. She'd drawn her service revolver and now braced it on the woodpile. It was thirty yards, but she could probably make the shot. Except . . .

"Where the hell are you," he called. He searched one way and then the other. "Where you hiding?" He tipped his head to listen.

Blind drunk, the stupid ass! Ada holstered her gun, moving as little as possible, and from her knees flung her hat toward the cornfield. Boniface wheeled and fired three shots. That made eight total, and that, she hoped like hell, was what a 30-30 holds. She dove for her truck, climbed in, and started the engine as Boniface fumbled to re-load. She kept her head down and wheeled the truck around, kicking up as much dust as she could, and bounced and careened back down the long meadow toward the stand of pines. She'd almost made it to cover when a bullet shattered her rear window and slammed into her radio. Glass shards flew through the cab.

She bounced and swerved and fishtailed through the woods and back over the chain barricade, but then slowed and caught her breath before leaving the grassy two-track to join the Forest Service road. Her retreat this time did not include wild splashing through the stream fords, nor did she race down the rocky road; she'd fixed enough flat tires and didn't need to break another one. She also didn't need to kick up any more dust, inasmuch as the shattered rear window was letting in plenty as it was. The wooded bends and the tight, brushy stretches she took more slowly until finally her shaking hands became too much and she had to stop.

At a stream crossing on her knees, she washed the dust and the grit from her face and neck. Her ear bled from glass shards, she discovered, and now, goddamn it, she had another stain to get out of her last good uniform shirt . . . and she had no hat! But the breeze was surprisingly cool there by the water, and birds sang as she hadn't noticed in the longest while. She took off her shirt and washed the blood from the collar in the cool stream, then took off her boots and socks and stayed twenty minutes more.

The hot, dry Basin Creek Canyon was behind her by noon, but she knew even before her tires hit the smooth surface of the highway she would have to return. She could not let someone take pot shots at the law. She was going to have to deputize a couple of men and come back for him, and they would likely have to carry Louis Boniface out in a tarp.

*Update 3:15 p.m. – Back at my desk, which
I don't hardly see enough of anymore, doing desk stuff.*

TEN DOLLARS FOR A NEW STETSON! But what could she do?—the stores would be closed all weekend, and she couldn't just go around out of uniform. She left the truck at the motor pool and begged them to fix the window first thing.

There was nothing in the Frigidaire to eat when she swung by, and she didn't want to pay for a meal alone at the café having just shot ten dollars on a stupid hat. So, she opened a can of peaches and ate them at her desk. Her heartbeat hadn't quite settled down nor had her hands stopped shaking, but that might have been from careening the truck through the winding Salmon River Canyon for the umpteenth time in a week. In any case, the peaches tasted fine, and she started a pot of coffee as well. She leaned back in her chair and rested her feet up on the oak desk.

She was going to have to arrest Louis Boniface, and it made her angry just to think about it. You can't shoot at a damned sheriff— not even an "acting" one. But that left her no further ahead in the case, and no one gave a hoot about a crazy moonshiner. Everyone wanted to hang somebody for the Neagle deaths, thanks to sheriff-candidate Jeff Banning's agitation, and she no longer had any leads that made sense.

She had Boniface, and he'd had some reason to shoot at Dolf Neagle a few years back—although recent events confirmed he didn't need much of a reason to start blasting away. In any case, Boniface had no opportunity. Eddy Asakura had means, vis-à-vis the poison plant he grew, and opportunity to kill Clifford Neagle, but he had no remaining motive. And she had Holland Riis-Moreau: a crook, a bully, and a man-whore vindictive enough to have her tire cut. His wife vouched for him with regards to Neagle, but of course, Sybil was a rich man's wife and desirous of staying that way.

Boniface denied—convincingly, she had to give him—a business operation with Riis-Moreau, or at least, "that was years ago," he'd said, and years ago did not align with the immediacy of the Neagle family deaths.

A little of the peach syrup in her coffee didn't taste too bad, and she had just lied to herself that she would eventually figure something out when Ethel came in with more bad news. While she was out, there had been a fight up at the Redfish campground. Lettie Nance, now apparently the acting police chief of Stanley as well as everything else, had taken care of it, but she'd also begged, according to Ethel, for Ada to do something about the growing evacuee situation out there. Something had to be done.

That, damn it, was all she needed! After all the miles and the blown tires and being shot at and shot at again, that was all she needed right then. Why in hell, she had to wonder, would anyone want her job? She'd just as soon let that idiot Jeff Banning have it; Banning and his *Blazing Six Guns* solution for Mr. Asakura, and his short-sighted army tents for displaced families. He'd never been homeless. He had never slept in his car and wondered where he would find his next meal or if there was anyone in the world who cared. They needed houses, these people—beds and kitchens, not tents, but where do you relocate whole families?

She sat up straight, laughed, and tossed the empty peach can into the trash bin. Her bootsteps echoed off the masonry walls, and she skidded around the marble halls, nearly knocking Ethel over at the clerk's door.

"I have to find some phone numbers Ethel." She could barely catch her breath. "Can you help me?"

Ethel did find the numbers with a few phone calls of her own, and Ada, clutching the slip of paper in her hand, hurried back to her office and dropped into her chair. She dialed the long-distance operator, and in less than a minute was talking to Jeanie Lamoille at the Minidoka camp.

"Hi, yes. Ada Reed here. I wonder if you and Mr."—she checked her notes—"Carl have a minute for me." She kicked her feet up on the desk and leaned back. "Yes, the lady sheriff. Yes, exactly.

I wanted to thank you both again for your help and to ask how things are going there?"

"Uh-huh, oh I bet! Listen Jeanie . . ."

It was a wild idea, but not a perfectly cockamamie one, and the more she discussed it with Miss Lamoille the more they both liked it. Lamoille even got her boss on the line for part of it. Many of the residence halls had gone to dust and vermin, Carl explained, but a few in close, where the returning veterans had stayed, were in pretty good shape. The kitchens were operable, and they ran the water and sewer regularly to keep them working.

"Hell yes," the suspendered superintendent told her, "We could put up ten times your number."

This would not be without federal approval, however, and Jeanie Lamoille bet there would be a hundred forms that hadn't even been printed yet.

That was disappointing. However, by five o'clock in the afternoon, and with a lot more help from Ethel and the long-distance operators, Ada had spoken with Senator Herman Welker all the way back in Washington. It was dinner time in Washington, but Welker remembered Ada from her picture in *Life Magazine*. Anyway, federal approval could be gotten, the senator was sure, but it wasn't a straightforward situation. The Interior Department was involved, obviously, and the Army somehow. It would have to go through a Senate committee, because everything this side of the second coming had to go through a Senate committee. But none of that could even be put on the schedule without an emergency declaration and a direct request from the governor of Idaho—and Governor Jordan hated her.

CHAPTER THIRTEEN

Saturday, 29 September, 8:00 a.m.
Telephone calls and meetings
Finding options for the fire evacuees

SATURDAY OR NOT, SHE WAS GOING to nail her rear end to the office chair till she got something done for the families at Redfish. It wasn't a matter of avoiding the Valley Creek case. She'd failed to get the necessary blood analyses for *anisatin*, but if Eddy Asakura had no motive, then Japanese star anise growing in his garden had little relevance. Nor really did she think the debauched Louie Boniface could have gotten himself together enough to murder Dolf Neagle. That made Riis-Moreau her new best suspect—but only by default. She would check with Ethel's niece's boyfriend and with Ephraim's barber's brother-in-law for any unusual meetings or movements out at the Obsidian that might have some bearing—but not today.

She would deal with all of them in due time, but today the displaced families needed her help more urgently, and she was on to something with Minidoka—using the relocation center as a temporary . . . relocation center. To that end, she stayed in all morning trying to work out the details.

Mostly she worked the phone, trying to find someone on a Saturday who could get her an interview with the governor. She called friends of Montgomery's from one end of the valley to the other. Unfortunately, a good number of Montgomery's friends had also been friends of the man whom she had shot and killed back in July. They proved not so helpful. She called the sheriffs of Lemhi, Butte, and Blaine Counties, but got only official front-office numbers from them. She even called the chairwoman of the Idaho Ladies' Auxiliary of the VFW, catching her at the Garden Club and in a disagreeable mood. The thing of it was, those who disliked her were not helpful, and those who liked her enough to help her were themselves not on the in with the governor's people.

She was getting to know the long-distance operators but accomplishing little else, and for that reason she might have been a little short with Cheryl Miller and Betty Hopson when they found their way into her office. They looked nice, damn them, with Cheryl in an autumn-floral shirtwaist dress and Betty flouncing a harvest gold fit-and-flare. Both wore tasteful heels, of course, and Betty just had to hang her new sun hat on the hook next to Ada's brand-new goddamned Stetson.

Ada rose from her desk, pushed back her straight, drab, lifeless hair, and smiled, sort of. "How can I help you?" she asked.

"It's a pleasure to see you, too, Ada."

The girls had come to see about an issue Ada had been hoping to ignore for a little while longer—maybe at least until after fire season. Betty got right to it. "Russia!" she explained.

It took Ada just a moment to catch up, but she nodded. "I know," she said.

"They've exploded another atom bomb."

"I know. I heard it last night on John Cameron Swayze."

"Are you building a shelter?" Betty asked her.

"No . . . no!" She shook her head. She knew from communications with the State and with federal agencies that there was no call for panic where they lived. The whole thing, in fact, was silly, what with very real dangers and very real displacements happening in her county. But it was serious, too, and a lot of her neighbors had been asking questions about the atomic testing and what they should do about it. She was scheduled to do a 'duck-and-cover' talk at the grade school in October.

Betty and Cheryl were mature, rational people, and Ada knew they were not given to flightiness; nor were they prone to drink in the morning—except sometimes at the golf course, for which they were not properly attired. People were scared, she knew, and it ran deep. She bit her lip and for a moment could think of nothing at all to say.

She needed badly to get back to her phone calls and fought not to show a growing impatience. But Cheryl stepped over just then with a pamphlet from the Civil Defense Administration. She said, "They have designs here for fall-out shelters. We need sirens. We have to have an evacuation plan!"

"Evacuate to where?" Ada asked, perhaps touchily. "We're already as far back in the . . ." She caught herself and said, "Cheryl, we are relatively safe here in the mountains. We're a town of six hundred people one hundred-fifty miles from Boise and two hundred-fifty miles from Butte Montana. We would not be a primary target in case of war."

Betty said, "Well, what about the atomic lab . . ." She waved her hand. "Oh, what is it called?"

"The National Reactor Testing Station. It's just over the hill," Cheryl said. "And it most certainly would be a primary target."

"That's in Arco. It's . . . ninety miles over the hill."

The phone rang, and Ada sidestepped toward it, but Betty stepped forward then with several sheets of paper.

The phone rang a second time. "It's a petition," Betty said. "Half the people in town have signed . . ."

A third ring. "Betty, that should go to the County Board, and Ethel will . . ." A fourth ring, and Ada dove and swept up the receiver. ". . . Ethel will have to . . . Hello? Hello?" The line was dead.

"Everyone agrees it's awfully important we act on these initiatives.

If you can get things rolling, Ada, I'm sure it will be remembered on election day." Betty's smile was serious and reassuring.

Ada willed a smile just like it. "Of course. I'll take it to Ethel for the necessary verifications."

She took the petition in hand, and in the same motion with her other hand turned Betty and eased her toward the door. She said, "I'm sure they'll want to take it up at the Board meeting next week."

"Are we taking up too much of your time, Ada?" Cheryl asked—not icily, but not so warmly either.

"No of course not . . . No . . ." She took her hand off of Betty's back and turned to Cheryl. "Not at all, it's just that I . . ." She lost her words for a second and nearly laughed. "Cheryl, doesn't Tony have a friend in the governor's office in Boise?"

"You mean his cousin Ned. Ned is Jordan's assistant manager of public relations, but I doubt he can help with evacuation . . ."

"I thought I remembered it so." Ada smiled genuinely. "You know, we have not talked in the longest while. Do you girls have time for coffee?"

BY EARLY AFTERNOON THE THREE LADIES had outlined a citizen's action program, and Cheryl had found Cousin Ned's telephone number in her address book. That would help a great deal, but now Ada really needed to get back to the phones.

Ethel saved her. She stuck her head in the door and said, "Sheriff, a call came in for you . . . Oh, I'm sorry."

"No, please, what is it, Ethel?"

"A Ranger McGann asked for you to meet him at the airfield, but I didn't get whether he needs help with a situation or if he was the situation."

"Tall Ranger McGann?" Betty asked. Cheryl gave her a look.

Ada practically dragged Ethel into the room, handing her the petition and introducing her to the ladies. She grabbed a few things from her desk, and with apologies and promises to discuss the need for a civil defense plan with the Board, she ran out and down the hall to the backdoor and skipped down the stone steps. Her red light was flashing as she pulled out of the motor pool lot.

Update 12:45 p.m. – Camas Airfield.
Looking for ~~tall~~ Ranger McGann

THE WHITE CLOUD RANGER STATION SWARMED with husky young men bare to the waist and heavily booted, shouting and rushing about, lugging crates and tools, and rolling barrels. Ada passed by the station, turning left at the highway instead, and drove a mile north to the Camas airfield. The airfield, too, appeared to be preparing for battle. She parked behind a garage-sized tin shack with an orange windsock waving high above it, flipped off the flashing light, and stepped into a crowd of ranchers, police, and even military personnel. The men milled uneasily in a rough ring in front of the pilots' shack, with District Ranger Ben McGann in the middle of the ring fending questions.

Ada made the mistake of asking a man near the back what was going on. He turned out to be the local newspaper reporter, and she felt like a total amateur when he scoffed and asked, "Aren't you supposed to know?"

McGann just then excused himself from the crowd with a promise of a general meeting when he got back. He headed for a line of planes parked along the runway and Ada quick-stepped to follow. He turned to scan the sky to the west, saw her, and waved her over.

"Greylock lookout called," he explained. "There's a fire in Basin Creek." He was sorting through items in a rucksack as he talked. "I'm going up to take a look. There's room in the plane if you want to come along."

"Did the Loon Creek fire jump the ridge?"

"No. That one's been laying down on its own, and even if it had flared up again, we'd have seen it come over the top."

"Lightning-caused, then?"

"There's been none."

Ada stopped in her tracks. "Oh damn!" she said. "Yes, I have to come with you."

She dodged back through the crowd to her truck and stuffed her camera, her duty jacket, and a canteen into her rucksack, then double-timed to catch McGann who was angling toward a single-engine, high-wing Beaver. The propeller was already turning. McGann showed her where to step and helped her to squeeze into the back seat, then folded himself into the front seat next to the pilot.

The plane was taxying before she figured out the seat belt, which she'd heard about but had never actually worn. It bounced to the far north end of the grass field, turned, and had started its takeoff before she could find places for her Stetson, her feet, and the rucksack.

They rose quickly from the grass runway and banked hard left, circling the upper valley and crossing back over the heart of Camas. "Damn!" she said.

McGann had put on a radio headset, but he leaned back and lifted an earphone. "What?"

"Nothing. Sorry." They'd passed right over her house, and she hadn't seen it. But the courthouse was easy to spot, and the fairgrounds, and Main Street; then the school, the fringing fields, the road up Garden Creek Canyon leading to the pass . . . She'd never flown before, although she didn't say so to the guys up front.

They climbed quickly and flew almost dead into the afternoon sun, and she wondered how the pilot could see at all with the glare. The plane didn't bounce as she was used to a car doing but jumped and dropped and dodged side to side. McGann held a map in his lap and talked with the pilot through the headset while Ada watched the creeks and ridges fall away below them almost too rapidly to track. The plane passed over Ramshorn Mountain, where the jumping and dodging worsened, then headed west-southwest toward a thick column of smoke rising and mushrooming a lot higher than they were flying. Their path took them eventually right down the upper Yankee Fork River, with Ada straining to keep track of landmarks. Her head and her stomach were starting to spin, so she raised her eyes to level, and found that it helped some. She also found it easier to navigate that way, by watching the distant objects approach more slowly. The top of Red Mountain stayed at two o'clock to her, and when the lookout on Mt. Greylock was off her right shoulder, she knew the Town of Custer lay directly below.

She tapped McGann on the shoulder, and he took off the earphones and leaned back toward her. "Is Custer in danger?" she asked. She had to speak loudly over the engines and the rush of wind past her window.

"Not likely," he yelled back. "The wind is from the northeast, so they should be okay."

"Are you doing okay?" she asked.

He nodded. "It's been a hell of a few days, though, hasn't it?" They crossed over the Yankee Fork valley, and the sun glinted off row on row of dredge tailings.

McGann looked tired but dashing behind his aviator sunglasses. "We need to talk, Ada," he yelled back.

"Yes, I think we . . . You mean, right now?"

"About what to do if this thing blows up in our face."

"Of course."

"The lookout says it started in upper Basin Creek, but a stiff nor-easter is fanning it right toward Stanley. We have to plan for a possible highway closure at least."

She shifted in her seat and had to nearly yell to be heard over the oscillating drone of the engines. "How long?"

"Three days. Two if the wind picks up."

"Damn, if it cuts the highway there, it cuts the state in half," she said. "We'll have no travel east-west or north-south."

"That's right. It'll be 300 miles to Boise by way of Arco. I thought you'd better plan right now which side of the fire you want to be on." He got back on the radio and, in a clipped, staticky give-and-take, sounded like he was giving directions to his crew chiefs.

When the plane crossed over the Basin Creek divide, the whole hillside to their left was ablaze. Ada barely remembered to get her camera out. Trees were exploding as the flames touched them, and flaming brush and branches swirled in cyclonic winds. They flew past the front edge of the fire and circled it counterclockwise. Downwind, though no closer than half a mile from the flames, the turbulence buffeted the large-winged Beaver until Ada was more out of her seat than in it. The air grew thick with smoke, and her bandana did almost nothing to cleanse it. She kept the bandana on anyway, to catch her stomach if the plane didn't at some point settle down.

Buzzing over the lower canyon, Ada spotted three parties high-tailing it down the dirt road toward the highway: hunters, she assumed. She didn't know what kind of vehicle Frenchy Boniface owned, but she was quite sure if he was in the shape he'd been in the day before, he wouldn't be able to drive it. The road fell behind them and disappeared quickly in the blue haze.

Through the whole circumnavigation McGann eyed the fire, traced their route on the map, and argued over the radio.

He turned back to her and took off the head gear. "Headquarters in Boise wants to fight this thing, but I can't see any place to drop smoke jumpers."

There was nothing but heavy forest and hills all around them. Crews couldn't even drive in, Ada saw, because they'd be driving up a narrow canyon right into the wind.

"I see nowhere to set a line until its right on top of Stanley," McGann said. He pointed the pilot due north, toward the source of the fire, then hung the headphones around his neck and stretched as much as he could in the small cockpit.

"Goddamn it," he said to Ada, "they've been talking for years about fighting fires like this from the air. Aerial bombardment. But that's all it's been, talk and study. I'd give anything for a fleet of water bombers right now."

They saw no one on the roads in the upper canyon, but Ada pointed down to the narrow point from where the burn appeared to have spread. "Can we take it down to get a look?"

McGann nodded and spoke with the pilot, and the plane began a steep downward spiral. "What the hell is that?" he asked.

"It's a moonshining still," she answered as they passed over from the north. "Did you see something? I thought I saw something lying there."

"I believe I did too. Let's take it down again."

A minute later, a second pass over Boniface's place confirmed their sighting, and they were able to get some photographs. The body—Frenchy's, she was certain—lay about twenty feet from the copper tanks and tubes at the edge of the hidden clearing. It wasn't just near the burn; it was the point-source of the burn.

McGann said, "I'll see if I can get a rescue team up here."

"You have other priorities," she said. "No one can help Frenchy anymore." She closed her eyes to the glare and said quietly, "*The fire you kindle for your enemy often burns you more than him.*"

"What was that?"

"Just something Maggie Li once told me." The plane banked and climbed, and the team headed east, back toward Camas. Although the air mostly cleared once they crossed back into Yankee Fork airspace, Ada fought her stomach the whole way.

The Beaver skipped on the runway, jolting her upright with an "Oh!" She'd ridden the last ten minutes with her eyes closed, rubbing at tears from the smoke and glare. The plane bounced and jostled to the end of the grass, then the pilot gunned the engine through a tight turn and taxied into line with three other planes. One of the planes was Forest Service green, a smaller one was State of Idaho white, and the third sported Army insignia and gun mounts under its wings.

Ada ignored them all and headed straight to the pilots' shack at a trot, feeling oddly rubber-legged on the firm ground. But when she opened the door of the shack, a whole platoon of citizenry was crowded inside, and there appeared only to be a men's lavatory and not a ladies'. She trotted to her truck instead and, passing McGann ambling to his rig, explained she would see him at the ranger station. She was confident she could make it that far.

Update 6:15 p.m. – White Cloud District Ranger Station
—Civil advisory meeting

THE MEETING ROOM AT THE RANGER STATION was filling quickly, with a noisy, jostling crowd spilling into the hallway. Although primarily to inform mayors, public safety officials, and law enforcement personnel about the fire bearing down on Stanley, other concerned citizens were not turned away. Mayor Applegate was there, as was Ethel from the courthouse. Ethel was talking and laughing with big John Hogan, the Forest Service wrangler. Ada weaved between elbows and backsides to greet Custer Police Chief Kellen Munson, who was easy to spot in his green and blue plaid, yoke-backed shirt.

He was leaning against a wall next to the water cooler. "Sorry about sticking you with the dogs again, Kel," she told him.

"They're fine for now. I got them out running yesterday. They're trained up pretty good and . . ." The mayor of Stanley, Lettie Nance, entered the room, and Munson stood up and cleared his throat.

He said. "How'd the fire start?"

Ada leaned in so her whisper could be heard over the hubbub. "It looks very much like it started at Frenchy Boniface's still."

"You going to try to mount a rescue?" he whispered back.

She glanced around and said in a normal voice, "From what we saw, there was clearly no need for haste."

"Oh. Jeez, that's too bad." He filled a paper cone with water. "You know the darndest thing, but I thought you said that trophy buckle you found on the Neagle boy—the one with Boniface's name engraved?—was for calf roping, 1946."

She pulled out her notebook and checked. "That's right. Why?"

"Well heck, Frenchy Boniface stopped competing after the war. At least I thought so. I didn't know he picked it up again." Munson shrugged and got another cone of water.

Ada shrugged too. With a new fire threatening, she had more than enough to deal with without getting lost in the weeds over a rodeo prize. "I'll check it out," she said.

"Maybe it was a fake buckle."

"Maybe so. I'll check it out."

State Police Sergeant Ken Blevins stood in the back of the room talking with a colonel of the Idaho National Guard. Ada avoided his glance. She ought to tell Blevins, but at the same time didn't want to tell him, about the anise plant in Asakura's garden—about the *anisatin*. It would be the professional thing—inter-departmental courtesy, and all that—but Blevins would go straight for Eddy Asakura; he wouldn't stop even to consider motives and alibis. She would have to tell him, but today she had plenty to deal with, with the new fire flaring up.

Before she could worry about any of it, the room hushed, and folks began to sit as Ben McGann stepped to the front. The ranger tossed his hat onto the nearest table and hung a map on the wall behind him.

He gave the talkers another few seconds to quiet, then said, "Let me tell you what the sheriff and I saw from the air." Ada sidled to the front and remained standing, but well off to the side with her hands stuffed in her pockets.

Munson jostled his way into a seat next to Lettie Nance. Jim Cummins sat on the other side of Lettie, Ada noticed. Cummins wasn't elected to anything, but he was one of the only sober citizens of Clayton, and apparently had driven in to represent that community. They all sat together at a table, and Ada thought they all looked a little nervous. The Guard Colonel in back folded his arms impatiently.

The fire, McGann told them, appeared to be heading right down Basin Creek Canyon toward the highway, and he expected on its current path it would cut the highway in a couple of days. The good news was the wind was supposed to back around and blow out of the east-southeast by Wednesday night. That would head the fire toward Valley Creek, and that would be the best outcome. That country was recently blackened, the ranger explained, and offered no fuel to keep the fire going.

Ada cleared her throat and looked squarely at Lettie Nance. "Get up to Valley Creek as soon as you can," she said—

"Louder!" from the back.

"—Tomorrow morning, if possible. If anyone has moved back in, it's because their place wasn't burned before. It could be in danger of burning this time."

Lettie said, "They're all asking about the Neagles. How is it they didn't make it out?"

Sergeant Blevins sat up in the back. Ada opened her mouth but didn't say anything for a second. "Tell them . . . warn whoever has moved back in to keep a watch out for the wind changes. If the wind turns as expected, it'll be coming right over Basin Butte this time."

McGann said the Forest Service would set up a command post at the airfield in Stanley. Asked if this fire was lightning-caused as well, he glanced at Ada, who tried to hide a grimace.

"We're still working that out." He handed Ada the pointer he'd been using, and said, "I'll let the sheriff say a few words."

Ada stared at the pointer then swung both hands behind her back and cleared her throat a couple of times. She kept her eyes mostly on the front table: on Applegate, Munson, and Lettie Nance as she began to speak. "Get your evacuation plans in order and wait for word from me or Ranger McGann. We'll have . . ."—she turned to McGann—"a good three-hour warning?"—he nodded—"before the fire cuts the highway. If it cuts the road, do not wait for word from anyone."

She looked again right at Lettie Nance. "Get your people headed over the pass to Ketchum. Not just to the campground at

Redfish—the fire crews may have to fall back to the campground—get them all the way over Galena."

Kellen Munson seemed calm enough, considering the situation. Ada told him, "You folks in Custer are in good shape for now." Munson nodded. She said, "Nevertheless, you might talk to them about boxing up a few things just in case."

At that point, the army officer lost patience. "Colonel Branson," he told the room by way of introduction, "Idaho Army National Guard." He shook his head and braced his hands on his hips. "This is not helpful, to say anyone is in good shape. The town of Custer lies right behind the fire. An unlucky shift in the wind and there would be nothing between them and a roasting. The fire could be on them in hours."

Ada tapped her leg with the pointer but dropped her eyes. "I see your point," she said. "But in fact, the Yankee Fork Valley is filled top to bottom with dredge tailings hundreds of yards across. They make a pretty good fire break, I think." She cleared her throat.

Colonel Branson gave no indication he'd heard her. "The Guard is going to set up roadblocks tonight. We'll close the highway at Torrey's Hole; turn everyone back."

"At Torrey's?" Ada asked. "That would isolate Robinson Bar, Sunbeam, and a half-dozen farmsteads. Maybe the roadblock should be moved forward to Sunbeam instead."

The Colonel said, "I'm sorry, who are you, pretty lady?"

She slapped the pointer in the palm of her left hand and looked squarely at the colonel. "I'm the sheriff," she said. "There are two exits at Sunbeam: both circle back here to Camas. Setting up at Sunbeam would allow us to keep our lines of communication open." It was a military expression she'd heard Montgomery use. It seemed to get Branson to listen, at least.

"We'll have to see about that," he said. He crossed his arms. "I'll have my men look at it."

When he'd started talking, Ada had felt oddly relieved. Like it was nice to have someone willing to take charge and give orders.

But the more he talked, the more she realized he didn't know the country or the people.

"We're declaring martial law immediately," the Colonel boomed.

The whole room glanced over their shoulders, then looked, open-mouthed, to Ada. She made an effort not to scoff because it would not be helpful, but God! This time she did not drop her eyes.

Picking her words carefully, she said, "Yellowpine County is five thousand square miles, Colonel." Branson's chin came up and his shoulders squared.

Ada said, "I don't mean to be argumentative . . ." She glanced over at McGann, who was leaning his shoulder against the wall with a 'don't look at me' look on his face.

"I don't mean to sound argumentative . . ." she said again. Munson and Mayor Applegate were sitting with their backs to Col. Branson looking fully appalled. "I'm just suggesting maybe a good approach might be to trust your rearguard and focus your forces for the attack." She swung the pointer to the map and the wind arrows McGann had drawn.

Chief Munson winked at her. Col. Branson said. "I'll consider . . . fine, we'll hold off for the time being. But it'll be hour to hour. The decision will be mine."

McGann cut in again. Roadblock or no, he told the folks, the highway might be cut by the fire along with all but radio communications. They needed to divide commands. Branson immediately claimed overall command. Ada nodded and suggested the Guard was best equipped to assist the fire fighters on the hot side.

"Agreed," Branson said. "We'll set up a little south of Stanley, down by . . ."

"The Obsidian Ranch has fields wide enough to land a plane." She bit her lip.

"What about me?" Sergeant Blevins asked her. "Which side should I be on?"

She would have expected the moon to fall out of the sky before she heard anything of the sort from the state trooper, but she nodded and said, "Ken, I know it's a longer drive home for you, but it's critical you work the Stanley side, to keep the evacuation routes open."

"That's what I was thinking."

The colonel asked, "What are you going to do, uh, Reed, which side are you going to be on?"

Applegate jumped up. "We need her on this side."

"Yeah," she said. "I guess I'll be the law on this side of the fire."

WITH THE MEETING ENDED, THE MAYORS and marshals gathered their notes, shook hands, and within ten minutes had moved out. Ada and McGann leaned on the split rail fence bordering the parking lot and nodded to each car and truck as it left. "So . . . anything interesting happen today?" he asked.

"Normal stuff." The moon in its first quarter was trying to lighten the eastern sky, although it would be another hour or so before it broke over the hills. Her throat was raw from the smoke she'd ingested during the plane ride, and she felt her whole body was made of wood.

"Dinner?" he asked.

"Huh!" She laughed because, God yes, she'd love to have dinner and a glass of wine. Just to talk—about anything at all except forest fires and suspects, and refugees. She'd love to sit with a second glass of wine and laugh and not care, and maybe get up and dance to something slow if someone dropped a nickel in the jukebox. She said, "Damn it, you know I can't. You know you can't either."

"No, you're right. I wish we could."

"I wish we . . ." She smiled and shook her head.

He took a few steps toward his truck. "Keep me posted . . ." he started to say. He stepped back to her and leaned in a little. "Let me know where you are Ada. I don't want to have to worry."

She nodded. "You too."

He had to be as exhausted as she felt, but he jogged the twenty yards to his truck. It made her smile. He hit his green flashing light as he headed out of the ranger station, and burned rubber southward, toward the fire.

Chapter Fourteen

Sunday, 30 September, 7:00 a.m.
The law this side of the fire

No ALARMS SOUNDED IN THE NIGHT; no sirens or telephone calls. No one had needed to wake her, and that was good. She got a pot of coffee boiling before first light, buttered two pieces of toast and stuck a slice of ham between them, then took her breakfast out to the bluff where she'd started most mornings since taking the 'acting sheriff' job. There she sat cross-legged on a flat volcanic ledge, closed her eyes, and tried to will the day to be a slow one. It was quiet on the bluff, but for mountain chicka-dees flitting among the sage and warblers perched in the scrub. As the sky lightened, the whole valley would come into view below her—sometimes with veils of mist hanging over the river bottoms. There was no mist today, of course, nor had there been for the last two months, and that lack of moisture was part and parcel of the fire season that had plagued central Idaho.

By 6:15, the sun began to make itself known on the far side of the Pahsimeroi Hills. The breeze on the bluff swirled cool and sweet, and the bird calls sounded clear as chimes. There wasn't a whiff of smoke, and but for the warming of plane engines down at the airfield, she could close her eyes, sip her coffee, and almost imagine the heart of her county was not ablaze.

But of course, it was. The Basin Creek fire was scary, but it would be okay. That is, the people would be okay in spite of the fire. It would cut the highway, most likely, but the road would re-open. If it made it to the Sawtooth Valley, the firefighters would make their stand at the river confluence. They would back-fire Stanley hill, sacrificing the cabins and goat shacks of Lower Stanley, but the historic timber homes and businesses of the mountain village would be saved.

She knew Ben would be fine, too, and she had to stop worrying. He was no fool, and as long as his supervisors in Boise weren't fools, the wind would back around and the fire burn itself into ground already blackened, and no one would get hurt . . . no one else, that is. She would have to go in and recover the body of Louis Boniface, but no one else had to get hurt.

It only took a few minutes for the eastern sky to brighten from periwinkle to a frightful coral color. Ada sloshed out her coffee, which had gone cold, drank up the clear air for another minute or two, then followed the trail back to start her day.

On such a rare morning, she would ordinarily have walked the six blocks to the office, but on this day, it was important to keep the pickup near her in case she had to leave quickly. She drove. Three blocks from her house she came upon an 'Ada Reed for Sheriff' sign someone had defaced. Long lashes were drawn above the two 'ee's of her name to make them look like Betty Boop eyes. She stopped the truck, pulled the sign from the ground, and replaced it with a new sign. She supposed the graffiti could have been worse.

She found worse at 3rd Street and Main. The two ee's in her name had been altered again, but obscenely in this case. She replaced that sign as well and determined that henceforth only capital letters would be used on her posters.

"YOU DID WELL LAST NIGHT, ADA," Mayor Applegate said as he stepped into her office like clockwork. He helped himself to a coffee with three cubes of sugar, then settled with a groan into the hard, wooden swivel chair facing her desk. "That Colonel Brassplate couldn't find his ass with both hands," he said. "Pardon the French."

"He'll be helpful if things go awry."

"His men will be helpful in spite of him." The mayor leaned back in the chair and scanned the room for a minute with his lips scrunched up and his fingers intertwined over his vest. He said, "You did good at the meeting, honey. People listened to you. I was proud."

"Thank you, Uncle Eph. Don't tell me you're thinking of giving me your vote." She grinned over her coffee cup.

"We'll see. I can't speak for Corrine, of course." He exhaled long and slow, made a puckering sound with his lips, then shook his head. "Ada, you're not doing well right now. You're losing the election. Banning's got you nailed in the papers over the fire refugees. You need to get behind that issue and find a solution."

"You think I'm not behind it? It's all I worry about day and night." She slunk down in her chair. "I think I have a chance to house them all at the Japanese Relocation Center down at Minidoka. It's not the Ritz, but there are facilities ready to use, and there's lots of room."

"Interesting. Bold. It'll catch some attention."

"I'm not doing it to . . ." She pursed her lips and shook her head. "It doesn't matter. The Interior Department can't say yes without the War Department, and the War Department won't say yes without a senate committee's blessing, and the Senate won't act unless the governor calls and requests it."

Applegate blew on then sipped from his coffee. "Have you talked to the governor?"

"Damn it, Jordan's a Republican. I'm sunk."

"Leaving aside your language for a moment, Ada, he's a politician first and a Republican second."

"I don't think he likes me."

"He hates you. You shot and killed his biggest donor. But hon, you've since been interviewed by every newspaper in the state and every magazine in the country, and you photograph well. I hear he's coming to Stanley to parade in front of the fire effort."

Ada said, "That doesn't help me a lot. I'm stuck on the wrong side of the fire."

"Well, maybe it's for the better after all. You know, Corrine is putting up plums and apricots today. Applesauce tomorrow."

He picked up *The Science of Wildfire Suppression* from her desk and busied himself with the graphs and photos, and Ada got her mind back to the Valley Creek deaths. She spent a full minute staring out the window considering the coincidences and connections between the people of interest in the case. She muttered, "It's a small county."

Applegate looked up. "It is a small county," he agreed. He went back to his book.

She wagged her head. "It's just a small goddamned county."

"It's a small county where folks watch their language."

Ethel poked her head in before Ada could apologize. "You done good, Fancy Badge!—oh, hello Mr. Mayor." She cleared her throat. "Uhm, Sheriff Reed you received a call from the town manager of Mackay. I thought you were out. He asked that you call him right away."

Mackay lay forty-five miles south of Camas on U.S. Highway 93. She'd been there once for a football game back in high school, but not since. The town manager, when she returned his call, told her there had been an accident on the highway, right downtown. A pedestrian had been struck and killed by a truck that morning.

"Isn't that usually handled by your local police?" she asked.

"Well, it generally is, Mrs . . . Sheriff. But the victim is Lance Harding, the former sheriff before Montgomery's time. I thought I ought to call you as a courtesy, inasmuch as it might be a fraternal thing."

"I see what you mean: being one of the force and all."

"I guess. We got him in a beer cooler right now. The Night Owl

Tavern; it's on Second and Main."

She thanked him again and told him she would be down directly.

Update 9:45 a.m. – U.S.-93 near Mackay. Pedestrian fatality

IT WAS FORTY-FIVE MILES SHE DID not need, with a forest fire burning its way straight toward Stanley, but she packed a lunch and set out in the county pickup. The main highway split two miles south of town, with Highway 75 heading west to Stanley, and U.S. 93 continuing south toward Arco. The southbound route was newly paved the whole way, and on that smooth hard surface she could almost hear herself think without a lot of rocks and gravel banging in her wheel wells. She found herself doing fifty miles per hour before she even realized it.

The highway ran straighter than nature would have it down a wide, sunny valley, with hardly a tree to relieve the eyes. The peaks of the Lost River Range towered over her left shoulder for most of the drive, and there broad alluvial fans spilled from one rocky canyon after another. Her thin, black ribbon of highway rose and fell over the toes of the fans, and her red pickup truck was often the only sign of human intrusion. At the foot of Mt. Borah, the road wound through the Thousand Springs marshlands, and her passing there raised blinding flights of ducks and geese.

The new highway turned to older, cracked pavement at the Mackay town line, where it became Main Street. Ada did not pull up to the Night Owl Tavern but continued two more blocks to where a crowd of six or seven citizens milled around barricades that closed off the entire road.

She had not met the town cop of Mackay, but she recognized him from what she'd heard. About seventy years of age, he was tall and wiry and no doubt a statue of a man in earlier days, although he'd begun to bend slightly in the middle. He wore a badge on his western-cut shirt he'd probably had to dig out of a drawer that morning.

"Paul Shelton." He stuck his hand out and gave Ada's an honest shake.

"Ada Reed. What happened here, Paul?"

"Witnesses say he just wandered into traffic—walked right in front of that hay hauler there." He pointed to a truck parked about a block up the road.

"Like he was a zombie," a boy of maybe fifteen said. He did his best zombie walk for her; Ada watched with a growing sense of unease.

"Like he didn't know up from down nor side to side," a woman said.

Ada caught her breath and looked up from her notebook. "Like he was hallucinating, maybe?" she asked.

"Maybe," the woman replied. "I wouldn't say a zombie so much as someone whose mind wasn't working properly."

A shiver worked right down Ada's spine. "I don't understand. You mean like he was drunk?"

"Harding—Lance—was never a day drinker," Officer Shelton told her. He eased her aside and said more quietly, "I mean hell, he could tie one on at night. Especially when Loretta wasn't around. But no, I never seen him drunk the next morning. Everyone who saw what happened says the same thing: he appeared not to know what he was doing."

"Is this his house?" Ada asked. It was a small, one-story clapboard cottage with a neat garden. The front door stood open.

"Uh-huh. Looks like he just stepped out and wandered into the road." The old cop squinted up into the sun. "His widow—it's Loretta; she was born in town, one of the original families—she's taking it pretty hard. She's sitting with his remains at the Night Owl."

Several cars idled on the far side of the barricade waiting to get through. Ada told Shelton he could take down the barriers.

He nodded. "Haven't used them since '43 – '44."

"What happened in '43?" she asked.

"We closed this road completely—it was Harding's idea—stopped all traffic from the south. The epidemic, you know."

Ada stopped, and again felt a chill. "Whooping cough?" she asked.

"It was bad down there on the Plain and we had no medication for it up here. You have to take care of your own."

She walked the two blocks back to the Night Owl and found Harding's widow sitting in the lounge rather than in the cooler where her husband was being refrigerated. Half a dozen old men sat around but at a respectful distance, talking low and shaking their heads.

"He was in good health," Mrs. Harding said between wiping at her eyes. She was a small, round woman with white hair surrounding a muffin face. "I wasn't home. I was in Pocatello last night sitting with my sister. I got back this morning and found everyone standing out front of our house. Lord, I never supposed . . ."

Ada asked, "Did Lance drink tea?"

"Tea? No, never."

"No, of course not. Did he . . ."

"And he was cutting down on the liquor as well. He went through a spell after he retired; everyone knows that. But he was cleaning himself up. We were going to church more this last year, and he almost never drank anymore—not heavily."

Ada promised to look in on her when the report was complete. In the walk-in cooler she found a man of seventy years or so; six-feet tall and maybe one hundred-eighty pounds, though not in fit shape anymore as he must once have been. He was laid out on a wooden door spanning two beer kegs. His hair was mostly gray, and his skin was thin and rosaceous, as a man just entering old age. There was a trace of blood on his chin, and more on the front of his shirt. It could have been from the trauma, but . . . she leaned down and sniffed. It was vomit, just as she'd found on Dolf Neagle.

It made Ada sick to do it, but she left a note pinned to the body instructing the coroner in Pocatello to test the victim's blood-alcohol level, and especially to analyze for *anisatin*.

Update 3:50 p.m. – Forest Service field command, Stanley

Hallucinating!—and yes, a bloody vomit. Damn, but it sounded much like the Neagle deaths, and it was all pointing again to Eddy Asakura's herb garden. Ada drove slowly out of town, unsure again of anything in the Valley Creek investigation. Unsure, except that Eddy Asakura had means and opportunity—at least in the Neagles' deaths; and now once again a motive—at least in Lance Harding's death. It was Lance Harding, after all, who had put Eddy in jail for rustling when the young man didn't even eat meat. But damn it, no motive anymore in Clifford Neagle's death! She drove on, alternately confused, worried, and sad through flocks of honking geese and trumpeting cranes.

A left turn at Thousand Springs put her onto the rocky, rutted Trail Creek Road toward Ketchum. It would have been more responsible for her to head straight back to Camas, but she was so far south anyway and had other things to deal with that she took the chance and swung west. Hopefully, the highway would stay open, and she could make a complete loop of it. An hour and a half later she gassed up in Ketchum and headed north on Highway 75 over Galena Summit and down into the Sawtooth Valley. All up and down the switchbacks of Galena Summit she dodged a rag-tag caravan of evacuees and sightseers.

The airfield sat on a rocky bench above Stanley, overlooking the broad meadows of lower Valley Creek to the north and the Salmon River to the east. A Forest Service fire camp was going up below and to the west of the airfield, and the place swarmed with yellow-shirted fire fighters and green-shirted supervisors. A lot of no-shirted young men swung sledges, hauled on ropes, and lugged crates and timbers as Ada weaved her way through the construction. Plywood walkways were being laid down to connect rows of green canvas tents, and pipes and hoses stretched out to connect water trucks to latrines and shower tents. She paused for a minute to watch a large mess tent be hoisted and staked. But she was in the way, and the whistles and cat calls that followed her grew embarrassing, so she hurried through to the airfield.

She ran into State Patrol Sergeant Blevins on the edge of the airstrip. He also was trying to stay out of everyone's way and greeted her almost congenially. Together they watched a small cargo plane land, yawing left and right to drop down onto the short gravel runway. It rolled up to their end of the strip, and they had to turn and lean away from the flying sticks and sand as the plane pivoted around and caught them in its prop wash. They both reached their hands to their hats.

"I tried to call you earlier," Blevins yelled over the engine noise. "Thought you'd be interested. A red and white, high-wing Cessna took off from the airfield this morning, first light. It headed south. Any guesses who?"

She shook her head. The cargo plane began its taxi, and in the heightened roar but calmer breeze she scanned the crowd of yellow shirts and khaki pants behind Blevins.

"The Cessna had a New Jersey registration," he shouted. "It was your rich guy, Riis-Moreau."

Ada froze. Holland Riis-Moreau was no longer her last best suspect, but she wasn't ready to clear him completely. She turned away with hands on her hips, took a deep breath, and as calmly as she could, said, "I'll be darned."

Holland was not her last suspect since she'd seen what she'd seen in Mackay that morning—the confusion and heedlessness indicative of *anisatin* poisoning. But Eddy Asakura was only half a suspect, because although he might have had a grudge against the old sheriff, he no longer had one against any of the forest fire victims.

In the case of the Neagle family, the vindictive Riis-Moreau still stood front and center in her lineup.

She had to wonder if she'd let Holland off the hook too easily. And if she had, if she'd let him wriggle away, was it out of fear and uncertainty about her husband and his questionable ethics? Was it out of shame over her faithless marriage? She couldn't tell herself no on either count, and it made her wince.

The plane's engine quieted, and Blevins said in a normal voice, "You talked to the guy again a few days ago, didn't you? You must have impressed him."

"I think I impressed him more the first time."

She crossed her arms and turned so Blevins wouldn't see the worry in her face. But it probably didn't matter. After what she'd found in Mackay, let him go. If Riis-Moreau had wanted to kill Dolf Neagle or Lance Harding—if it was about cheating, either with his wife or with his money—he would want it to be obvious, a message for the world to see and understand, not made to look like an accident. He certainly wouldn't kill subtly, using poisons or hallucinogens. Let him go, because it all seemed to be coming back to Eddy Asakura, damn it.

Blevins was checking his watch and scanning the skies. He said, "You don't look concerned. You don't think, anymore, Riis-Moreau might have killed Dolf Neagle?"

No, she didn't, but . . . "It's entirely possible, Ken. He's such a moral cesspool it's hard to judge." She needed Blevins to believe it for a little while longer.

"It wasn't his money clip?"

"It was." She needed him to believe it until she could deal with Asakura without the State Patrol's ham-fisted help.

"But you don't think his wife was whoring around with Neagle?"

Whoring around? Ada thought. *The woman was all alone and abused and betrayed by her husband.* She said, "Sybil was . . . seeing the boy, and Holland knew it, too. But Ken, we have nothing more on Riis-Moreau. We can't act on it."

"Not with him way the hell and gone in New Jersey, we can't." Blevins shook his head and scoffed.

And that was fine; let him think what he thought of her. Yes, she had compromised because of Montgomery, but without harm to the investigation. God, she hoped it had caused no harm. She'd compromised half her life for Montgomery Reed, but that would be the last time. Just bring him home from the war safe, and there would be changes. "It'll work out," she said, mostly to herself.

What must have been the Forest Service command center was going up on a slight rise on the west flank of the gravel bench about two hundred yards from where they stood. Tent flaps were being tied back and tables set up. The two of them watched and waited in the smoky breeze for another ten minutes while Ada weighed the risk against her responsibility to share information with the State Patrol Sergeant. She asked, "Do you remember Lance Harding, the sheriff before Montgomery?"

"Sure. Lance is a good guy. I like him."

"I'm sorry then. He was killed this morning. Stepped into the highway out front of his house and got hit by a truck."

"I'll be damned. Any unusual circumstances?"

She hesitated just a moment. "Huh-uh. Just an awful accident."

She turned and they both watched a twin-prop sweep around a distant piney knob to start its approach. "Do you have to drive all the way to Pocatello tonight?" she asked.

"Fortunately, no. The state springs for a room in Ketchum. You?"

She kept her eyes on the plane and said, "I have to get back, and anyway I'm all done in."

"No rooms here anyway."

Neither made mention, but it was the governor's twin-prop touching its wheels and blowing back twin eddies of dust. Before it had even slowed, Blevins touched the brim of his hat and hurried off in the direction of the command tent.

Ada did not wait for the entire entourage to deplane, but hustled back to her sheriff's pickup where it was parked among a tangle of visitor's vehicles. She climbed inside, checked that she wasn't being watched, then reached into the jockey box for a small makeup case. Using the rear-view mirror, she powdered her face, boldened her eyes with a bit of mascara and an eyebrow pencil, then daubed on a modest but attractive red lipstick. She smacked her lips and saw in the mirror it wouldn't do. So, she removed the modest lipstick with a tissue and applied a deeper red.

That would do well enough, she supposed. She brushed the wind and road dust from her hair then tucked in her uniform shirt tight as a drum, snugged up her belt, and set the new, ten-dollar Stetson on her head. She arrived at the command-center tent as the governor began to speak.

Blevins, who had beat her there, was being handled by one of the governor's aides—a young, bespectacled man over whose shoulder Blevins watched with noticeable impatience. As she walked by, Ada said, "You're Ned, aren't you?" She winked when the young man smiled and nodded.

In addition to officers and rangers in the tent, there were reporters from all over the state and maybe half a dozen from the wire services. Ada scanned the crowd, finding and greeting one reporter she remembered from the aftermath of the Yankee Fork case. In just a couple of minutes four reporters stood around her with their pencils to their notepads. The governor, speaking from up on a plywood dais, noticed the commotion and met Ada's eyes.

She let him finish his remarks. Then, with a pleasant but serious air, walked up and onto the platform, shook the governor's hand, and said loudly and slowly enough for pencils to get down every word, "Governor Jordan, I can't tell you how much it means to the people of Yellowpine County, your coming out here as busy as you are, and bringing such strong offers of assistance." He and she continued to clasp hands as they turned and smiled for the half dozen photographers.

The governor didn't miss a beat. "We're here to do everything we can for you, Sheriff Ada." The crowd seemed to fade back, and she was amazed at how almost genuine the governor's smile looked in the flash of the cameras.

"Well, there is one immediate and growing need," she said, again clearly and deliberately. "But I believe you are the person capable of resolving it with a signature." The governor leaned in and the reporters stepped closer. Blevins scowled from the back of the tent, his stance wide and arms folded across his chest. But Ada kept a smile plastered on her face, and before she left the stage, the governor had nodded approvingly, and all the reporters had jotted down her plan to use the internment camp at Minidoka to house the fire refugees.

She found Ben McGann behind the headquarters tent, where he was helping to wire up a two-way radio. He had not been among the uniformed persons at the press conference, a fact for which Ada was most grateful. As she came nearer, yellow shirts and green uniforms turned, and hats were snatched from heads. McGann saw it all and fought back a laugh, then explained to the others he had to talk logistics with the sheriff, and the two of them stepped away from the gawking eyes.

Alone on the boardwalk, he said, "Well, it must have been you I heard up on that stage, buttery tongue and all. And don't you look…"

"Don't say it."

"… all that and more." He smiled. "Really, I thought you were great."

"I feel dirty. For a minute today I was never going to compromise again, but I guess I blew that." He looked at her, puzzled, but she just laughed. "Anyway, I think it worked; we may get some help for the people who lost their homes."

A gas generator started up, turning them away and down another plywood path, which they followed deeper into the camp between bunk tents and tool sheds. "How about your day?" she asked.

"Not so bad. The wind is trying to back around toward the west, as the meteorologists predicted. That'll make it a good day, all in all, if it works out." He scanned the sky and his whole bearing seemed tired. She wished she could tell him to rest and not to worry so much.

He said, "So, you just came by to see the Governor?"

"I was down south today in Mackay. A pedestrian death, a former lawman."

"Sorry to hear it. Any unusual circumstances?"

"Yes, and it has me worried."

They wandered up by the water truck, stepping over hoses that snaked down to the shower rooms and to the mess tent. "The National Guard helping out?" she asked.

"Branson isn't so bad. His intentions are good, and if things go to hell, it'll be good to have him here."

"I suppose it will." She smiled because Ben was a generous person—maybe too generous. And when he stood tall and scanned the skies, as he was doing just then, he reminded her of an old-time movie poster; or maybe like a hardy woodsman come to the rescue, as Sybil Riis-Moreau had intimated. She laughed but only shook her head when he asked her why.

They took in the hills together, and the forests and the rooftops of the old town. "Are you staying the night?" he asked.

The question caught her mind straying along similar lines, and she stuttered, "Is the highway open east?"

He scrunched his lips and nodded. "For emergency traffic, but it's not the safest. I'd rather you stayed."

She stared a moment, not really sure if she'd understood, then looked away. "I ought to go, Ben," she said.

"I know. It's tough, isn't it?" He put his hand on her shoulder, and said, "There's no food to be had in town, so come by the mess tent before you leave. I'll buy you dinner."

She glanced around. "Do you think that's a good idea?"

He raised his brows in surprise—or maybe disappointment, or possibly just confusion. She said, "Sorry, I just meant, you know how people can be sometimes when they've too little to occupy their minds, getting all catty and stupid over the simplest and most innocent things. It could look . . . you know . . ." It was definitely bewilderment, on his face. She stuck her hands in her pockets and pulled them out again. "To some people, I mean, getting the wrong idea when there's nothing whatever . . ."

"Ada, It's just a plate of hash."

She dropped her head, stuck her hands back in her pockets, and willed a look of composure. "Well then," she said, "How can a gal say no to an offer like that?"

Update 8:15 p.m. – Driving through to Camas, if the fire lets me

The Salmon River canyon was so thick with smoke that evening Ada could hardly breathe, but the guardsmen at Lower Stanley waved her through, telling her only to keep a steady pace and not to stop for anything. The visibility improved a little by Sunbeam, so after checking in with the National Guard team posted there, she swung north along the Yankee Fork. The road through the narrows was as treacherous as ever and kept her focused, and she had put Sergeant Blevins, and the governor, and even tall, woodsman McGann out of her mind by the time she got to Custer.

Chief Kellen Munson had been watching the two orphaned hounds for four days, and that was a rotten thing for her to stick him with. And the truth was, she'd gotten used to having them greet her in the evening and . . . drool and take up the whole kitchen floor. She kind of missed the company.

It was past eight o'clock when she rolled into town. Munson's pickup truck was parked at his place of residence, and he was in the backyard splitting firewood. He left the maul in a block of wood and met her at the gate. The two dogs trotted over as well, practically stuck to Munson's heels.

"I'm sorry Kel," she began, "It was never my intention to dump these dogs on you. I got busy faster than I expected to."

Munson turned a quarter turn and crossed his arms. "It isn't me needs an apology," he said. "Dogs can't be dumped like loads of baggage. They're sensitive creatures."

She'd not come prepared to defend against that line of accusation. "Uhm . . . You're right, Kel, I was selfish. I didn't consider how they might take it."

He lowered his voice. "They just lost their brother, their master, and their home!"

"I know. I was . . . Maybe I should get them to the shelter in Camas, after all. They'll make sure they get adopted to good, responsible homes."

Munson yanked off his hat, revealing in the bright moonlight a tan line and a head of thinning brown hair. He slapped his leg with the hat. "They'll split them up! Ada, no one is going to take on two full-grown hounds, the way they eat. Do you want to split these guys up after all they've been through?"

She raised her own hat and raked her fingers back through her hair, blew a long breath, and . . . And just off the back porch of Munson's house a brand new six-foot by four-foot wooden dog-house sat between tall poplars. It had a shingled roof and fresh-painted siding. An old, braided rug covered the ground out front, and there were feeding bowls on either side of the door.

Ada stuck her hands in her pockets and turned away for a minute. "Oh, damn it," she said, but then smiled. "I'd grown kind of fond of Mutt and Jeff."

"I've been calling them Zephyr and Blaze."

"They would be a lot better off with you, wouldn't they, Kel?"

"It isn't for me to say, Ada. They're properly your dogs now."

"But we both know they would. And you wouldn't mind either, would you?"

He shrugged. "They ain't been no trouble."

She arrived at her house after ten, exhausted from the drive but confident she and the governor would find some relief for the fire-displaced families. She was confident, as well, she'd done right by her two canine dependents—leaving them with Kellen Munson. She was less confident regarding the mysterious deaths of Lance Harding and the Neagle family, and not confident at all of her own heart, or that she had her hands on the wheel of her own careening life.

CHAPTER FIFTEEN

Monday, 1ˢᵗ of October, 8:10 a.m.
No news on the fire.
No progress to speak of re the Valley Creek fatalities.

ADA WOKE IN A SWEAT AND TOSSED FOR WHAT FELT like half the night. It was the fire, yes, but it was everything else, too. Had she found unusual circumstances in the town of Mackay? God yes, she had—inexplicable behavior, hallucinations, an unwillingness or inability to get out of harm's way. It was all too similar to the four Neagle deaths, and it all pointed to Eddy Asakura.

The problem that kept her awake, though, was it all pointed too neatly to Eddy. The subtle, enigmatic means of death; the cold, dispassionate revenge; it fit perfectly into the cliché of a mysterious oriental: a ninja assassin. If someone had wanted to frame Eddy Asakura for murder, he couldn't have done better if he'd left a samurai sword in the victims.

She didn't roll out of bed until after seven, and she barely got to the office by eight. Her workday began in the high-ceilinged and echoey clerk and recorder's office, where Ethel provided her first with coffee to pry open her eyes, then with a thick, string-tied file folder. Inside the folder, Ada found the details of Sheriff Lance Harding's arrest and prosecution of Eddy Asakura. It had happened five years earlier, in summer of 1946, and the charge was rustling and butchering a calf. Courtroom testimony showed Asakura could not have been within twenty miles of the discovery of the animal's entrails, but that detail seemed to have evaded the jury. Lost on them also was the fact that the Japanese American didn't eat meat. Harding's testimony and the black eye he sported were convincing enough, and so Asakura, also bruised and cut, had been taken off to jail, where he sat for three months. This was nothing new, she'd already known Eddy had reason to hate the old sheriff.

"Ethel," she asked, "do you remember Lance Harding? I'm wondering who else might have disliked him. Disliked him enough to . . . even a score with him."

"Bump him off?" Ethel, who had been reeling around the room with a watering can, sat at last with a coffee of her own. She said, "Harding was a bull of a man; tougher even than your Montgomery." She counted on her fingers a short list of men in the county who might have held grudges. "But," she said, "grudge or no, folks respected him—or most did."

Ethel began shuffling a thick stack of papers, sorting and validating them with a rubber stamp and ink pad. She stamped several pages with rhythmic fervor, then paused to say, "Louie Boniface never got along with Sheriff Harding at all, and they fought the one time."

"Wait, Boniface fought Harding?"

The stamp stopped in mid blow. "The fight didn't last long, and Louie rested and recuperated in the slammer for a couple of weeks. But wouldn't Boniface have been dead before Lance Harding passed away?" The thumping of the stamp resumed.

Ada nodded and somewhat absently said, "Yes, he certainly would have been." Harding hadn't passed away so much as took leave of his senses and stumbled to his death. Just like the Neagles: erratic and irrational. It occurred to her Louis Boniface had also been acting erratically before he died. He'd been nutty as a fruitcake, in fact, both times she'd seen him.

There was something wrong about it, and she hopped down and paced the clerk's office. The old moonshiner had been half out of his mind when she'd seen him last, shooting blindly and rambling—hallucinating?—about charges and accusations no one had made against him. Could Frenchy Boniface somehow have been another victim? "Was it right under my nose; did I miss it somehow?" she said aloud.

She turned back to Ethel, "What about Riis-Moreau, did he have trouble with Harding?"

Ethel kept stamping. "Nothing I'm aware of. I think Holland is careful about keeping his nose clean in Idaho; keeping the Obsidian Ranch a safe haven."

Ada blew a raspberry sound and held up her fingers to count: "Boniface and Asakura had grudges against Harding, and Boniface and Riis-Moreau had grudges against Dolf Neagle. It's Boniface in both cases, but he's dead."

"As a doornail," Ethel agreed.

It could still have been Asakura, Ada supposed, although he had no remaining grudge against Clifford Neagle. She thought a moment and asked, "Ethel, did Eddy Asakura have any kind of run-in with Louis Boniface?"

"I don't think so. They're hardly birds of a feather, if you know what I mean."

"Who hated Louis Boniface?"

Again, the rubber stamp paused over its target. "Except for revenuers and sermonizers, I'd say everyone loved Frenchy."

Perhaps not everyone, however. Holland Riis-Moreau may well have held a grudge against the old moonshiner—by reason of a bad business turn if not by reason of Holland's mis-adventurous wife. It made her sick to think the man she'd let slip away to New Jersey might again be her number-one suspect.

Ethel finished her paperwork and gathered the pages into a neat stack. Ada wished she could do the same with her own loose ends. Her head spun. She had three probable murders now, and three stubbornly imperfect suspects.

*Update 9:05 a.m. – Consulting with my good friend
Sergeant Blevins of the Idaho Highway Patrol*

"LANCE HARDING WAS A FRIEND OF MINE!" The words were delivered just a decibel or two below a shout, and they preceded Sergeant Ken Blevins through the door by two or three heavy steps. Ada was at her desk, slouched under the gaze of Harry Truman with a library volume of *Medicinal Herbs and Home Curatives* pressed to her head. She slid the book into her desk drawer and sat up just as Blevins stomped in. He squared his shoulders and took a wide stance.

He had swung through Mackay after they'd talked at the airport, he told her, to pay respects. He'd talked to the witnesses, seen Lance's body. He'd seen the note she'd left pinned to the body, and he'd had his office look up *anisatin*.

"Hallucinations? Are you kidding me?" he all but yelled. "I asked you if there were unusual circumstances. You lied to me!"

"I didn't lie. I withheld certain speculative notions for a short period . . ."

"From a Japanese spice plant! Did you know Asakura traded blows with the deceased."

"I know."

"Did you know it took Harding and a couple state troopers to subdue that bastard? I was one of those troopers, damn it. He is one dangerous son of a bitch!"

Ada considered the ramifications of that last bit of information but let it go for the time. She said "I checked the court records. There was not a piece of admissible evidence against the man. He didn't even eat meat. Why was he ever arrested for cattle rustling?"

Blevins scoffed and tossed his hat onto the spare desk. "Let's take your point, *Acting* Sheriff. The kid was wrongly accused, beat up, and sentenced to jail even though he was innocent. I feel bad for him, but that's a pretty strong motive to kill the man who done it, wouldn't you say?"

Yes it was, damn it, but . . . "A lot of people got sideways with Lance Harding."

"A lot of people don't study the art of assassination. And it sounds like Lance was disoriented and hallucinating. Didn't it even occur to you maybe that's how the Neagles bought it too?" Blevins snatched up his hat and moved to the door. "You should have told me about the Japanese poison."

"I'm waiting for the blood work. There's no evidence yet anybody ingested poison, or even that anyone was . . ."

He didn't let her finish. "I wondered why you didn't care when Riis-Moreau got away. You knew then it was Asakura!"

"It's more complicated than that, damn it! You move too fast, Ken, without thinking things all the way through."

"And you move too slow, and more people die. Or has that not been made plain enough to you?"

The gloom that had been growing since she'd looked on Lance Harding's body suddenly made it hard for her to breathe. She had moved slowly back in July, and a young man she might have saved had died; and then another. Now here she sat acting like she knew what the hell she was doing. Maybe they were right after all, and she was no lawman. Maybe she'd merely been lucky before.

"Are you going to arrest Asakura again, or shall I do it?" Blevins stood half in and half out of her office, his voice booming through the halls.

She stood and shook her head. "Put out an APB for Asakura, but don't . . ."

"I know where to find the son of a bitch!"

"No, not in my county. You have a personal grudge against the suspect. You just told me so yourself."

She'd almost forgotten the physical run-in she'd had with Blevins in July, but his sneer told her he hadn't. "I'm not bound by jurisdiction anymore," he practically hissed. "If you want to bring him in, do it before I find him. If he gets away, I'll see this county throws you out on your ass!"

Update 10:15 a.m. – Have to check things out down south again. I don't know, I think I need to talk with the Mackay cop. There are coincidences . . . Maybe I missed something.

SHE'D MADE THE TRIP TO MACKAY ONLY THE DAY BEFORE—she was driving in circles. But she gassed up and swung her pickup onto the paved highway south from Camas. It had nothing to do with Blevins' threat because, frankly, getting thrown out on her ass sounded like a pretty good option right then. No, it had to do with the old cop in Mackay. He had said something odd, and it struck a chord: *We closed this road for the epidemic—it was Lance's idea,* he had told her. The epidemic he referred to was the whooping cough—the same that had swept through the Minidoka internment camp. It wasn't much of a lead, but she wasn't demanding a lot of new leads just then.

She drove straight through, getting to Mackay by late morning, and found the cop, Paul Shelton, at his place of business: a radio and TV repair shop on Pine Street. He pinned on his badge, put a *Back Soon* sign in the window, and walked with her.

Blevins had been there not eight hours after she'd gone, Shelton told her, and he had paid respects then made some calls on his radio. He'd escorted Harding's body down to Pocatello with his red light flashing.

Main Street was quiet but for a lone pickup truck easing through southward. Half the shops appeared to be shut down. Her boots and his echoed on the sidewalk. "Business not so good?" Ada asked.

The old cop shrugged. "A little slow. Kids don't stick around anymore. Off to Boise mostly. Some go to Denver, some to Butte. It's television, I think. Gets everyone to thinking there's something out there."

The sound of geese reached them from over the rooftops and drew the attention of both to the eastern sky and the limestone crags towering over the town. "There ain't nothing, you know—out there," he said. "But who listens?"

The police barricades were down when they got to the site of the accident, and the witnesses had got on with lives behind curtained windows. A grain hauler rolled by headed for the elevators at the north end of town.

"It was in December of '43," Shelton said. We closed the road coming up from the Snake River Plain, but heck, it didn't affect all that much traffic. With gas rationing, no one was really travelling in those days. We were able to open it back up a month later when they'd got the whooping cough under control."

"How did they do that?"

"They eventually got the antibiotics to put it down."

"Harding set up the barriers?"

"Him and me, but I mean we weren't the only ones. Blaine County, Lemhi County, they all stopped traffic up from the plain."

"Did you ever meet a man, a Japanese American by the name of Asakura? Then or recently?"

Shelton cocked his head. "I'm pretty sure not."

"Did you see any Japanese persons try to come through here during the time of the barricades?"

"Mrs. . . . Sheriff Reed, I can confidently tell you I've never seen a Japanese person at any time here or anywhere except, you know, in movies and magazines." He gave her an embarrassed smile. "It's not our demographic."

Ada stuck her hands in her pockets and for several minutes the sky above was noisy with birds in south-bound V-formations. Shelton was patient and lit a smoke. She waited for things to quiet. It had just seemed somehow connected. "I'm sorry Paul, for bothering you. I don't know what I was thinking."

He said, "It's an odd line of questioning, all in all."

"It's an odd case." She hesitated, but only for a moment because Paul Shelton wasn't just a nice guy, he was a cop like her. She said, "Did you hear about the family who died in the Valley Creek fire?"

"Sure. But what does that have to do with Lance's roadblock, the whooping cough, and . . .?"

"There are some similarities in how Harding and the Neagles died."

"By a hay hauler versus a forest fire?"

"Subtle similarities. Plus . . . one of the fire victims was a guard at the Minidoka internment camp, and one of the suspects . . ."

"Of Japanese descent." Shelton whistled and stuck his hands in his pockets, "Yeah, I can sort of see that circle."

More geese honked in the valley to the west, and they both lifted their eyes to it. He said, "I used to be an okay cop, I thought." He raised his hat and wiped his head with his sleeve. "There was a time I could almost put two and two together."

"It's not like an Agatha Christie novel, is it?"

"It never was."

"What are you thinking, Paul?"

"I don't know a damned thing, Ada. Pure speculation. But maybe you should talk to a doctor down in Jerome."

"What doctor?"

"You'll find him at the County clinic down there. Fielding or Felton, I think. I expect he'll have some information along your general lines of inquiry."

Update 3:30 p.m. – County clinic, Jerome, Idaho,
to see a Dr. Fielding or Dr. Felton, I think.

THE JEROME COUNTY CLINIC WAS A two-story brick building, and it would have been avant-garde back in the '20s. Honeysuckle vines clung to the north and east walls and juniper trees trimmed tall as rockets lined the walk. Ada parked on the street in front, stepped out, and stretched her back one way and the other.

Her uniform drew stares from pedestrians on the street when she stepped out, and then from the patients in the lobby, and finally from the girl at the desk. "Nurse?" She held her Stetson in her hand.

"You're a real sheriff?"

"Yellowpine County. I'd like to see a Dr. Fielding or Felton, please."

The nurse had her wait in the lobby for fifteen minutes with a mother and her three coughing children, then led her to a mahogany-paneled room where she waited more comfortably for another ten minutes.

Doctor Feldthaus was a busy man, but he offered her a cup of coffee, which she accepted. He wasn't sure he could be of help, he explained as he poured himself a cup. "I remember Paul Shelton. Good man, but I don't know why he sent you here." He was an older gentleman with white hair and deep worry lines creasing his brow, but spry enough, and straight as a broomstick.

"You got your town through the epidemic of '43," Ada said. "Jerome stopped the whooping cough before anywhere else in the valley."

"And I'm still proud of that. We passed quarantine rules, mask ordinances. That's what a doctor does—or it used to be; he takes care of his community." The old man walked over and put his arm up on the windowsill.

Ada stayed in her seat and drained the coffee cup. But an uneasiness that had started on her drive south from Mackay made the coffee sour a little in her stomach. She already knew the answer to her next question. Paul Shelton had known it too, she'd seen it in his eyes, and others would have known. She asked quietly, "Where did you get the medicine?"

The question seemed not to surprise Feldthaus. He scanned the high bookshelf, as though he wanted a volume up there. "The government eventually distributed a supply . . ."

"Eventually?"

"Initially, I was able to get the antibiotics on the um . . . they call it the black market. I wasn't going to be too proud; folks were sick."

"It came from the camp; the internment camp?"

The old man ran his hand over the books. "I didn't ask a lot of questions, but generally—yes." He turned then and rested his hands on the back of his desk chair, facing Ada. "They had a big supply out there and, hell, folks in town were suffering—good folks whose husbands and sons were off fighting for our country."

She cocked her head, unsure what to say to that. He noticed.

He said, "Look, the whooping cough probably started in the camp anyway. There was no cleanliness among those people."

The old doctor should have shrunk after a statement like that; he should have cast his eyes down and apologized. But he stood there tall and proud as ever. She fought to keep calm, though, because she needed a little more from him. "Your supplier at the camp—was his name Neagle? Clifford Neagle?"

The doctor crossed his arms. Ada said, "He's dead, if that's your hesitation. I'm working on a murder case, and I have to have an answer, please."

After a pause, he nodded. "Neagle was a warehouse worker, and we'd had some dealings previously; bandages, needles; little things going to waste anyway."

She tried to stay professional, but damn it, she'd driven too far, and had too much coffee on an empty stomach; and she'd seen and heard more than enough. She slammed her cup on the desk and stood. Her hands went to her hips. "Two dozen people died in that camp because you accepted pilfered medicine. Twenty-four American people," she couldn't help but add, "whose sons and husbands, damn you, fought for our country too!"

He took one step back, but then raised his palm skyward, like a diviner. "Don't you lecture me, young lady. You would do the same thing for your people."

She stomped to the office door and turned. "Not that."

Feldthaus brought his hand down, slapping the chair back. "You would—you'd save your people first. Or is that just a dress-up uniform you're wearing?" He marched over and pushed the door open for her. She didn't move, though his reach brought him inches from her. He smelled of astringent. In the sunlight from the high windows the skin of his face was translucent and veined. His white hair was thinning, and the scalp underneath pink. She had admired the man when they met. She'd gotten up and shaken the hand of the doctor who'd served his community so selflessly and . . . honorably. She looked at him now with nothing so much as dismay.

He said, "I did what I had to do. You have nothing to charge me with."

"Charge you? Don't you get it, old man? Those internees out there, those families—they were your people too."

SHE FOUGHT TEARS ALL THE WAY TO HAILEY, gassed up in Ketchum at the last station open, and was fighting mad before she made Galena summit. There was your damned motive! Eddy never suspected Clifford Neagle of shooting his father. Hideo Asakura didn't die trying to escape, he died breaking into the warehouse. He died looking for the medicines Neagle was pilfering and selling; the antibiotics that might have saved his wife.

Update 9:30 p.m. – No way through.
Staying in Stanley for the night.

"YOU'RE DRIVING IN CIRCLES." BEN MCGANN's smile was warm, but the worry in his eyes and the fatigue were easy to see even at the darkest edge of the camp.

"I know. Shut up." She returned the smile, but quickly let it fade. The anger she'd felt coming over Galena Summit was now an ache in her chest and a weariness so deep she could barely raise her head. "Ben, I think I'm going to have to arrest someone for the Neagle deaths."

"A guilty party, hopefully."

"It'll be easy to get a conviction."

McGann turned and studied her face—or tried to in the bare starlight. "That isn't always the same thing, is it?" he asked.

She didn't want this job. She didn't want to have to fight with Ken Blevins, or argue with the county Board or the damned newspaper, or pretend to be in charge when she wasn't. She didn't want to have to arrest Eddy Asakura who was, too, a victim of sorts. "I don't know. I'm just so awfully tired of thinking I always know better."

He stuck his hands in his pockets. "Recent history supports that hypothesis."

Her smile came back—even a bit of a chuckle. The drive and then what she'd found in Jerome had done her in, and Ben was easy to talk to. She had hurried up to the Forest Service command tent and been so relieved to find him there. Then she'd stood in the lantern light stuttering some reason to be stopping by and bothering everyone. He'd come up with an excuse to step away for a few minutes.

Lights came on in a couple of tents in the camp and went off in a couple others. McGann stood silhouetted by the ghostly glow of the granite peaks, and for a few minutes the ranger in him considered the breeze and the dryness and even the smells in the air. Someone somewhere got a transistor radio tuned, and the tinny sounds carried over the sage . . . and then the long roads, and the anxious hopes she'd held out for Eddy, her empty house and empty weekends, and now her damned empty marriage suddenly became too much. She hugged her arms close around and tears couldn't be helped.

He noticed. "You've had a rough couple of days. I'm sorry."

"I'm okay. Let's not talk about it." Because she was barely okay standing near and letting him study the wind. She didn't want to talk about any part of her tough days, or her nights, or her life that was a goddamn mess. She really needed a hug and wished she and Ben were closer, but she only wished it for a minute, because that wouldn't work at all and then where in hell would she be? They stood side by side, and the evening breeze was blowing down off the high peaks and not smoky at all, and in the clear air the stars reached right down to the lights of Stanley, and they all blurred together.

He said, "I'm afraid you can't get through the canyon tonight. It's too dangerous."

"I don't want to . . . I'll stay here tonight." The mountain air had turned chilly, making her shiver, and she looked away. "I mean, Lettie Nance has a small room back behind the grocery she lets me use if I need it. It's . . . I'll be fine."

McGann waited for the fire boss to blare something over the PA system: a loud, metallic, *Able Crew on standby till midnight; Delta Crew hit the sack.* He took off his hat and said, "I wanted to tell you, to ask you . . . be careful, Ada. Promise me you will?"

She nodded, and he did put his arms around her then, and she hugged him back. He said, "This thing could blow up in our faces."

"I know."

"I don't want to have to come looking . . . I don't want to have to do the paperwork on you, you know?"

She smiled for him, and they started back toward camp to the transistorized strains of *Unforgettable.* She said, "Don't you go getting yourself killed, either. Okay?"

"It's a deal."

CHAPTER SIXTEEN

Tuesday, October 2nd.
Stanley back to Camas
Barely making it through.

THE SMOKE HAD CLEARED ENOUGH BY 9:30 the next morning that the Guard allowed traffic through, but only following behind pilot vehicles. She was warned at the Sunbeam checkpoint that even that passage was provisional, hour to hour.

From Sunbeam all the way to Juniper Flat she followed a logging truck that swayed under its load until Ada feared she would be pulling the driver from the river. The whole damned county was in a rush—some coming and some going, and the rest, like her, running in circles.

There'd been a siren in the night. She was lying awake worrying about Eddy Asakura and whether he could really be a killer, and about Inga who loved Eddy and had already lost one young man she loved. She'd worried about Montgomery, if he was safe in Korea and whether she should even give a damn, but then of course she should but what was going to happen when he came home? She'd even laid awake worrying about Sybil Riis-Moreau, too hurt to stay but too scared to leave the man she was married to. She'd worried about everyone but Ben McGann, although it was him called to danger. Out of nowhere she'd heard the siren blaring over the whole town, and she'd heard the engines start up and the shouting and running of men; and she had cried. But then she was so awfully tired she'd fallen asleep and woke cold and alone.

She backed off from the logging truck and drove more slowly, choking and tearing up from the heavy smoke. At the turnoff to Juniper Flat, she let the engine idle while she stepped out and stretched. Eddy Asakura would have to be arrested. The circumstances of Boniface's death made no sense yet. But the testimony of Dr. Feldthaus, that Clifford Neagle stole the medicines that might have saved Asakura's mother, took things out of her hands. Given Blevins' threats, the sooner she went in to arrest Eddy the easier it would be for everyone. But she didn't think it wise to go in alone. If he refused to come out with her, he would just get himself into more trouble. It would be better for everyone if she had a deputy or two with her.

She stood in the late-morning sun with the river splashing behind her, pondering her next move. Then that decision, too, was taken out of her hands.

Update 12:00 noon – The highway has been cut.
Have to get word to canyon residents.

ETHEL GRIMES' VOICE CRACKLED OVER THE RADIO, startling Ada so that she reached in and grabbed at the microphone, but then dropped it and had to open the door and duck under the steering wheel to retrieve it. "Come again, Ethel?"

The fire, Ethel explained, had exploded into the canyon of the Main Salmon, sending fire fighters scrambling in both directions. Traffic was stopped at Stanley and at Sunbeam.

Ada formulated her plan while speeding down-canyon to Clayton. There she set up barricades to west-bound traffic and asked the part-time and partly sober constable to man them, to warn away traffic, and to keep an eye out for Asakura's vehicle coming out. She requisitioned a tank of gas at the mining company office, then raced back up-canyon to Sunbeam with light flashing and siren blaring. The only traffic she passed coming the other way were a few Forest Service and National Guard rigs.

At Sunbeam Junction a half dozen cars were lined up in the west-bound lane, waiting to get through. Asakura's red GMC pickup truck was not among them, nor was Blevins' black-and-white. Ada parked in the tavern lot next to an army deuce-and-a-half and trotted up to the barricades. She was stopped by a National Guard captain waving around his pistol.

"Put your gun away, captain," she said as she approached.

"Who the Sam Hill are you?" There were a couple privates with rifles guarding the corners of the barricades, and a couple more hauling jugs of water up from the river.

She pinned on her badge. "I'm the sheriff who's telling you to put your gun away. You can't shoot a fire, for heaven's sakes. Why are these cars here?"

A horn honked, and two or three of the drivers leaned out the windows. It was mid-afternoon, and hot as hell in the canyon, and the smoke helped nothing. The captain looked like he might sell insurance in his day job, and like he wished to God he was back doing it. "The cars are being held until we have further information as to the situation. Who . . .?"

"What do you know so far?"

"About 11:45 we got recon that the fire had broken over the ridge in two places near Mormon Bend."

"Damn! Has it jumped the river?"

"No information on that, Ma'am."

The wind was gusting mostly down canyon, but the clouds showed winds aloft to be mostly to the south. "Do you have radio communication?" she asked.

"None down here in the canyon. We ramble a messenger back and forth to Custer where they have reception. As to the vehicles . . . Ma'am, I'm waiting for confirmation to release them."

"When was your last communication?"

"About an hour ago."

"Well, if there's fire in the canyon at Mormon Bend, there is no way they will get it mopped up and safe for through-traffic today. There's nothing of concern eastward, so send the cars back to Camas. Tell them they can catch 93 south or north from there."

The captain looked her over, not argumentatively but a bit perplexed. "It's all right Captain," she told him. "Colonel Branson and I are like Fred and Ginger as far as command structure. Do as I say, now."

ADA HELPED TO TURN THE CARS and get them headed east, then followed the convoy out as far as Robinson Bar. She stopped there and informed the residents the highway going west was cut, and that the highway in either direction would be dangerous with emergency traffic and equipment. The fire, though moving away from them now, could turn without warning. From Robinson Bar, she drove to Peach Creek, Torrey's Hole, and then Juniper Flat, always with the same warning.

A light breeze was blowing over Juniper Flat and the air was fair to breathe, although the smoke roiling up in the west made for a frightful red sky. She talked to half a dozen residents before working her way back into Asakura's farm near dusk. This time when she shut off her engine, she stuck handcuffs in her pocket and belted on her gun. She resisted the impulse to check the back of the house first, and instead walked straight up the steps and knocked on the door. The table and chairs she'd shared with Eddy a few days earlier were still out, although a different teapot and different cups made up the setting. There was no answer at the door. She did step around to the side, then, and checked the garage. The old GMC pickup was not there.

Ada was sitting at the table on the porch jotting notes in her book by the fading orange light when she heard and then saw Inga Nilsen approaching from the cottonwood tangle. She'd expected her and rose from the chair. The younger woman said nothing but walked up the steps and stood staring into the trees. She had been crying, but her eyes were dry, and she'd brushed and put up her hair. She wore a blouse made of fine silk.

"He's not here," Ada said. "He could be in trouble."

Inga nodded. "The state cop, Blevins, was here late yesterday with an armed trooper."

"Did they take him?"

"No. Eddy had gone earlier, before noon. It is *Obon*, a Japanese holiday. He didn't say where he was going, but there was talk around the flats yesterday about Harding, the old sheriff, being dead. It worried Eddy. He told me to stay here. He doesn't want me to get hurt." She crossed her arms as if taking a stand. "I would have gone with him," she said.

The neighbor lady across the field stood on her porch, arms folded and making no pretense of being busy. "She can go to hell," Inga said. "I don't care anymore. Eddy cares, but I don't."

"Were you with Eddy at the lake on the days in question?" Ada asked. "I'm afraid it's an official question, and it is awfully important."

"Yes, of course I was with him." Inga picked up a porcelain cup from the table and touched it to her forehead. It was an antique piece, delicate, and masterfully painted. Inga said, "You have someone to hold you, someone who cares. You wouldn't understand."

"Yes, I would. I do. I understand completely." She stared for a moment through the branches of the elms into the hazy yellow sunlight, then stepped forward and took Inga in her arms and held her for a minute. "We're all looking for the same thing," she whispered.

She sat the younger woman down at the table and found her a handkerchief. Then, because the emergency was behind her now, literally, and there was nothing more she needed to do in front of her, she sat down too. "How did you and Eddy come to know each other?" she asked.

Inga smiled even while wiping at her eyes. She said, "Well, at first I didn't really meet him at all—for a couple of years I just watched him from across the orchard. He was angry, I thought, or crazy. He worked like a madman, sunup to sundown with an axe or a shovel, seven days a week and twelve months a year. But he turned that old wreck of a farm into something right in front of my eyes. I mean, the house was falling down. He'd bought the place for nothing at a sheriff's auction, and the fields had all gone to brush and weeds. But it's something now, you can see for yourself.

"The neighbors didn't like him being here. Everyone said he was angry after the war, and they said it was because his side lost. You know how people are. But he was, I guess, loud and stubborn sometimes, too, and that's probably why he ended up in jail."

Inga seemed pleased to be talking about it, and Ada realized she'd probably not been able to say a word about Eddy Asakura to anyone before this. She asked, "Surely you talked across the fence now and then?"

"We did, I guess. We must have. But most of that time I just watched him from my place. And he watched me sometimes too; I saw him looking now and then. But then one morning, and this was in the fall because the leaves were all yellow and blowing around, I opened the door to a knock, and Eddy was right there on my front porch. His hands were clean and he was dressed nice, and he handed me a five-dollar bill." Inga laughed and covered her face for a moment before continuing. "It turns out, he had put up some beehives, and he'd been selling honey in town. He said it was mostly my orchard his bees were making their honey from, so he owed me a share of the profits.

"Well, that was just silly, wasn't it? But he brought a jar of honey with him, too, and I had just baked bread, so I brought out a plate and some milk, and we sat there in the blowing leaves talking for hours." She looked down for a moment and smiled. "And do you know what, Ada? I fell in love right there on the porch."

Ada smiled as much as she could for the young woman, but it hurt more than she would have expected to hear the story and see the glow on Inga's face. She envied everything Inga had, even if it was a furtive and dangerous love. And then her stomach began to ache because she knew she was going to have to arrest Inga's young man. She jumped up to go, and both women stared and were embarrassed to see the gun strapped to her hip. Inga said, "Eddy is a gentle man, but . . . I don't think the gun will help you to talk with him. I think he's very good at . . . not being taken."

"I won't wear the gun. I promise."

"I don't know where he was going; I would tell you if I did. But *Obon* is a time for homecomings, for visiting with ancestors. Please find him before Blevins does."

Update 7:40 p.m. – Trying to get home, if I can find my way.

THERE WAS NOTHING MORE SHE COULD do that night. If Eddy Asakura had gone through the canyon, she could not find him from this side. He was on his own. Blevins would have radioed, probably, if he had re-apprehended the suspect—unless he'd managed to kill Eddy in the process.

She drove home slowly through smoke so thick she could barely see the road under her headlights. All day it had been like this, and all day the same thoughts had unsettled her until she could hardly breathe. For the tenth time she wondered what the siren had meant and to what ranger duties it had called Ben. She hadn't heard from him all day, and she had no idea where he was when the fire exploded in the canyon—if he was safe. And then a pang cut through her like a knife because she hadn't heard from her husband either—in almost two weeks. It was all just a goddamned mess, and she didn't know how she was supposed to feel or how to make any of it work. She supposed Inga Nilsen felt much the same, but that didn't make it better.

She tried the AM radio and laughed when she found an Omaha station even down in the canyon—a lucky accident in the stratosphere. It was Nat King Cole again, and even though the music was staticky and faded in and out, she hung on the station until there was not a note left to hear.

A half-moon broke out of the smoke as she entered the Camas valley. It had been so long since things were clear that the moon, though pretty, seemed incongruous somehow: hopeful, but mis-timed, out of place.

The lights were on in all the businesses as she drew near to town. She dried her eyes and cruised slowly up Main Street. Across from the bus station teenaged girls sat with teenaged boys, eating and laughing at the drive-in. That, too, felt foreign to her. It was a scene she'd known a thousand times, but tonight it seemed distant and strange, and Camas could have been any town in the country for any belonging she felt.

The houses were lit in her neighborhood, as well, and moon-light washed the lawns and gardens. It was a tidy neighborhood of driveways and elms, and she knew she should be grateful she had a home, even if it wasn't perfect, even if it was . . . his home, not hers. The curtains of the houses were not yet drawn for the night, and she didn't mean to snoop, but from high in the sher-iff's truck through the windows of the homes a mother bathed a child; a shift worker—she knew his name—sat for a late meal; a family sat in front of the Jack Benny show. They were all her neighbors, but their lives were those of strangers, and it hurt like hell to think it might have been her life, too, if things had been different.

Ada turned off her headlights and let the pickup coast to a stop in front of her darkened house, then sat with her head down on the steering wheel for a minute longer, wondering if what she was giv-ing up was worth it; if anything she was doing was helping anyone. Her arms and shoulders ached, and her throat was raw from the smoke; the feeling of wanting to cry hadn't left her for a week, and . . . and her damned house was not dark!

She raised her head and glanced around. It should have been dark, but through the gap in the drapes she saw the kitchen light was on. She was certain she'd not left it that way, although she hadn't been home in two days.

She'd promised Inga she would not wear the gun, but her light was on, and it shouldn't have been. She eased the truck door closed. There were cars parked at the curb up and down the street, but damn her, she didn't know her own neighbors well enough to know which belonged or if any didn't.

There was no one in the kitchen when she peeked in from the back yard. She entered through the door as quietly as she could—with the gun and holster on her hip. She pushed the door closed without a sound, and at that moment heard or maybe felt a bump in the rear of the house. She drew the revolver and held her breath.

There may have been a soft footstep; possibly a door latch clicking. Gripping the pistol in her right hand, she decided not to flip off the kitchen light—it was too late for that. She wasn't sure, then, whether to draw back the hammer of the gun—if it would make a loud click, or maybe it would cause her to overreact and shoot too quickly. She decided to kneel back by the Frigidaire and keep her thumb on the hammer but not draw it back.

All of that she considered in the two seconds between the latch clicking and the bathroom door opening wide enough for a person to edge into the hallway. Even in the sliver of light from the bathroom door she could see Sybil Riis-Moreau's face was bruised, and her lip cut.

Update 9:30 p.m. – Found my way home after all.

"NO, I'M AFRAID THE LAW CAN'T DO A DAMNED THING about that. I'll do everything I can for you, Sybil, but the law's not helpful in that regard. You have to either leave him or fight back."

They sat in the kitchen where the light was best. Ada had cleaned Sybil's face, then found Munson's witch hazel in the cabinet and dabbed a little on the cuts and bruises.

"Is that what you did," Sybil asked. "You fought back with Montgomery?"

No, she had cajoled and placated and given in; she'd run and hid out for days, but . . . "No, honey, never. But it's not going to be the same anymore."

"Well, I can't fight Holly, and I'm afraid I'm not going to leave him, either."

"It never gets better, you know."

"Oh, I know."

They shared a can of Dinty Moore stew because that was nearly all Ada had in her cupboard. "I can't leave him, we both know that." Sybil said. The spoon hurt her lip and she ate slowly.

Ada said, "Well, he's flown away anyhow. His Cessna was seen leaving yesterday afternoon."

"I thought he might. The army in the front yard made him nervous."

Sybil had run from her house the previous morning and had slept the night on Ada's couch while Ada slept in Stanley. She would not be going back any time soon, with the highway cut, so they both settled in for a visit. They finished the small meal in near silence but for Sybil softly humming a tune. Ada rinsed the bowls in the sink, but then there was a clumsy moment.

"Come on," she said, trying hard to smile. She got into her pajamas and found another pair for Sybil, who'd run from her home with nothing but the house dress on her back and what was in her purse. Ada put a stack of records on the Magnavox and poured two glasses of brandy. She sat in the big stuffed chair and Sybil curled up on the couch as Doris Day began "Sentimental Journey." The song made them both laugh, and they lit a candle to soften the suddenly harsh moonlight through the windows.

Ada struggled for a minute with how to tell Sybil that Louis Boniface was dead. It was apparent she had known the man, but Ada wasn't really sure how things had sat between them. In the end it had to come out.

Sybil quieted at the news. After a while, she said, "I was young when we were together. He was ten years older than me in years and more than that in experience, and I didn't have a snowball's chance in hell against him back then. He was like a force of nature." She threw her head back and chuckled, then said quietly, "I hope he's at peace."

Ada said, "The timing of his death. I'm sorry but I have to bring it up. The timing is suspicious, with Holland flying out the very next day."

"But you said he died in the fire."

"We haven't been on the ground yet. We don't know if there are . . ."

"Bullet holes?"

"I suppose."

"You want it to be Holland."

"Honestly, Sybil, I don't want it to be anyone it isn't. In this case, I just hope it isn't someone I think it is."

"Okay then," Sybil said. "Let's start from the beginning. Holland loved that old bastard. And me and Frenchy? Hell, that was thirty years ago." She sighed and brought her feet up under her. "It's hard to believe it's been so long."

She had grown up in Hailey, a grocer's daughter and a home-coming queen. Hailey is where she'd met Louie: at the Wood River Roundup. He was All-Around Cowboy and she was all-around good looking. She smiled, then laughed. "But it's true," she said, "I was a looker back then, and built like a brick shithouse. God, what I wouldn't give for your waistline now, Ada. But anyway, Louie wasn't no pretty boy, but he sure knew how to get and hold a girl's attention.

"And Lordy, what a whirlwind! We spent that whole summer together—or most of it because he was riding the circuit. By the fall, though, it was evident he could fight as ardently as he made love, and I eventually shook him off and moved to New York. My father was happy enough to pay for it just to get me away from my cowboy. I didn't see Louie again for, oh God, twenty some years.

"He didn't marry the very next girl to come along, but damn near. She left him, too, eventually, and I guess he lost his daughter. He got to be a drunk, and I suppose he got to be mean when he was drunk. That was years later, of course, while I was in New York—which is where I met Holly."

Ada got up to change the record and to freshen their drinks. When she sat again, Sybil continued: "I know what you think, but Holland Riis-Moreau would not be jealous over a beau from thirty years back. But he did suspect I'd wanted to buy the Obsidian because Louie was here. And maybe he was partly right. But it wasn't the man anymore, and Holland understood that. It was the times, you know? Back when I was young and poor, and who gave a damn because I was pretty and I could dance till sunrise then kiss and love till noon. Maybe I came back looking for the girl I used to be."

"Did Holland buy his moonshine?"

"Sure, he did. But there was never enough for a big operation, and Louie couldn't stay sober enough anymore to ramp up. So, it was more of a hobby for Holland. And he got a kick out of the 'old coonass,' he called him. He liked to go up there and play moonshiner and mountain man. Louie was Holland's only real friend in Idaho."

CHAPTER SEVENTEEN

Wednesday, October 3, 7:35 a.m.
Two weeks since Neagles found dead in Valley Creek.
Fires still burning, though the winds may have turned.

SHE WOKE COLD AND FOUND SYBIL gone from the couch, and she panicked for a moment thinking the woman had changed her mind and tried to get back home. But she heard and then found her in the backyard bringing in an armload of firewood. Sybil had already got the coffee pot perking on the electric plate.

"I should have had such a good roommate in college," Ada said.

"You went to college?"

"Mm-hmm. Three years."

Ada made poached eggs and toast, then apologized because Sybil had to dunk her toast in the coffee so it didn't scratch her cut lip.

When she'd washed and dressed in a clean uniform, she told her guest, "I'll be home earlier this time, and you should count on sleeping here again due to the highway closure. The TV gets channel seven if you fiddle with the antenna, and there are some garden vegetables in the Frigidaire."

Sybil smiled in spite of her cut lip. "I'll make a soup for dinner. I mean, if you like soup."

"I love soup."

SHE INTERCEPTED ETHEL GRIMES on the marble steps of the courthouse at 7:30, as the sun was peeking over the Pahsimeroi hills. "Good morning, Ethel," she sing-songed.

"Morning, Fancy Badge. Good lord, Ada, do you ever sleep?"

"Oh God, how bad is it?" She leaned to catch her reflection in the window glass. "I've missed the Avon Lady for six weeks straight. I have nothing to put on my face."

"You looked pretty good in the Idaho Falls paper yesterday—shaking hands with the governor, no less."

Ada pushed her Stetson back and gave Ethel a broad grin. "Yeah. As I explained in great detail to the Camas Currier the other day . . ."

Ethel let a grocery truck roar by on Main Street. "They finally gave you an interview?"

"I gave *them* an interview; an exclusive. I said, 'I'm confident the governor is onboard with my plan.'"

Ethel turned the key and shouldered the massive oak door. "You actually said, 'my plan'?"

"Uh-huh. 'My plan to aid and temporarily house the families displaced by these hellish fires.'" Ada crossed her booted ankles and pretended a curtsy.

Ethel's laugh carried right down Main Street. "Won't that frost Jeff Banning," she said. "That rusty old tangle of barbwire!"

Early morning at the courthouse was usually the most pleasant part of the day. Some days it was the only pleasant part. The hallways were cool and dark, and but for her and Ethel's footsteps on the marble, wonderfully quiet. She could hear a couple maintenance guys clanking away in the basement, but the secretaries wouldn't be in for another half an hour. The arrival of court clerks, waterworks guys, and deputy regulators, and the attendant slamming of doors and rattling of windows, would start a half hour after that. The supervisors, judges, and citizen supplicants would show up around nine o'clock.

Ethel unlocked her office door, dropped a pile of mail on her desk, and took a watering can around to the begonias and geraniums that grew everywhere there was not a stack of papers. Ada said, "Ethel, could you help me? I need to start the paperwork for an arrest warrant. I think Judge Stavig is in today."

"Edwin Asakura?"

"I'm afraid so."

"I can do that." She interrupted her watering to hand Ada a manila envelope that had been delivered to the outside box. "It looks like you have a special delivery from Pocatello," she said.

"It's from the State Morgue. I've been expecting it." Ada set the envelope down and took the coffee pot to the janitor's closet to fill with water. She made coffee while Ethel sorted the remaining mail. While the pot perked Ada opened the envelope and read the lab report on Lance Harding. She read it three times and heard nothing else Ethel said for a good minute afterward.

It was impossible! The lab had found no *anisatin* in Harding's blood. Blood-alcohol levels were normal, as well. There was elevated formic acid in the serum, but no sign of *anisatin*. None!

"I have a problem," Ada said, leaning on the counter and dropping her head to her fists.

"Of course you have."

"Eddy Asakura hated Lance Harding. He hated Clifford Neagle too, and they're both dead." She stuck her hands in her pockets and raised her head. "The problem is, I now have no physical evidence whatever to tie Asakura to either of the deaths."

"Stop the paperwork?"

"For now. I may need the warrant yet; I don't know."

She hopped up and sat on the clerk and recorder's counter, as confused as she'd been since the Yankee Fork case. Yes, Harding could have been a straight-up accident, and Boniface might have been too. But the circumstances—the heedlessness and disorientation—were too similar to the Neagles, and the Neagles certainly did not die by accident. She supposed someone could be framing someone else—it was still there to be considered. But although the case was confusing, she did not think it needed the complication of an Agatha Christie plot.

"Give me a second," she said. She scooted down and hurried to her own office for the laboratory reports on Dolf, Clifford, Irma, and Mooch Neagle. Returning almost at a run, she laid the earlier reports out on the clerk's counter next to the new report on Harding. They were not all that similar, but she hadn't expected them to be in most regards. There had been no buildup yet of alcohol in Harding's blood as there had been in the sun-fermented family members. And of course, severe blunt force trauma as the cause of Harding's death made for a considerably different report than suffocation and immolation.

In fact, there was no similarity in the reports at all, except—and maybe this was worth looking at—except for elevated formic acid in the blood serum of all the deceased. Dennis Mink had noticed the formic acid in the Neagles' blood workups and had found it odd. He'd wondered if it was related somehow to the carbon monoxide buildup. But there would have been no carbon monoxide in Harding's case.

Now Ada was more certain than ever all of the deaths had to be connected—and accidents miles and days apart are not connected. It had to be homicide, and someone had to be consumed with loathing to bring about that much death.

She pushed the reports aside and hopped up to sit on the counter, again counting on her fingers. Asakura had reason to hate both Harding and Clifford Neagle. But Asakura had no interaction whatever with Boniface, and besides, the physical evidence against him had just evaporated. Riis-Moreau may have resented Dolf Neagle but had no run-in with Harding, and he apparently loved "the old coonass," Boniface. It was Boniface who hated both Harding and Dolf—but who hated Boniface enough to kill him, other than a couple of dead men?

She twisted back Ethel's way. "I asked before, but who had it in for Louis Boniface?"

"Everyone loved Frenchy."

Yes, everyone loved Frenchy now, except maybe Frenchy himself. She scoffed, but in fact she'd never seen such—the hair rose on the back of her neck—she'd never seen such self-loathing as Boniface had shown.

"Damn me, Ethel!" she said.

"Start the paperwork again?"

"No!" She slid from the countertop and grabbed up her papers. Again, she'd not seen the signs in front of her face. Frenchy Boniface was a desperate man, tormented by something in his past. And unstable as he was, it would have taken very little to push him over the edge to homicide. Hell, the man was on death's door himself!

She needed to look closer into what Boniface was up to and with whom. Mostly, she needed to get into the law enforcement records kept in her own office. But dashing out Ethel's door, she nearly bumped into her election opponent, Jeff Banning. "Excuse me, Jeff," she said. "I'm in a big . . . I'm in a . . . Excuse me!"

Banning was a leather-vested rancher two decades her senior and half again her weight. He didn't budge but glared at her and said with an unnecessarily loud voice, "A big hurry to get where? Asakura was identified yesterday morning going through the checkpoint at Sunbeam. You can't get through that way anymore."

"Not now, Jeff. There are important things I have to look into."

"Five deaths, all attributable to your Asian friend, and you have other things to look into?" He swept his gaze down the hallway, noting an audience leaning from doorways and pausing on stairs. "What is more important than protecting folks from a cold-blooded killer?"

She feinted to his left then swung around to dodge by his right. "All I can tell you is your friend on the Board is behind in his information," she said, backtracking down the hall. "Although I'm sure he'll fill you in as soon as he knows something."

Back in her drab-green office, she got another pot of coffee started on the hot plate, then commenced to turn the file cabinets inside out. She was elbow deep in ten years of murders and misdemeanors, barfights, and dog bites when she finally came across the run-in Boniface had with Sheriff Lance Harding.

Harding had confronted Boniface at the Rod and Gun Club in Stanley, where the man had been drinking and fighting most of the morning and waving a gun around. He'd even taken potshots at a young Dolf Neagle. Harding disarmed him easily enough, and the other patrons had returned to their beers at the bar while Harding sat down to have a smoke and talk it over with the Frenchman. But Boniface wasn't ready to let bygones go. His hackles were up. Harding must have said something, and Boniface knocked the sheriff backward right out of his chair. The fight didn't last long once Harding got back to his feet. He kicked and beat Frenchy so severely the other patrons had to pull him off. He cuffed him, kicked him some more, and threw his ass in the slammer to await trial.

Okay, she already knew Boniface had reason to hate Harding. But what was the fight about? Ten minutes later in another folder labeled "B" for Boniface, she found that Louis had earlier filed a missing persons report for his daughter. Clipped to that report Harding had noted that "the little whore probably left town with the latest of her drunken cowboys." If he'd used the word "whore" at the bar as well, it may well have precipitated the fight.

She fished from the evidence drawer the box of personal items found on the Neagles. Leaving the few items from Mooch, Clifford, and Irma in their envelopes, she spilled Dolf's things onto the desk. The wallet held nothing new of interest. The money clip was, for now, a red herring. The ring and the box of water-logged Sen-Sen she also set aside. It was the damned belt and buckle—that was the connection. She flipped over the buckle: *L. Boniface 1946.*

She was back in Ethel's office in short order with the belt and buckle in hand. She said, "There was a fight between Boniface and Dolf Neagle. The result of Neagle's philandering, I think Kellen Munson told me?"

"That was five years ago, but . . . Yes, I believe Frenchy accused Dolf of ill-treating his daughter."

"Exactly. Where can I find that daughter?"

"Louise? Why, I've not heard heads or tails of her in years."

It took a second, but, "Louise?—you're joking! Her name is Louise?" Ada leaned heavily on the counter for a minute, then raised her head and said, "Ethel, could you get me a long-distance phone number?"

Update 9:55 a.m. – Back in office, back on the phone.
Running in circles again.

SHE WAS NOT RUNNING IN CIRCLES so much as running up and down the hall with clerks and secretaries and supervisors craning out their office doors to see what the slamming and boot-clomping was about. At her desk, controlling her breathing, she let the clock tick around to 10:00 a.m., which she guessed was a reasonable hour for an off-season rodeo association front office to be open but not yet gone to lunch. By 10:05 the operator had connected her with the secretary of the association.

The secretary couldn't help Ada very much at all, but she put on, after a ten-minute long-distance wait, a Mr. Prescott. Prescott was the man in charge of awards and certifications for the Idaho Stampede. Though he must have been eighty years old, he turned out to be an encyclopedia.

"I've heard of you Sheriff Reed," he said by way of hello, "Hell, I thought I'd never see the day. But how can I help?"

Ada blinked her eyes and sat up. "Yes. I have a trophy buckle, Mr. Prescott . . ."

"Just Prescott."

". . . apparently issued by the Idaho Stampede, and I'd like you please to verify it." She turned the buckle in her fingers as she described it in detail.

His voice was rocky as a bad road, but he spoke slowly and

thoughtfully. You're sure it's from '46, the numbers aren't rubbed away . . . ?"

"The buckle looks in pretty good shape: *L. Boniface, 1946.*"

Old Prescott was sure Frenchy—Louis—never competed after '42. "Broke his back," the man said. But then he whistled long and low and told Ada she had herself an interesting artifact there in her hand. "The buckle was clearly not awarded to Louis. And I'll be darned, but that buckle was awarded to his daughter, Louise Boniface, in 1946."

"But it's a horseman throwing a rope, and a calf . . ."

"Women's Breakaway Roping. Yessir, Louise won it all that year. She was a chip off the old block."

Ada half listened as she examined the belt and buckle more closely. The leather was not shiny with wear; it was not the Neagle boy's everyday belt. But neither was it brand new. The leather was tooled with his name on the back, and the strap had been riveted around the bar of the buckle for some time. The metal itself was slightly worn where it had been clasped and unclasped. The buckle was not new on the belt; he had not recently received the thing.

". . . It's a shame what happened to her," Prescott was saying.

A chill gripped Ada from head to tailbone. "What do you mean? What happened?" she managed.

"Well, hell. I mean . . . that would have been the last time Louise competed. A shame, too, because she was popular on the circuit. An easy gal to talk to—and to look at."

There was silence on the line and for a moment Ada thought she'd lost the connection. But Prescott said, "I guess she passed away in Denver not long after that—January of '47, I believe. Story is . . ." He cleared his throat and there was another long pause. "Naw, hell, I don't know any story. I don't know anything more about that."

"I'm conducting a murder investigation, Mr. Prescott."

"I'm sorry, sheriff, but I got no more gossip or rumors to share in that regard."

Prescott wouldn't budge for her, but it took Ada a short ten minutes to reach the sheriff's office in Denver. The Denver County switchboard was then able to connect her with the City of Denver Police Department, District 2. The officer on duty there didn't recall the case, but while Ada again held the line, he found a detective who did.

"Almost five years ago, but yes, I remember some of it," the detective told her. "Louise Boniface, nineteen years of age, Idaho address. She died as a result of an illegal medical procedure, if you understand my meaning. We get young girls coming to the city now and then for that purpose."

Ada held the phone to her forehead and breathed deeply. She didn't want to ask because she knew the answer and didn't want to hear it. But she braced her elbows on the table and said, "For what medical procedure, specifically?"

"Well, Ma'am, and I wouldn't repeat it straight out to a lady if you weren't a law officer yourself, but the fact of it is, it was one of those backroom places a woman seeks out sometimes with regard to an unwanted pregnancy."

"I see."

And that was it. It was so matter-of-factly laid out; the whole thing was so goddamned matter of fact she could scream. "What, um . . ." It took her a moment to draw in a full breath. "What was done with Louise's body?"

"I believe her father came down from Idaho some weeks later to collect her remains."

Ada sat a good ten minutes after thanking the officer and hanging up the phone, unable even to get up and pour a coffee. If Louise had died in Denver in early January, as the officer said, it would have been while Boniface was locked up in Harding's jail. Any chance Frenchy might have had to save his daughter, Harding had denied him. And if he thought Dolf Neagle was responsible and then just discarded Louise . . . *Oh, goddamn them all!*

She stayed at her desk and cried for Louise, whom she'd never known. And then she cried for Frenchy Boniface because she knew how her own father would have died a hundred deaths over something like that. She cried for the Neagles, the whole family—even Dolf; and then for Harding, bully that he was.

Then she sat ten minutes longer trying to put away her feelings and be matter-of-fact like all the other goddamn cops. It all made sense from a human standpoint, but of course, not from a detective standpoint. That is, there was motive and then some for Boniface to kill Dolf Neagle and Lance Harding. He had to loathe them. But the means to commit the murders was doubtful, and opportunity seemingly impossible.

Ada jumped up and, touching at her eyes, returned to Ethel's office. "It was hers!" she said as she stepped through the door. "It was Louise Boniface's buckle the whole time! And God, wait till you hear this . . ."

Ethel hung up the phone and turned with a perplexed and worried look. "Sheriff," she managed, "there's been another death."

ACTING SHERIFF ADA REED GATHERED HER THINGS into her rucksack, stuffing in her jacket, gun, canteen, and a Forest Service road map. What else? What would she need? She had no idea where she would end up on this outing, or when, so she threw a can of peaches in, too. The truck was fueled and serviced, and the motor pool boys had left it out front.

But Jeff Banning stopped her again with a booming rant everyone in the hallways and half the people behind office doors could hear, "Sergeant Blevins and the State Police are going to take Asakura dead or alive. A Yellowpine County family murdered, and a Yellowpine County officer murdered, and it's a damned shame we have to rely on the state to do the job. I guess our TV-star sheriff might break a nail or something."

She had no time for this! She exhaled hard, turning just her head to look the guy from top to toe. She'd known him her whole life—not him in particular, but him in a general broad-brimmed, small-hatband sense. Him in the sense of a backslapping old boy with a wide stance and a narrow mind. She knew him inside and out. "Jeff," she said in a voice almost as loud as his, "you're a tack-hammer man in a double-jack county."

She brushed him aside and took the courthouse steps two at a time. The light on her truck was flashing and the siren wailing as she pulled onto Main Street.

Update 1:00 p.m. – Lester Booley's residence, Mosquito Flats

A TANGLE OF DIRT TRACKS OFF THE Mill Creek Summit road had her skidding in circles again, and forty minutes under a flashing light and a blaring siren put her nerves on edge, so she was nearly at wits end when she finally found Mosquito Flats and the Booley farm. She took just enough time for a couple of deep breaths before stepping out into the hot afternoon sun.

It was a hard-scrabble place with a log house that had been added-on to several times, a couple lean-to goat sheds, and half a dozen automobiles in various states of broken-down. A sturdy-looking two-story barn dominated the farmstead. It was to the barn that Mrs. Booley led her, to see the son who had managed to kill himself.

They walked briskly, scattering chickens and goats, the woman clasping her elbows and saying nothing. Lester's mother might have been on the near side of fifty, but there was a used-up air about her. She stood straight, but thin and dry, in a threadbare housedress. She'd been crying but was beyond that by the time Ada got to her, and was now more angry, wide-eyed, and belligerent. "What the hell was he thinking?" she cried at last as they entered the darkened barn, "That he could fly?"

Lester, the young man she'd confronted in the park ten days earlier lay dead on the floor of the barn. Though smart-alecky and disrespectful, the poor kid was barely twenty-three years old, and it made Ada sick that he could be so young and so dead. His skin was flushed, and there was bloody vomit on his clothes. "Did he think he could effin' fly?" Mrs. Booley wailed, drawing out the shrill challenge. It appeared the boy had fallen—or jumped—from the loft and broken his neck.

"What had he been acting like before?" Ada asked.

"Like a damned fool, that's what!"

"Had he been acting . . . crazy?"

"Lord, yes! He was wailing' and swearing all night, stumbling around and smashing things. He got himself drunk is what I think. Drunker'n a circus monkey!"

In the loft, Ada found an unmade cot and a table with a wash basin, a pack of cigarettes, and a set of keys. A change of clothes hung on hooks. "Did he live up here?" she called down.

"In the summer times. He always moved down to the house soon as the weather turned."

She found bloody vomit on the floor of the loft, and a quart jar, mostly empty, of a clear liquid next to the bed. She smelled the jar and jerked her head back. It was strong alcohol. "Did your son—did Lester ever have any run-ins with a man named Frenchy? Louis Boniface?"

"Not run-ins. They got along fine."

"Did he ever have any dealings with a Holland Riis-Moreau?"

"The rich man? No, he didn't ever say so."

Ada found the lid to the jar, screwed it on, and climbed back down the ladder. "This is important, Mrs. Booley. What was your son's association with Frenchy Boniface?"

The belligerent denial had almost played itself out in the woman, and a quiet desolation was beginning to take hold. "He . . . He ran errands for Frenchy." She spoke quietly, even plaintively. "He delivered things, and Boniface paid him to do it."

"Delivered what things?"

Lester's mother didn't answer, but Ada knew. What else was Boniface delivering but his so-called peace offerings. "*To the folks with whom I have quarreled,"* he had told her, *"Those who may have gotten a short measure of truth and justice."* The trophy buckle was never his gift to Neagle, how could it have been? Louis would never have sent such a keepsake to the low-life who betrayed his daughter.

Ada breathed in deeply and asked, "Did Lester ever deliver to the Neagle family, over in Valley Creek?"

The woman dropped heavily onto a hay bale and rested her head in her hands. "I expect so. He was friends with Dolf Neagle. He was upset when he heard Dolf had passed." She grasped her elbows and stared off into the scrub woods. "He delivered a number of gifts in the last couple weeks. Big gifts. Whole cases of Frenchy's product."

"This product?" Ada held up the Mason jar.

The woman shrugged. "So, maybe Lester measured out a little from each—no more than his share. So what if he did?"

A station wagon pulled up beside Ada's truck. It was from the mortuary, and Doctor Mink rode in the passenger seat. Mrs. Booley began to breathe heavily. "I could have done more for the boy," she moaned. "I could have looked out."

Ada turned back and shook the woman by the shoulders. "Who else did Lester deliver to?" she nearly shouted.

The woman looked up, confused by the sudden harshness.

"Who else?" Ada insisted.

"I guess, Harding, the old sheriff. And I believe he said the mayor in town: Applegate."

Uncle Ephraim!—Damn it, he'd prosecuted Boniface back then!

Update 1:55 p.m. – Mill Creek Pass to
Lower Custer and Maggie Li's kitchen

ADA BOUNCED AND SWERVED DOWN Mill Creek Pass to the Yankee Fork Road. She raced west toward Custer although it killed her not to be racing east toward Camas and her Uncle Ephraim. But Ephraim would not drink a gift of moonshine—probably not anyway, and certainly not to a drunken state. God, she hoped not! She had to warn him, but she had to get to Eddy Asakura, too, before the State Patrol got to him.

She tried to raise Ethel on the two-way radio, but the damned thing was still out; Frenchy's bullet had gone right through it, and she'd got the rear window fixed but not yet the radio. She hurried down the winding road with one foot pumping the gas and the other riding the brake, trying to find a speed that would save a couple of lives without breaking a tire on the rocks.

She made it to Custer, siren whooping and lights flashing, on four good tires and a cloud of dust. She hit the brakes and skidded to a stop in front of the jailhouse. "Get in!" she yelled to Munson, who had stepped out to see what the clamor was about.

"Ada? I'll just get my . . ."

"Never mind, don't get in!" she shouted through the open window. "Get on your radio, or your telephone, or whatever you have, Kel, and call the courthouse in Camas. Have someone track down Mayor Applegate. It's life and death. Track him down and warn him not to drink anything he might have received as a gift."

"What the . . .?"

"Just do it, Kel, find Ephraim!" She pulled away, sending gravel flying, and sped out of town, westward to the ruins of Chinatown. Margaret Li had been a geochemist in her earlier life, and she was the only person Ada knew who might answer her questions now, with no time to lose. Weaving her truck between debris piles and trenches, Ada came to another skidding stop in front of the woman's green clapboard cottage. She flipped off the siren, grabbed the quart jar on the seat, and quick-stepped over the plank bridge.

ADA TOOK A STEP BACK. "AND what is that?" she asked.

"It is sodium hydroxide. Some call it lye or caustic soda; I prefer the chemical name." Margaret Li swirled the vial to dissolve the powder. "And then a few drops of iodine . . ." She carefully squeezed a dropper of deep yellow fluid into the vial and swirled it again. "And there you have it."

"There we have what?" Ada leaned in a little but saw only a slight yellow tint in the test vial; no other change.

"Nothing, as it turns out." Li set the vial in the rack and screwed the top back onto the iodine bottle. "Nothing, and that is not good."

"I sometimes think you try to be mysterious, Maggie, and I haven't time . . ."

"Ethanol—drinking alcohol—will go cloudy when titrated in this way. The less-desirable methanol will remain clear, just as you see."

"So, it's . . ."

"Methanol."

"Wood alcohol? But that's . . ."

"Poisonous. It is the first vapor to come off in a distillation, but it is easy to control if the moonshining fool knows what he is doing."

"Boniface was a pro."

"Hmm." The old woman eased herself onto a kitchen chair. "In any case methanol will kill you if you ingest enough of it. Most times, the unlucky victim will pass out before that. Just a moderate amount, however, will cause your insides to bleed, and of course you will go blind."

"Blind!" Ada said.

"Not while you're drinking. But after a few hours, as the methanol is metabolized to formic acid, the damage is done. You lose your sight, and the loss is irreversible."

Blind! They were not mad or hallucinating; they were blind—Lance Harding and the Booley kid as much as the Neagles. Ada brought her truck to a stop in front of the jailhouse once again and leapt up onto the boardwalk. "Kellen . . . Chief, did you get hold of the mayor?" she called through the door. "Was Ephraim at the courthouse?"

Munson was hanging up the telephone. "He wasn't there, but Ethel Grimes thought maybe . . ."

"You have to go, Kel. Get in your truck and track him down any way you can. It's methanol—wood alcohol. Frenchy Boniface was sending out gifts of tainted liquor to all his old enemies."

Munson thought a moment and whistled. He grabbed his hat and hurried to the door. "Where are you headed, Ada?" he yelled.

She was already at her truck. "Through the canyon, if I can." She tossed her hat in the cab and climbed in. "If it's passable. I have to find Eddy Asakura."

CHAPTER EIGHTEEN

Wednesday October 3rd—addendum
3:00 p.m.
Into Valley Creek, if I can get there.

ROCKS BANGED HER UNDERCARRIAGE and crows scattered from the road in front of her as she raced down the Yankee Fork valley toward Sunbeam. She should have seen it, and she cussed herself for not. Boniface, in his despair, had to be drinking his own poison liquor, even knowing what it would do. He'd taunted her: "It's a good batch, won't you try some?" He'd tilted his head, watched her from the corners of his eyes. "And Dolf suffocated slowly?" he'd wanted to know. "Good! And he was wearing the buckle? Oh, that's fine!"

The rabbit's foot jerked and slapped side to side till it broke its string and fell to the floorboard. She should have seen it, damn her, and but for her own biases she might have. She'd been prejudiced by Asakura's differences, too ready to doubt what she didn't understand. She'd been prejudiced by what she saw in Riis-Moreau too, ready in his case to hang him for what she did understand all too well.

She met a Guard vehicle coming the other way around a tight curve in the lower canyon and had to brake and swerve nearly off the roadway. She turned her red light and siren on, then, and slowed a little through the turns. Flat tire be damned, she had to be careful now not to put the truck in the drink.

The Neagles hadn't had a chance; it was so easy now to see it. All four of them were deep in their gift of liquor the night before and had awakened sick and stone blind. They'd heard the fire coming; had smelled it, had felt the winds rush as the firestorm sucked in air all around. They'd felt the heat but had no way to flee. Mooch had thought of his hounds and rushed to save them, but he could not find the key to the kennel. He'd gotten hold of a prybar and let them out, almost too late, but then had fallen, unable to help himself. Dolf, car keys in pocket, also knew there was no way to run. He'd thought of the well at the last minute, had found it easily enough, and had taken refuge down inside. But the smoke found him even there. Irma had laid herself down in her bed, and the old man, Clifford, resigned himself to his end as well. He'd felt his way to his rocker on the porch and waited for the flames.

Her wheels drifted around the last turn, and she saw the barricades were still up at Sunbeam. No traffic waited, but the National Guard captain and his men stood at the ready. Her rapid approach caused two of the guardsmen to wave their arms and rifles. She skidded to a halt, flipped off the siren but left the red light flashing. Leaning out the window, she demanded, "What's the condition of the road, Captain?"

He touched the bill of his cap. "Ma'am. I've received no orders to let anyone pass."

"Do you remember me, Captain?"

He put his foot up on the running board. "Sheriff uhm . . . Ginger." He nodded.

"Close enough. What's the condition of the road through to Stanley?"

"Well, I guess with the change in wind they were able to put down the fire along the corridor, and they're mopping up now."

"Good. Open up. This is an emergency."

"I can't let you through ma'am. Direct orders."

She was preparing a good cussing out when the roar of a diesel engine made the captain back off a step. They both turned to see an army deuce-and-a-half round the corner from the hot side and ease up to the barricade. Two privates pulled the barricade back for the truck to pass, but Ada did not yet back out of the way. She got out of her pickup and climbed onto the running board of the guard truck to talk directly with the driver.

He'd come through from Stanley that afternoon. "The town's fine," the corporal told her. "Flames never got two miles from the structures."

"And the highway?"

"Well, it's hot going, but they've knocked the flames down and cleared the debris. I got through okay. There's still an axe and shovel crew in there working it."

Ada climbed back in her pickup and backed enough to let the heavy truck pull through. But as it passed, she jammed it in gear and swung around the back side of the truck, driving through before the barricade was back in place. She hit the siren and sped around the bend with the guardsmen shouting and waving in her rearview mirror.

The road was untouched and free of traffic as far as the mouth of Basin Creek, and she was able to gain some time, speeding through some stretches at up to fifty miles per hour. Beyond Basin Creek, though, the presence of panicked wildlife and wind-fallen trees caused her to slow. A few miles past the junction she found herself in a hellscape, with standing trees afire on the hill to her right. Her face felt the heat of the flames from a hundred yards. Embers glowed, and ash blew up in swirls.

Yellow-shirted crews were mopping up at Mormon Bend, where the oiled gravel road base had caught fire and was still smoking. Crews were swinging axes and shovels on both sides of the road. The boys were blackened from head to foot, their sooty faces streaked with sweat. But they waved her through with smiles and even managed a catcall here and there. She waved and continued on, but half a mile beyond the bend there were carcasses of deer floating in the river. A bear and her cub clung to an island in the stream. The baby was singed and bawling, and the mother pacing angrily.

Near Stanley she met traffic coming the other way—they were more crews heading into the fire zone. She was waved out through the barricade without question.

The town itself was given over completely to yellow-shirted fire fighters and the fatigue-clad guardsmen. She wanted badly to stop and ask about Ben McGann but didn't dare spend the precious minutes it would take. He'd promised he would be careful, that he wouldn't take chances, and he'd made her promise too; they'd sworn to each other. Still, she wished she could see he was okay.

She hurried on, but then, damn it all, at the intersection of the highways she was waved over by State Patrol Sergeant Ken Blevins. He looked rough, like he'd slept in his uniform and hadn't shaved. He spoke just as roughly. "I didn't expect you back on this side, Madam Sheriff. What brings you around?"

She stepped out of the cab and tried to talk with him. "We had it all wrong, Ken, it was never Asakura, it was . . ."

"I'm through with your damned theories and postulations. Did he circle back home? Did you get him?"

Blevins hadn't caught Eddy either; Ada had to bite her lip to not show her relief.

He stared her down. "Where is he then?"

"Frenchy Boniface . . ." she began, but he spun away from her with his hands on his hips. It was no use, he was not going to listen and he was not going to work with her. "Asakura's left the area for a while," she told him. "It's *Obon*, a Japanese holiday." She leaned on the fender of her truck and crossed her arms.

"He's on goddamned holiday?"

"*Obon* is supposed to be a time for homecomings and ancestors."

Blevins' eyes narrowed. "Homecoming and ancestors? Hell, he's gone back to Minidoka!"

She nodded. "Possible." And though in a terrible hurry, she crossed one boot over the other and stayed leaning on the fender of the pickup. She said, "There's nothing I can do. That puts him out of my jurisdiction."

"It doesn't put him out of mine!" Blevins hopped into his cruiser and flipped on the flashing red light. And that was exactly what Ada needed him to do: to chase off to southern Idaho and leave her the hell alone to bring in Eddy Asakura her way.

But she couldn't do it. It would be unprofessional, and as much as Blevins was a ham-fisted pain in the neck most of the time, he was a cop, and an honest one, and she owed him more respect than that.

She marched over, leaned with her hands on his open window, and said, "Shut your damned trap for a minute, Ken, and listen!"

Once he'd shut up and loosened his white-knuckle grip on the steering wheel, it took her just two minutes to explain. When she was done, he whistled low and long and asked her if she thought it was still worth him checking down around Minidoka.

"It's worth a look," she said. "I have to make it in to Valley Creek Lake. I have reason to believe he might be holed up there."

Blevins scanned the sky over her shoulder. "That's not far out of the fire's path, Ada," he said. "You be careful, you hear?"

Update 5:15 p.m. – To Valley Creek Lake,
hoping to find Mr. Asakura

WHEEL TRACKS MARKING THE VALLEY CREEK road told of a panicky exodus the night before, when the wind had changed. However, by the time Ada worked her way in, only two trucks passed her coming out, both loaded up with tools and bedding and barnyard animals. They were the stragglers among the lucky families who had skirted the previous fire but now saw themselves directly in the crosshairs of this new one.

She'd almost expected to see green shoots on the hills since the victim recovery nearly two weeks earlier. Of course, there had not been a drop of rain, so the canyon remained as black and gray as before. Nothing had changed, either, in the sense of godlessness pervading the place. The smoke grew heavier as she drove in, and there was no doubt as she continued northward into the old burn that she was downwind of another major fire to her right.

The vehicle tracks thinned the farther in she drove until there were none at all, and from there on she knew she was on her own. There was no sign Eddy Asakura had passed through, either. However, new ash covered the road—deposited from the surrounding hills by the swirling breezes. If he'd come two days before, his tracks would have been buried. She kept driving in spite of a growing sense of dread, because it was her fault Asakura had gone into hiding. She'd brought her suspicions back to him— the star anise in the tea. He was no fool, and when word reached him about Harding, he'd fled. He would not have gotten the warning of a change in wind and would not know to evacuate.

The truck bounced along, the tires eerily quiet over the ash. The sun hung in the sky in the west so that the day stayed bright but for the haze. The daylight, though, was misleading, and possibly because of it she didn't pay attention to the towering wall of brown smoke growing in the east. But when the road bent hard in that direction, she could no longer miss the columns of smoke and the mushroomed ceiling spreading out above her. She kept driving, now more urgently, bouncing and jarring past the turnoff to the Neagle's homestead—continuing eastward in the direction of Valley Creek Lakes. The wind grew and whipped around, dropping ash like a snowstorm.

She passed from the older burn back into unburned forest, where the road ended a half mile into the woods. There, at last, she found Eddy's old GMC pickup hidden back in the brush and covered with a heavy dusting of ash.

Update 5:45 p.m. – Afoot

THE COLUMNS OF SMOKE HAD GROWN MILES HIGH, but they were staying south, keeping to the far side of Basin Butte. If the wind direction stayed as the meteorologists predicted, the fire should stay on that side of the butte or come over the top at worst. It should stay well south of upper Valley Creek.

Nevertheless, she hurried. She rifled the rucksack, keeping with her the canteen of water and the jacket, but stowing the gun and holster under her seat, where she also found the rabbit's foot. She tossed it into the pack along with her notebook, the flashlight, and the can of peaches, and slung the pack over her shoulder.

Bolts of lightning lit up the roiling mountains of smoke four miles to the south. It was 5:45 P.M. The upper lake lay two miles above her, and she had maybe two hours of daylight. She started up the trail straight away, knowing she would have to keep a good pace.

But the trail faded quickly to a game track overgrown with brush and crisscrossed with deadfall. Within a mile she found she was without a trail at all and having to stay nearly in the creek bed to find her way. The smoke, too, was increasing and it grated at her throat and made the going more difficult. But there was just another mile to go. It was 6:30 P.M.

By 6:45 the climb had steepened, and smoke was blowing in heavily, causing her to cough and stumble in the murky light. It was no use pretending otherwise; the wind had come around and was blowing out of the southeast—toward her now. The hazy air was suffocating, and she wiped sweat and grit with her bandana. She wanted badly to know what was happening to the south of her, but the brush was too thick. There was no doubt, though, nothing good would be coming behind the smoke. She wet the bandana in the stream, tied it over her nose and mouth, and continued on. The lower lake couldn't be more than a quarter mile upstream, and there she could take refuge.

She nearly cried when she broke out of the brush into the clearing of the lower lake. There was no water! She found just a broad marshy flat where the shallow lake should have been. The hot summer had dried up the lake, and she would find no protection there at all. Standing in the clearing dumbstruck, her eyes and lungs burning, she was now finally able to see the fire storm to the south—and for the first time the red flames at the base of the smoke. It was no more than a mile and a half away, and it was coming right at her. The setting sun was a faint red disc at her back. Her watch said seven o'clock.

She sprinted around the muddy marsh, burning and abrading her throat in the effort, then spent a precious ten minutes finding the right inlet stream, the one that would take her to the upper lake. If Asakura was up there, he was in better shape than she. If he was not, she couldn't help him, but she had to get to the lake. There was no hope anymore of going back.

With no other trail to follow, she again had to push her way up the over-grown channel. The ravine ran due east; the fire was approaching at an angle from the southeast, and she could hear it now even above her own wheezing and coughing. It was a freight train, now less than a mile away and eating the distance between them.

The last pitch was steep, and she climbed hand over hand in places through the narrow ravine, getting soaked in the stream and torn by brush. But she topped the ledge and stood on the rocky basin floor just as the trees on the ridgetop crowned in flame. Gusts of hot air blasted her, bending her over as she struggled forward. Through swirls of clear air she spotted the lake fifty yards ahead, and made a dash for it. But she was coughing so hard she fell to her knees and threw up. The ground around her glowed an eerie reddish gold, and it felt as though her wet clothes were boiling on her. She rose one more time and sprinted for the water, threw off her pack, and dove in.

A coughing fit underwater nearly drowned her. But she found her feet and stood, struggled for breath, then waded in chest deep.

Breathing there was no easier, with clouds of smoke snaking over the surface of the water, and waves of heated air whipping around.

Within minutes the fire crested in full force and engulfed the lake basin, leapfrogging around and completely surrounding her. The roar of the wind and the shriek of boiling sap were deafening. Trees exploded one by one, searing her face. The sun went down quickly or was masked by the smoke. The only light came from the fire and the glow it made in the enveloping pall.

The lake water was cold and made her shiver, but the air was impossibly hot, so she dunked herself time and again. Each time she came up the air was too hot to breathe and there was too little oxygen to it. Her breaths wheezed through her throat and it felt like her chest was bleeding. A wet bandana held over her face helped to cool the air some but did nothing to provide more oxygen. Her head began to float and the lake surface to spin, and it occurred to her, dreamily, that the carbon monoxide was building in her blood just as it had in the Neagles'.

A bright flare seared her face and she dunked again. As she came up for air a fire-tornado snapped a flaming tree from its roots and whirled it high into the air then dropped it into the lake a hundred feet away. It was the last thing she saw.

Chapter Nineteen

Thursday, 4 October, About 6:00 a.m. I think.
(Timex not as waterproof as advertised.)
Taking stock, then heading back to town with prisoner.

Her own coughing woke her. She was shivering violently, and scraped and sore from the rough rock on which she lay. But she turned over and found the rock warm to her cold side, and that stopped her shaking. However, every breath cut at her insides like a knife.

On her knees, she immediately heaved over in a long coughing spell that ended with her trying to empty her stomach. The sky above was clear, and although the sun would not top the ridge for a couple of hours, it was light enough to see every detail of her surroundings. She was kneeling in the middle of a cauldron of ash and embers. But for a thin lacing of green along the outlet stream, all the color had been burned from the place. There were black, and gray, and the dull umber of volcanic rocks, and nothing else until her eyes lifted to the blue of the sky. A convocation of tree trunks stood on the surrounding slopes, absent branches, smoldering and smoking. Ash puffed and swirled everywhere. Other than that—other than ash, smoldering logs, sky, and stone—there was water, and she kneeled on a rock surrounded by it.

The water tried to reflect the blue of the sky but was choked with floating debris. Half-burned branches and bits of black charcoal bobbed in the waves, and a few white-bellied fish floated at the shore. Ada stood, wobbled, and when steady on her feet, waded to shore then staggered the fifty yards to the edge of the lake terrace. Below her, the ridges and vales were blackened as far as she could see. Pockets here and there billowed with smoke, but the conflagration was spent; it had burned itself out of fuel in the night.

She found her hat on the way back to the lake. The ten-dollar Stetson had caught in a tangle of brush in the outlet stream and had singed along with the foliage. It hurt her throat to laugh, but the brim was burned in scallops on one whole side, and the crown showed finger holes right through. She stuck the thing on her head anyway.

Her rucksack was not where she had thrown it down but sitting on another flat rock by the water's edge. Where she went to retrieve it, she found the shrine. It was a simple thing, and she might ordinarily not have noticed it: just a dozen flat stones stacked into a three-tiered pagoda. She sat down with legs crossed, found her field book and pen inside the pack, and began catching up her notes. But she jumped up again at the welcome but altogether startling sound of a human voice.

Eddy Asakura shouted and waved from halfway around the lake. She waved back, and he started toward her along the bare, rocky shore carrying a string of fish. Taking his time, he stopped now and then to poke with a stick at an interesting bit of cinder in the waves. He tipped his hat to her as he approached. "Are you okay, Mrs. Reed?" he asked.

"Yes, thank you," she tried to say, although her throat was too scratchy to say it clearly.

He put down his catch and sat on a rock near her, and they both listened to the breeze for a minute. Asakura bent down and drank from the lake with his hand. "May I ask what brings you up here, Sheriff?" he asked.

She laughed, clutching her chest for the pain. "I came to save you."

"Oh. That was kind."

They said nothing more for a couple of minutes. He helped Ada to remove and empty her boots, and when she'd wrung out her socks and settled again he asked, "May I offer you breakfast?" He held up the string of fish. "I will start a fire and cook them if you prefer."

"No thank you, I . . . you mean you'd eat it raw?" She grimaced. "Thank you, but I think my throat is sore enough."

"As you wish." He laughed and set to work quietly skinning and fileting the trout on a pine board and cutting the flesh into strips as Ada returned to her notes. The only sounds were the lightest ripples of water on stone, Eddy's knife at work, and the muffled pops and crackles in the embers on the hillside. But it had been nearly a day since Ada had eaten anything at all, and with time the idea of raw fish lost some of its horribleness. She eventually tried a bit and found it slid down her sore throat easily. She accepted another, and then another.

A light breeze cleared the smoke from the lake basin, and the morning brightened. Asakura listened to the ripples for a while longer, then said softly,

> *"Dew slakes blackened earth.*
> *Life ascends; a seed remains*
> *in ashes still warm."*

"Is that a poem?"

He sighed. "I suppose not."

"Eddy, I spoke to the old doctor. The medicine that treated the epidemic in town was taken from the internment camp. I'm sorry about your mother. She did not have to die."

He bowed his head. "One died who might have lived; another lived who might have died. *Shouganai.*"

"And your father was shot not trying to escape but trying to break into the warehouse for medicine."

"Yes. I had to be told by others after the camp had closed its gates that Clifford Neagle stole the medicines and sold them." He gazed for a moment over the debris-choked waters. "In the end," he asked, "how did Neagle die?"

"He'd been poisoned; he was blind and could not run."

"It is an awful thing, to be blind."

Ada said, "He sat as the fire bore down on him, and he waited for it. He did not run blindly but sat on his porch and accepted his fate."

Asakura nodded. "That much, then, I shall respect about the man, even if I cannot forgive the rest."

The valley lay quiet and lifeless below them, a smoking wasteland; and farther, miles beyond the blackened earth, more trouble was roiling in the west. "I don't think it's our duty to forgive everything," Ada said. "There are things I've forgiven—too many times. I won't forgive them anymore."

He laughed and cut another slice of fish. "You would not have made a good internee."

"I would have been a troublemaker?"

"Yes, I believe you would have been."

She thanked him for the fish but searched in her pack for . . . the peaches! The can was bulged out and still a little warm. Asakura opened it with his knife, and they might never have tasted anything so sweet in their lives. The syrup soothed her throat.

THEIR VEHICLES WOULD HAVE BEEN DESTROYED in the fire, so they decided to take the high road out, down the Basin Butte Road. It was eight miles—maybe ten, but there might be fire crews mopping up along the road. There would be no shade and no water for most of the way.

They climbed slowly at first, up the steep highwall of the basin, and stopped to catch their breath once they'd gained the ridge road, and to look back on the lake below them.

"What will be done with me?" Asakura asked.

"There are still some stubborn folks who will need convincing. Be patient. Be a willow this time, not an oak."

"Easy to say."

"Eddy Asakura, I'm arresting you for fishing without a license."

He laughed. "What is the point of that?"

"While you're my prisoner, no one can touch you."

A small bird flew below them: a mountain bluebird, and it circled the lake basin, catching the sunlight on its wings. They both followed the bird's flight until they could no longer see it.

"Surprising," Ada said.

"Beautiful." He watched the trail of the bird for a moment longer, then nodded. "I see your point, Sheriff, but you are one and they are many."

She swung the pack onto her shoulder. "They're not going to screw with me," she said.

EPILOGUE

Saturday, November 10, 1951
Moving day.

THERE ONCE HAD BEEN BARLEY WAIST-HIGH to a girl in coveralls, and wheat by the wagonload. But with years the fields had dried and packed hard, and she stood waist-deep now in weeds instead. Her father had killed himself trying to keep the weeds down. She and her mother had worked themselves to tears fighting the weeds. But it had only taken looking the other way for a moment, pausing with shovel in hand, and nature's disorder had reclaimed the land. The farm she looked over now was exactly as she remembered it, but everywhere different—smaller, perhaps; poorer, and dustier. Even the dirt-brown hills that had bounded her childhood were different. Rilled and dotted with sage, the hills looked the same, but they would never be so imposing as they once had been—now that she'd seen the other side of them. She'd seen the other side of a lot of things, she supposed . . . and of a lot of people.

The dry summer had caused the leaves of the cottonwoods to die on the branches, and they rustled and rasped in a late autumn breeze. Sheriff Ada Reed leaned against a split-rail fence, and her uncle Ephraim, Mayor Applegate, leaned with her as the sun continued a long afternoon descent. Down by the barn, Kellen Munson called and waved. He was ready to start cooking, and she waved back and gave a shout. She could always count on Kellen to help—there was no other side to him. He'd brought Lettie Nance with him from Stanley, and Lettie had brought a potato salad.

Cheryl's husband, Tony, and Betty's husband, Ken, were wrestling and heaving her Frigidaire up the back steps and through the kitchen door. She hoped the old wooden porch didn't collapse under them. She should help. They'd all been so sweet to come when she'd called, to help move her things from the house in Camas and to help her celebrate. Ada knew she should help. It was her moving day, after all—her choices, and her changes.

Applegate stepped his foot up onto the fence rail and bit down on a stem of grass, and that country pose in a three-piece suit caused her to turn and stifle a grin. Her uncle had, in fact, received a 'peace offering' from Boniface although, thank God, he was not a drinking man and hadn't opened it. Ada caught him before he might have 're-gifted' the moonshine. Since then, Ephraim had been accommodating and helpful in her decision to move to the farm, if still a little puzzled and concerned by it.

But he took in a deep breath of the country air and said, "I think I haven't been back to this old place, sweetheart, since your dear mother passed."

She said, "I barely have either, Uncle Eph. We only stayed another year or so after that. Montgomery, as you know, was not of the farming temperament."

They both quieted. He asked, "How are things between you and Monty?"

"Not so good, Ephraim."

"I thought not. I'm sorry, honey."

"He's been reassigned to Tokyo."

"Oh, well, that's good. When did it happen?"

She took a letter from her pocket and turned it over in her hands. It was the first from Montgomery since she'd sent him a package with socks, hand balm, and Sybil's engraved cigarette lighter. She said, "Almost two months ago, as it turns out. He only now got around to telling me."

She had to pause a moment so her voice wouldn't break. "He let me go on worrying and praying as if he were still in combat."

Applegate opened his mouth, utterly taken back, but found no words at all. To Ada, though, it was par for the course. Montgomery had never really forgiven her for shooting his friend, although the man was guilty as hell. He'd never forgiven her for running for sheriff in her own name—and especially for questioning how he had done the job when he was sheriff. And he'd never forgiven her for the other thing: the childlessness. She said nothing more about it to her uncle, but stuffed the letter back into her pocket.

Applegate said, "On a happier note, congratulations on your refugee assistance program."

It had all come together a few weeks earlier, while the valley still stank of smoke, and passions still burned over the Neagle and Harding deaths. The governor had come through with an emergency declaration. In Washington, a Senate committee had approved action, and the Department of the Interior had opened the old internment center at Minidoka to the families who had lost their homes in the fires.

Applegate said, "The governor is getting a lot of mileage out of it. You should have him eating out of your hand."

"It's enough he doesn't hate me so much." She raised her eyes to the sound of honking geese. "It's enough the families have roofs over their heads."

"Just in time," Applegate said. "Winter is coming."

"Yes." The hills to the east, unimposing as they might be, wore a dusting of snow, and she felt the damp coolness of it when the wind rushed down the slopes. She said, "Winter is coming, and it will be cold."

She'd had the oil tank filled and the furnace checked, but needed to get in a cord of wood. It would be cold, and it would be lonely for a while, too. But this was where she belonged. The smells of soil and woodland, and even the sound of the dry cottonwood leaves told her she was home.

"It's going to take a lot of work to make this the farm your father was so proud of," Applegate said.

"Yes, but that will have to wait for another time. I'm going to be awfully busy for the next three years."

She was going to be busy because damned if she hadn't won the off-year election for sheriff. They'd counted the ballots three times because the margin was just a handful of votes. Her uncle claimed it was his and Corrine's support that put Ada over the top. But Applegate smiled whenever he said it, then told anyone listening that it was damned-good police work on her part. The Canyon Currier, in an uncharacteristic flurry of fairness, had written so highly of her Valley Creek investigation they'd put her election almost within reach. Almost, but in fact it was Kellen Munson who got her over the top. He'd been shrewd enough to deliver absentee ballots to the fire refugees at the Minidoka camp.

And as far as the 'damned good' police work . . . She hadn't done that all by herself, either. They had made it out to Stanley together, she and her 'prisoner' Eddy Asakura. Thirsty, tired, and black with soot, they had picked each other up and kept each other going through the hot ashes and deadfall. The others had worried sick over her—Blevins, Munson, and McGann—when they saw how the fire had swept over her tracks. But she and Eddy made it down off the mountain, and State Patrol Sergeant Blevins drove them to Camas in his cruiser. Word somehow got to town before they did, and a mob had gathered at the courthouse. The people of the valley wanted to hang someone for the murders, and there had been a lot of shouting and some shoving. In the end, it was Blevins, swinging the butt of a shotgun, who cleared the way for them through the mob.

Ada had worried long hours and wondered how ignorance can breed fear and fear breed hate. But in the end, the folks of

Yellowpine County had been reasonable jurists. They listened to her testimony, saw the evidence pointing to Frenchy Boniface, and returned no indictment of Eddy Asakura. Now Eddy was there for her moving day, too, and he'd brought Inga, and they were carrying in box after box of dishes and linens.

A burst of laughter reached her from down in the farmyard—a sound she hadn't heard in that place in years. It was Betty and Cheryl carrying on with Sybil Riis-Moreau, and they were all laughing so hard they had to twist to contain themselves. Sybil had driven down alone in her Cadillac, and she'd brought a bottle of champagne for the house. She'd not started comfortably with the other ladies; she'd smiled a lot, not sure what to say. And she was over-dressed a bit, in a western outfit and fringed jacket that made her look a little like Dale Evans. But the get-up included cowgirl boots, not high heels, so she found her footing there in the barnyard in no time. Ethel was there, too, and talking with Maggie Li who had baked biscuits and bread. They had all come to help and to celebrate—all except Ben McGann, who was not there.

An evening breeze moved down off the hills and stirred the dry leaves around her feet, and she shivered and worried again that maybe Ben had made a decision and would not come. He had worried himself to death for her, she understood that. He'd been in the command tent cataloging the personal effects of a firefighter, a young man who was lost in a flare-up at Mormon Bend, when two weary and blackened survivors, singed and streaked with soot, stumbled into his camp. Ada had gone straight to a water hose and drank long and deep, then handed the hose to Asakura. As she straightened up, she spied McGann atop the rise standing at the tent opening. Their eyes met for just a second, but in that time . . . well, things had been rocky between them since. Now he wouldn't come, and her evening would be blue, and her other friends would notice.

She pushed up onto the fence and hooked her boot around the bottom rail, and there she sat letting Ephraim chat away. She let the light soften and the air cool, and she let her friends' husbands do all the lifting and Kellen do all the cooking.

Once they'd wrestled in the heavy furniture and the appliances, the men popped the tops from bottles of beer. The boxes were all in, too, and she felt a pang of guilt for doing so little. But the grill was smoking, and she could smell the chicken from where she sat, and already Sybil and the girls were clinking their wine glasses.

She drew her boot up to the second rail and held her knee in her laced fingers and watched. And then a smile came to her, big and bright, and she jumped down from the fence. A plume of dust approached over the tops of the alders and they heard Ben McGann's Forest Service rig rattle and rumble over the cattle guard.

Applegate cleared his throat. "Ben, uhm . . . Ranger McGann seems an awfully nice fellow, if somewhat tall and . . ." He cleared his throat again. "I wonder, though, if some people might get the wrong idea, you working closely—as your duties require you to do, of course—But you know how some people can be when they haven't got brain cells enough to rattle around. It could be misconstrued, it could be . . ."

"Thanks for helping out today, Uncle Eph," she said. "And please thank Aunt Corrine for the preserves." She took his arm, and they started back along the fence line toward the house and yard, to her waiting friends.

There would be interesting days ahead, she knew. And they would be cold, some of them, and lonely, and not always so easy. But you can't get where you're going till you leave where you've been. The sunlight through the branches made her smile.

Roger Howell was raised in a loosely knit working-class and often not-much-working-to-be-had-class family in numerous towns in Idaho, Montana, Oregon, and Washington. Stories around campfires and wood stoves told of brawling uncles, lost gold mines, and friends and family who had gone away—to war, to jail, or to start somewhere better. Those stories made the years of the forties and fifties seem to Roger a lost romantic age. And it is. America then was suddenly safe and prosperous, but frozen with paranoia over atomic bombs and flying saucers. A good and innocent people thought they would save the world, but along the way sowed deep prejudices they didn't yet understand. In any case, all those romantic tales of friends and family seemed to happen just before Howell happened along. As a consequence, the midcentury years have always tempted him, so that his own stories, even after four universities and an international career as a geologist and engineer, tend to be of the small towns of the Northwest and of the time and the simple folks who only just preceded him.